THIS CLEARLY WAS THE LIFE
JESSICA WAS NEVER MEANT TO LEAD

Just a short while ago, Miss Jessica Eastwood had never known anything but the simple country surroundings that had been her home while her father was fighting for country and king.

Now the father she adored was dead, and Jessica found herself in the very middle of the shallow London society he had done his best to protect her from.

She was an heiress to a fortune that attracted hunters as honey drew bees. And she was dazzled by a lord who believed she should act the perfect lady while he enjoyed a shocking relationship with a woman who was everything a lady was not.

Jessica had to learn what her soldier father surely knew—that all was fair in love and war. . . .

RED JACK'S
DAUGHTER

More Delightful Regency Romances from SIGNET

Red Jack's ❧Daughter

Edith Layton ❧

A SIGNET BOOK

NEW AMERICAN LIBRARY

For Adam:
If music be the food of love . . .

1

It was a warm wet evening in early spring and Lord and Lady
Swanson's grand ballroom was crowded, close, and pervas-
ively damp. Yet there was not a lady present who was not
thrilled to be in attendance. Unfortunately there was also
scarcely a male present who did not at least once cast a longing glance over toward the tightly latched windows. But not
only would it have been social suicide for a fellow to approach
an exit, in many cases actual homicide might have resulted if
any gentleman attempted an escape from this night's magnificent affair.

The bone-chilling freak winter of 1814 was at an end and
this evening's fete was one of the last great social events of
the season. The new crop of eligible females who had been
launched the previous autumn now had only a few short
weeks in which to make their conquests. Clearly, they needed
assistance.

Their mamas, elder sisters, and aunts who were crammed
into the vast room with them knew that this late in the season, declarations might be wrung out of reluctant suitors
only by a kind of plotting that would put Wellington and his
staff to shame.

Thus, while the Incomparable, the Honorable Miss
Merriman, flashed her magnificent eyes and flirted with four
young gentlemen, wise mamas knew that the Incomparable
could legally wed only one of them. They knew full well that
the other three would soon be fair sport for their as-yet-
unattached and not quite so incomparable young daughters.
Now was the time to gild their tender young lilies with talk
of dowries, lands, and handsome annuities.

Papas were there too, in great numbers, to verify fortune
and acreage, along with uncles, brothers, cousins, and family
friends, all weaving tight nets to catch possible suitors.

7

Although most of them would rather have been any other place in London this evening, as they valued their necks they were gracing this final great ball. It was their duty to be part of this babbling, pressing throng and it was very fortunate that neither Lord nor Lady Swanson could read lips or minds.

"Gad," Sir Selby whispered to his companion, "must be a thousand here. Isn't there some sort of law against such crowds?"

"Only if someone's giving a political speech," his secretary answered lightly, watching his employer mop his brow again.

"Devil of a thing," Sir Selby complained as he replaced his damp handkerchief in his pocket. "Hot as Hades, between the musicians and the talk, I can't hear myself think. Lady Grantham is giving me dagger looks and he ain't here yet. Tell you, if he don't show, you'll have to step in for him."

The slight, pale young man smiled apologetically. "I'll be happy to, sir, but I don't think that's what the Lady's after."

"Blast, don't I know it?" Sir Selby grumbled. "I know Alex of old. It isn't like him not to show. But I brought you just in case."

The slight gentleman bowed as much as he was able in his cramped space.

"I'll be happy to help, sir, and moreover, I do think Miss Eastwood is a charming companion. But I can do little more than enable her to stretch her legs a bit. My appearance with her on the dance floor will do nothing for her socially."

"Be better than her sitting there like a log all night," Sir Selby groaned. "Damnation, Lady Grantham will have my head on a pike. Is she looking this way, lad?"

"She is looking in no other direction," the young man replied with a hint of amusement in his voice.

Sir Selby chanced a glance over to a corner of the great room where he knew Lady Grantham was sitting. Although she was half in shadow, he could see even from a distance that the Lady was definitely glowering at him.

Sir Selby looked hastily away. He was a stout elderly man with a round pleasant countenance, and what little remained of his hair was silver. He carried himself ramrod-straight as befitted a military man, although he scarcely came up to his slight secretary's shoulder. He had faced cannon, Napoleon's troops, and the furor of battle, and still he had feared none of them so much as he did risking another look back at Lady Grantham.

"She still looking?" he asked.

His secretary nodded.

"Gad," Sir Selby sighed, "it's almost the shank of the evening. I told Alex the importance of it and he hasn't shown his face. I didn't think him so unfeeling. I hope he hasn't come to harm."

"Not he, I think," his secretary replied. "It's only that it is early hours yet, for him."

"Aye," sighed Sir Selby, and he lapsed into silence as he watched the dancers swirl about the floor.

None of the ladies looked so well as they had when he'd arrived, he thought with relief. The heat and the dampness had taken its toll on all the careful coiffures and gowns. There's many a lady here that looks like a dowd now, he thought, brightening a little, even the beauties are looking a bit blown. All to the good for our gal, he thought happily.

But after a half-hour had gone by, which Sir Selby verified for the fourth time by his pocket watch, he sighed again and managed to wedge the watch back into his fob pocket.

"It's now or never, lad," he said in hollow tones. "The Regent will be coming soon and that'll put paid to the dancing. Then they'll trot out the supper for him, and by the time the music strikes up again it'll be too late to make much of an impression. You're for it, lad. I hope you can cavort like a lamb, they're starting up a country dance. Now shake a leg and get to it. Alex has let us down and you're our only hope."

It was at that moment, while the sets were beginning to form for the new dance and weary couples were retreating from the floor, that there was a momentary but distinct lull in the general conversation. It were as though there were suddenly a refreshingly cool wind blowing over them all and heads turned toward the doors. They had opened the doors and a little fresh air had got in, for there were new arrivals. Sir Selby turned. He could see, even from that distance across the room, who had entered.

"You're saved, lad," he said happily. "Run along if you want. No need for reinforcements now."

His secretary bowed and gratefully took himself off into the warm night, which was several degrees cooler than the vast room. Sir Selby began to edge toward the entrance to the ballroom.

The new arrivals were greeted with much enthusiasm. They were intimates of the Regent's set, and they were notorious, all of them. The Earl of Trent would be in great demand in the card room, for he was a gamester. Baron Bly attracted all the married ladies, for he was a great flirt; and the Marquis of Bessacarr would cause much comment, for he was such a mysterious, elusive fellow. But it was Lord Leith who caused all the females in his vicinity to sigh.

Sir Selby made his way toward him through the throng, stepping upon a few slippers where he had to, causing sharp pains in a few ribs where he must. He had many years in the military to guide him, and where he had to push over heavy ground, he did so with impunity.

"Alex," he finally said as he came abreast of the lofty newcomer, cutting into some raillery he was having with another guest.

"As you see," Lord Leith replied, bowing, and excused himself deftly from the gentleman he had been chatting with.

Sir Selby nodded happily. "Right, come with me," he said abruptly, starting to lead Lord Leith through the crowd back toward the far wall.

"Softly, softly," Lord Leith said smoothly, and laid a restraining hand upon the older gentleman to stop him. "Don't rush your fences, old friend. It will appear uncommonly odd if I enter and rush to an unknown's side. Let us have a glass of something first. What are they serving in this tropic zone?"

"Don't see why you're complaining," Sir Selby said as he changed direction and cleared a path toward the refreshment table. "You've done time in India. Punch," he said absently, handing a cup to his friend. "There's something in it, but not much."

Lord Leith sipped at his cup and smiled down at those acquaintances who hailed him. "I believe one could hatch eggs in here without hens. Have they bricked up all the windows?'' he asked in an undervoice.

"Just about," Sir Selby said, draining his cup. "They're expecting Prinny, and they know how he detests drafts. So they're keeping it nice and stuffy so that he won't bolt the moment he gets here. They've even got a fire roaring in the card room.''

Lord Leith sighed. "He's more likely to drop from the heat, but I can see their point. Still, it won't help them. I've just come from dinner with our Prince, and for once he's more in the mood for sleep than for applause. He'll be here, take his bows, and then take himself off and they'll have gotten their guests into a lather for nothing.''

"For pity's sake, then, Alex, drop a word in Swanson's ear before I melt," the older man begged.

"Alas, no, dear friend. I'm mute. For who's to say that some full-blown flower won't catch Prinny's eye and make a liar of me? No, I fear you'll have to soldier on and pray that someone is pushed through a window in the crush to get to our dear Regent.''

"Well, then," Sir Selby said with decision, "let's get on with it.''

Lord Leith laughed. It was such a rich, amused chuckle that several present, who were not already covertly watching the tall gentleman that had just appeared in their midst, found their eyes turning toward the deep pleasant sound.

"No, no," he said, sobering, in a lower voice. "That wouldn't do at all. You said it must seem casual and unrehearsed. I fear you will have to tolerate me for a little longer, and then, when enough time has elapsed, we will seem to just drift unknowing toward my dear aunt and your protégée. Then, and only then, shall I happen upon her, and then, instantly smitten, I shall beg you to make me known to the child.''

"And dance with her," Sir Selby added insistently.

"In transports of delight," his tall companion agreed.

Sir Selby, a man of action, stood back on his heels and waited impatiently while his friend engaged in light discourse with another guest. He occupied his time by puffing out his cheeks; when that palled, he paused for a moment to gaze up at his young friend. In doing so, he realized he was only following a general trend. For there were many others, notably female, who were doing the same thing.

It was hard to ignore Lord Leith, Sir Selby had to admit to himself, if only because he was perhaps the tallest fellow in the room. As a man who had once commanded many men, Sir Selby had to acknowledge that the lad was also well-set-up. Alexander, Lord Leith, was, for all his height, well-proportioned, graceful, and lithe. His closely tailored evening clothes showed that his shoulders were wide, his waist narrow, abdomen flat, and legs long and well-muscled. Sir Selby nodded to himself in approval and unconsciously pulled in his own considerable stomach.

But it was Alexander's face that commanded attention, Sir Selby decided, gratefully letting out his own breath. A generation ago, the older gentleman mused, a face like that need only have shown itself in the heart of Paris and the mob would have gone wild. "Aristo!" the rabble would have shouted after just one look, and the fellow would have been trussed up on a tumbrel on his way to Madame Guillotine before he could have uttered a word in defense. For it was an aristocrat's face, from its long, high cheekbones to the straight long nose, to the well-proportioned sensitive mouth. Six years in India had not ruined the clear white complexion. The long eyes, so heavily lidded that one would think the fellow dozed when he was not speaking, could open upon the world with a clear, knowing gray gaze. A considerable number of debutantes had practiced saying shocking things just so that they could witness the spectacle of those eyes widening in surprise, and a few had rued the day they had when that bland but chilling gray gaze had locked on to them. An equally impressive number of their bored and wedded sisters had refined upon the notion of witnessing those eyes closing at closer range, as close perhaps as the next pillow. But if any of them had achieved that goal, none knew of it. Lord Leith was a great favorite of the ladies, but the females he consorted with were not equal to that noble designation.

His curling light-brown hair was far too long for fashion. Yet while most of the young ladies present would tease their fathers for clinging to so antique a style, the thought of Lord Leith catching up those wayward curls with a black riband was enough to make them catch their breath. He wore no such thing, though, for he was always just in, while out of fashion. The Beau himself had said that with that face and those funds, Leith was his own fashion.

As Sir Selby watched and Lord Leith appeared not to, the Incomparable Miss Merriman tossed her raven tresses and turned her back upon the most eligible of her suitors so that the tall gentleman could catch her best profile. Lady Emmet emitted such a shrill giggle that her fiancé thought she deemed him a great wit, although her smile was all for Lord Leith's amused regard. Miss Timmins, who had nearly worn out her dancing slippers this evening with her vivacity, sat demure as a gray mouse and willed an air of forlorn dejection as Lord Leith's glance swept by her, for she had heard he had a secretly tender heart. Sir Selby felt his own heart sink as he saw the ravishing widowed Countess of Keswick give his young friend a look of unmistakable invitation.

"Now," Sir Selby said hurriedly as he noted Alexander's appreciative reciprocal smile, "you promised."

"Yes," Lord Leith said bemusedly, "so I did."

As the two made their slow and seemingly aimless way into the crowd, the taller inclined his head and said softly, "Really, you and Aunt do me much honor. You truly believe that if I ask the chit to dance, it will launch her into the social whirl?"

"Not *a* dance, Alex. Two. And so it shall. For she hasn't a prayer otherwise. Mind, you are not to dance with any other twice neither, for that would take the shine out of it. And," the older gentleman said, pausing for a moment as their path was blocked beyond even his maneuvering ability, "act as though she's your idea of something wonderful. And so she is. Can't judge everyone by outward appearances," he added on a note of complaint, never seeing the taller gentleman's slight grimace at his words.

"I've known her since she was breeched, and she's a lovely child. She's only come to town a few weeks past and I want to do everything in my power to see her make a good match. Mind, she's not to know a word of this," Sir Selby said, suddenly wheeling around and facing his companion, "for she'd have my head if she knew."

"She doesn't wish to be brought into fashion, then?" his companion asked with disbelief.

"Not she," Sir Selby said, shaking his head emphatically. "All she's got on her mind is coming to London to find the legacy her father's supposed to have left her. But if I know my man, he's not left her a campaign medal to polish up. No, if she's here to seek her fortune, it'll have to be on the marriage mart or not at all. And you're the lad to get her noticed. But don't drop a hint of my part in this, she's sharp as tacks."

"I've a lamentable memory, sir. I've forgotten just why I'm so enamored of her." Lord Leith smiled easily. "Which one is she?"

"Over there, in the corner, next to your aunt. In the shadows. Blast the girl, a fellow would have to have a torch in hand to see her properly, much less notice her enough to scrape up an introduction."

Lord Leith glanced casually to the sidelines, where he at once recognized his aunt, Lady Grantham, attired in several shades of purple. A young person sat her her side. She seemed to be dressed in too much gray fabric and to have no hair at all, rather only a gray lace cap atop her head.

"I thought she was a companion," he breathed. "Tell me, is it the light or is the young lady I am about to lose my head over scowling? No, not scowling, sneering?"

Sir Selby employed his limp handkerchief again and blurted, "Devil take it, Alex. You're too used to females throwing themselves at your feet. No reason she should be simpering just because you've tossed her a look."

"No, indeed," Lord Leith agreed calmly. "Just give me a moment to collect myself." He gazed over at his aunt again. "Tell me," he asked Sir Selby, "you say her father saved your life when you were soldiering together?"

"Twice," Sir Selby said tightly.

"Ah, well, twice," Lord Leith sighed. "Then I fear I am about to experience that phenomenon I have always scoffed at—love at first sight. But," he cautioned as he approached his aunt and the white-faced solemn figure seated by her side, "only to the tune of two dances. Not even if he had saved *my* life thrice will I do more than to lead her in to supper after that."

"Aunt," said Lord Leith, coming forward with every evidence of delight, "I had no idea you would subject yourself to this crush. When Selby told me you were here, I hastened to your side. What brings you here? I thought you were through with such pastimes."

"And so I was," Lady Grantham said in a clear carrying voice, "after I got Nettie and Lydia popped off. But I wanted to show my dear young friend here some of the high points of London fashion. She has only just arrived from the country and I thought she might be amused by tonight's entertainment."

Lord Leith looked over toward Lady Grantham's companion and thought that so might one show amusement at one's own execution. The light was too dim for him to make out her face with clarity. What he saw, however, was not encouraging for the charade he had promised Sir Selby. Her face was a white oval, the nose seemed small and straight enough, the lips compressed as if by effort; it was only her eyes, large and dark with a curious upward slant, that promised any attraction for him. But they were wide and unblinkingly assessing him. As he had noted before, her hair had been skinned back and was covered with what looked like a table doily, but was most likely some sort of lace cap. Curious, he thought, for the face was young, yet the cap signified spinsterhood.

Seeing the two younger parties appraising each other in silence, Sir Selby broke in. "Alexander, I'd like to make you known to my dear old friend, Captain Jack Eastwood's daughter, Miss Jessica Eastwood. Miss Eastwood, may I present Alexander, Lord Leith."

"My nephew," Lady Grantham assisted.

"Delighted." Lord Leith smiled and bowed, taking the young woman's hand.

But Miss Eastwood sat dumb as a stone and only gave a sharp nod.

As another small silence threatened, Sir Selby prepared to leap into the breech again. Damn, he thought, fellow's supposed to be a terror with the ladies, and he makes me do all the work. Lord Leith, however, for once disconcerted by the fierce and uncompromising stare he was subjected to, was trying to think of some way to approach the young woman conversationally so that he could then smoothly ask her to dance with him. It was difficult, he thought, a small smile forming on his lips, to feign sudden rapture for a basilisk.

" 'Red Jack,' that's her father, y'know, served with me for many years . . . on the continent, on the peninsula. He was a hey-go-mad fellow. Best of fellows. I miss him frightfully. Fell at the Battle of Vitoria. Just last year, you know," Sir Selby put in.

"So sorry," murmured Lord Leith while Lady Grantham glared at the perspiring Sir Selby, who had all unwittingly brought down a funereal atmosphere upon them. Miss Eastwood bowed her head for a moment to acknowledge Lord Leith's sympathies. In that brief moment Lady Grantham fixed a look of such annoyance on Sir Selby that he began to talk further in a hearty voice that sounded foolish even in his own ears.

While Sir Selby improvised wildly about battles and sport he had shared in the ranks with his dear "Red Jack," he became aware that there was once again a great press of people around him. A great many, it appeared, were curious as to what could be holding Lord Leith's attention for so long. An interested crowd had formed in their vicinity, and even the Incomparable Miss Merriman was now holding court not two paces away. Now, Sir Selby thought as he wound his reminiscences down to a halt, now would be the time for him to haul her off to the dance floor.

"Miss Eastwood," Lord Leith said quietly, a moment after Sir Selby had subsided, "the musicians are tuning up again."

Miss Eastwood looked up mutely at Lord Leith. A strange quiet had fallen in their corner of the room. It seemed a fair number of the guests in their vicinity had muted their own conversations and a few were frankly goggling, trying to see whom the lofty Lord Leith was addressing.

"Never saw her there at all," one vagrant masculine whisperer complained.

"Miss Eastwood," Lord Leith continued, "would you do me the honor of taking this dance with me? It's not a waltz, so there can be no question of impropriety," he added to fill the silence Miss Eastwood seemed to have no idea of breaking.

At length, she spoke. Her voice, though low and husky, was clear enough to carry in the eerie stillness.

"Lud, no," Miss Eastwood said abruptly. And then, after a hesitation, "Thank you."

She had done what no debutante in three Seasons had achieved. For a moment Lord Leith's gray eyes opened wide, but he made no other movement for a small space of time. Then, recollecting himself, he bowed and without another word strode off as the voices around them rose to a babble.

Sir Selby, however, was not struck speechless.

"Damnation!" he blurted.

"I think," said Lady Grantham, who was now truly in several shades of purple, "we shall leave."

Miss Eastwood looked about in confusion as she rose to accompany the elder woman. "How else should I have said it?" she asked.

"As 'yes,' " Lady Grantham said through clenched teeth, " 'Thank you.' "

2

"The cut direct," Lady Grantham moaned as she sat upright and held on to the door strap in the swaying carriage. "It only needed that, the cut direct."

"But," Miss Eastwood said softly, sitting across from Lady Grantham and watching her in the glow of the coach lamp with growing consternation, "I truly did not wish to dance with him."

"One might have said," Lady Grantham went on, addressing air, " 'Oh, but I cannot, for I've hurt my ankle.' Or one might have claimed one was still in mourning, although that is patently untrue, or one might even have laid claim to dizziness."

"Could even have pretended to swoon," Sir Selby grumbled from his corner of the carriage.

"Or one might have claimed fatigue," Lady Grantham went on, "or declined sweetly and requested a lemonade instead. Or cited the excessive heat, or even"—and here even Lady Grantham's voice grew a trifle wild—"claimed a prior commitment. But a bald, 'No, thank you.' It is beyond comprehension."

Miss Eastwood's pale face grew whiter.

"Terribly sorry . . . I didn't realize," she began, but then hesitated, for she did know and was thoroughly ashamed of herself for lying. "The fellow popped up from nowhere. He startled me badly, frightened me, in fact," she said.

And so he had. She had spent the interminable evening sitting next to Lady Grantham, scarcely heeding all the gossip she was receiving about the unknown persons who swam about the overheated room before her. She had grown by slow degrees from startled panic at the sight of so many exquisitely dressed people, to silent criticism of their obvious flirting and maneuvering, to contempt for their giddiness, to grudging admiration for their social grace, right back to startled panic when the imposing figure of Lord Leith had loomed up before her. She had long since reconciled herself to being an observer, an invisible person who could not be touched by anything but the warmth of the room, when he had startled her badly by asking her to dance. It had been the farthest thing from her mind and had chased away all judgment. She accepted that she was not the sort of female to attract such a gentleman, felt that there must have been some mistake, and knew only one thing for a certainty: that she could not stand up with him.

"Nonsense, Jess," Sir Selby said. "You've more bottom than that. Never saw you frightened yet."

"I shall dash off a note of apology," Miss Eastwood declared staunchly.

"Saying what?" Lady Grantham asked acidly.

"That I am sorry I discomposed him, that I—"

"Discomposed him?" Lady Grantham hooted. "Alex? As if some chit refusing him a dance could even touch him! When he's got the pick of the crop panting after him. No, you're best off to forget it. But you've knocked all your chances into a cocked hat, my dear."

"Ma'am," Miss Eastwood said quickly in a gruff little voice. "I'm terribly sorry if I've overset your plans, but it wouldn't do for you to think I've overset mine. For I've no illusions upon that head. It was kind of you to seek to assist me, but I well know that I'm not cut out for the social life. I've come to London solely to clear up matters of my father's estate. I told you how it would be, and though I thank you, and truly, for your attempts in that direction, and for putting me up, I pray you understand that I know I'm not cut out to be a figure of fashion."

It was a neat gentlemanly speech, but as it came from the lips of a young lady who had not even reached her majority, Lady Grantham only heaved a great sigh.

"Dear Ollie," the young woman went on, looking over to Sir Selby, "I know you both meant it for the best, but as you see, I've made a muddle of it. It won't do. When I wrote to you originally, I only wanted the direction of a good hotel. All your plans have been noble, letting me stay at Lady Grantham's, attempting to introduce me to other young people, but I can only embarrass you further. I thank you from the bottom of my heart, Ollie, and I apologize sincerely, but I think you'll agree that it's best you let me find my own way.''

Before he could answer her, the coach rolled to a stop. As Lady Grantham alighted, still shaking her head, Miss Eastwood stayed Sir Selby for a moment. She whispered, with just the hint of a sob in her throaty voice, ''Truly, Ollie, old friend, remember what Red Jack used to say, 'A fellow can't do more than his best.' And you've done it.''

A moment later she was out of the coach and following her hostess up the steps.

Miss Eastwood excused herself quickly from a distracted Lady Grantham and took the stairs to her room with unbecoming haste. Once there, she commanded a sleepy lady's maid. ''Amy, pack. That's right, and at once. I want us to be able to leave at first light. No, I'm not bosky. Just pack us up and be ready to come with me in the morning. We're going to a hotel as originally planned.''

After her maid had left with a minimum of explanation offered and a maximum of doubt manifest in her expression, and after Miss Eastwood saw that her bags were neatly packed and stacked at the entrance to her room, she allowed herself to relax at last. She was a young woman of resolve and felt infinitely better now that she had things in hand at last again. In fact, she mused as she stripped to her shift and cleaned her face vigorously with cold water, she felt better than she had in days.

She would thank Lady Grantham fulsomely in the morning and she would pen a very neat note to Ollie once she had settled into her rooms at the hotel. Then she would take up her vigil again, live quietly and comfortably until her father's solicitor contacted her, and only then would she decide what she would do with her fortune. This decided, Miss Eastwood hurried, as was her custom, into her night rail, plucked off her detestable lace cap, and began to undo the tightly woven strands of her hair so that she could brush them out.

It was only while she was brushing her long hair out that Miss Eastwood allowed herself the luxury of remorse. For Red Jack had always told her a fellow might wallow in regret in private but must never let anyone else see his indecision in public.

My dear Red Jack, Miss Eastwood thought sadly, how shall I get on without you? She had, in fact, been going on without him for most of her young life, though she chose not to remember that. Her childhood had been a solitary one, for governesses had been dispensed with early on, her neighbors had been too far-flung for the frequency necessary for close associations, and her mother, an almost mythical person, she had not seen since infancy. Her father's visits home had enlivened her life and influenced her as no other events had done. But they had been all too brief. It had always been too short a time before he was packing up his gear again and striding off to the wars, which had begun before she was born and still wore on now that he was gone.

She had sensed early on that those reprieves from the battles, which were his occupation and passion, were too long for him even as they were too short for her. For while he appeared to be easy and complacent in her company, she could never hold his interest above a fortnight. Still, he said he loved her, seemed to enjoy her company, and she knew no other ambition than to be his constant steadfast soldier.

It had been a summer's day, two years past, that she had her last look at him. A sweet day, far removed in time and place from the gaiety of the Swansons' ball and London. She had stood upon a rise near the house and waved her handkerchief till she could no longer see the blaze of his hair, nor the receding shape of his mount. Then she had turned and gone sorrowing back to Oak Hill, and somehow she had felt, had known, that the sight of his retreating form was the last she would ever have of him.

Not that she had any real thought of death, nor had any gypsy premonition of disaster teased at her as she had sat in the kitchen and helped Cook shell peas for dinner. But he had been different with her all through his visit this time, and she had seen that things had changed between them forever. It had troubled him from the first; now it nagged at her.

He had looked the same when he had marched into the house—without warning, as he always did—set down his bags, and cried a great "Halloo." She had run to meet him, flying down from the bedrooms, where she had been airing sheets, and had flown straight into his welcoming arms. He had swept her up as he always did and spun around and around with her. And then, dizzy, laughing, he had set her aside and looked hard at her, as he always did. But this time his blue eyes had widened and he had drawn in his breath and had said in a strangely solemn voice, "Lord, Jess, you've changed."

He had not. He was still dazzling in his red uniform, still splendid, compact, and trim, and bronzed from foreign suns. It had been two years since he had seen her, but still she looked at him with puzzlement, for nothing appeared different to her.

He stood staring at her with an indecipherable expression on his face and then gave her a strangely crooked grin. "It's your mother. You're the image of her now. My little Jess has turned into a woman behind my back. Now how could you do that to your dear old papa?"

She had looked down at herself and then back up at him, color flooding her cheeks.

"I'm still Jess, Red Jack. Never say you don't know me."

"Oh, I know you, Jess. How could I miss, with that hair of yours? But for a moment there you gave me a turn. When I left you were my straight little soldier, and now . . ." He smiled again and gestured toward her.

She had retreated from him then, even though she led him to the parlor for their usual renewal-of-acquaintance chat. She had taken tea with him and then dinner, and he told her wonderful new stories. Yet even though she had been awaiting his return these many months, she could not wait to get back to her room alone. And once there, she had laid her head upon her pillow and wept. She had honestly not seen the change as he had, she had honestly never wanted to, nor dared. There had been hints from the housekeeper, and looks from various males in the district. She had felt the difference but had avoided all acceptance of it. But she was, after all, Red Jack's daughter. She could not lack courage.

When all the house was still and she knew he had at last gone to his room and his rest, she had lit a few more candles and shut the windows and pulled the curtains close around them. After she had locked the door and listened to the old house creak down for the night, she had slowly stripped off her clothes and finally bravely faced herself full in the mirror.

He was right. It was not Jess there. Not this creature with the long hair waving and streaming about that lush, unfamiliar figure. It was an apparition, surely, that confronted her. She gazed at the reflection of two high-pointed breasts, a curving waist, a thicket to match her head between two long and tapering legs. Not Jess, surely not. Her face grew warm as she stared at those breasts; it was as if she were looking at some forbidden secret exotic picture, and she was both ashamed and aroused by what she saw. Whatever else she saw, it was certainly not Jess Eastwood, and she decided with determination, it would never be.

In the morning, he seemed more at ease with her. In many ways for the rest of that leave home it was as if the two years had never happened and she were still fourteen and still his little soldier. They rode together, they hunted, they fished, they took long rambling walks about the countryside while he told her stories of all the far-off places she had longed to see. In the evenings they sat before the fire and she listened to his tales, filled his glass, and laughed at his drollery till she was weak. As always, she secretly hoped he would tell her that he was, at last, selling out.

For he had told her a lovely anecdote about dear old Ollie and then had said casually, "Don't think we'll be seeing much of the fellow anymore. He's quit the cavalry, now he's come into a fortune and a title. So jolly Captain Ollie is now 'Sir Selby,' and don't you forget it, Jess. I imagine he'll be busy doing the pretty in London. Can you just see," he had crowed, "Old Ollie a proper 'sir?' "

She couldn't, remembering the merry fellow who had soldiered with her father and enjoyed so many leaves at home with them, but she brushed that information aside and waited for his next comment. He sighed, stared into the fire, and dashed all her hopes with his next words.

"No, even if I should come into an earldom, I could never so change my life. And there's little likelihood of that. So don't fret. It's Captain Eastwood's who's your pa, and proud he is of it too. I'm a military gent, Jess, and it's a life suits me to the ground. I only wish you had been a boy so you could taste it too. It would suit you as well, Jess."

She had agreed and took up her part again and begged again, as she always did and had done for the over a decade, that he take her with him. He had played his role as well and patted her head and told her once again that the tail of an army was no place for a female. But had she been a boy, he sighed with regret and left his statement unfinished, for they both knew there was no answer for that. Instead, they had gazed at the fire together till the last logs crumbled to ash.

He had been home for only two weeks when she saw he was eager to be off again. Too soon, they had parted with a wave and a hug and a smile. She had done the best she could and he had never said a word, so she must have done well. For she had bound her breasts around with a towel and worn her dresses loosely and dragged back her hair and wrenched it into tight braids wound around her head. Only once his gaze had gone to her hair and she had said lightly that it was cooler that way. He had grinned at that. She was his little soldier again.

Red Jack was a poor correspondent. She had only a few short letters of his to show for all their years of separation. But, she reminded herself, straightening and attacking her heavy hair with her brush again, she did have that last letter in hand. That last letter was the reason she sat here tonight in Lady Grantham's best guest bedroom.

It had been delivered late but at precisely the right moment. She had come home, angry and discouraged after a terrible row with Cousin Cribb. It had been over some paltry thing, repairs for the stable or renovation of the parlor, even now she could not remember. But she could never hold her temper around either Cousin Cribb or his wretched wife. It was not only because they had been so quick to come and take over Oak Hill after Father had died, she told herself repeatedly. Even she could see that though the laws of inheritance were unjust, they were the law of the land, after all. And Jeremiah Cribb, although only a distant cousin, was her closest male relative and thus had clear claim to her father's entailed home.

One look at the seedy fellow, though, and she had known that even Oak Hill's commodious rooms could not contain the two of them. She had requested and received, with obvious relief on both sides, permission to take up residence in the cottage. Even though she was still under age, there was no one in the village who could not understand the situation. For she and Cousin Cribb fought constantly, and she had begun to seriously wonder how she could make her way in the world when the letter had come.

She had stood in her small parlor and read it with tears flowing down her cheeks. He had fallen over a year before, and it had taken this long for the missive to reach her. It was so brief that even though she had it still she had no need to refer to it. It was graven in her mind's eye.

Dear Jess,

Everything's going well but the fighting is fierce. Don't worry, though, for I've the luck of the devil. Speaking of which, it occurs to me that I've been a devil of a papa to you. But I've put things right at last. If anything should ever befall me, rest easy. Red Jack don't forget his own. I've settled a neat future for you and it's in safekeeping. If I should stick my spoon in the wall, contact old Jeffers in London. He'll have the direction of your future well in hand. And you'll be a lucky rich young thing indeed. The best part of it is that it isn't entailed, nor can any other soul lay a finger on it but you. But that's grim speaking. I'll see you in the spring. All my love to my brave little soldier,

Love,
Red Jack.

She had written to Mr. Jeffers immediately and anxiously awaited his reply. When it had arrived, requesting that she come to London to discuss the matter, she had fired off another letter to the only other soul she knew in London, dear Ollie, now the impressive Sir Selby. All her bags had been packed when his letter came, ebullient and loquacious as ever, castigating himself for not inviting her sooner, felicitating her on her inheritance and enumerating all the jolly times they would have together.

She had both letters in hand when she marched back to Oak Hill to speak with Cousin Cribb. Her father's letter was not for his eyes, though; she would not give him such a glimpse of her greatest treasure, even though he was nominally her guardian.

He sat behind the high desk in the darkened study and fingered the letters for a long while before he spoke. His wife sat in a deep chair to his side. Mathilda Cribb was a massive, round woman, but there was nothing jolly in her countenance. Though she seldom spoke, her husband never made a decision without looking in her direction. It was eerie how the pair seemed to communicate with so few words.

Jessica sat up straight and met his long gaze without flinching. He was a small, crabbed-looking fellow, a shopkeeper who had worked hard all his life to no apparent avail. Oak Hill had fallen to him by chance, and it was the greatest luxury he had ever known, though it did not seem as if he greatly enjoyed it.

"Folk will talk about me letting an eighteen-year-old miss go to London by herself," he said at length.

At least, Jessica breathed to herself, there would be no dissembling between them.

"Not at all," she said, raising her chin, "for I won't be by myself. I'll take one of the maids for propriety's sake."

"Not that," he said, waving her answer away, "but staying with an older man. He's unwed, I take it."

"I shan't stay with Sir Selby. I will take a room in a reputable hotel," she answered promptly, though until that moment she had not realized that anyone could ever put such a construction upon her relationship with dear Ollie.

Cousin Cribb grunted, then stole a look at his impassive wife.

"This legacy," he began. "What do you suppose it to be? Your father left nothing to me that wasn't in the entail. He hadn't a groat of his own. Ran through his money like he ran through his life, heedless."

Jess contained herself with effort. Nothing could be more ruinous to her purpose than a squabble now, and well he knew it, from the bitter glint in his eye.

"I have no idea. But whatever it is, the letter clearly states that it cannot be considered part of the entail," she replied. "I'll take nothing that is rightfully yours. You can have your man of business see to it."

"So I shall, so I shall," he brooded. "Go then," he said suddenly. "I'd be a greater fool to keep you here. There's no love lost between us. The daughter of a gallant captain never could bring herself to be civil to a mere shopkeeper. So go. My only worry was as to how it would seem. We must be seemly now that we're masters of Oak Hill, eh Tilda?'' He laughed. "No matter that it's a great barn of a place, with no money to shore it up, no matter, eh?''

"Thank you," Jessica said quickly.

"But it will be seemly," he went on, "for one would worry about most chits haring off to London by themselves, but we won't have a care about dear Jess, will we? No life of sin for her lays waiting in the wicked city. For who'd have her, eh?'' he asked his wife. Her reply was to heave a great chuckle.

"I'll go now," Jess said politely, though she was sure the tips of her ears were glowing red.

"Go to the devil," he muttered, "but if you come back penniless, with his babe in your basket, I'll turn you out. And none will dispute me on that."

"I hardly would journey all the way to London for such a treat," Jess blurted, goaded beyond her control.

"No, not when Tom Preston could oblige you right here and save you the journey. That is, if you paid him enough," he chortled, pleased with the expression he saw in her eyes. It was like him, too, this ability to see into all unswept corners.

"I'll leave," was all Jessica could reply. And without waiting for his answer, she did.

Most young woman of eighteen would have been in raptures over the prospects of a trip to London. They would be anticipating new clothes and the excitement of new friends and flirts. Jess was content to pack her meager wardrobe of oversized, unstylish garments, and to dream of only one thing: her visit to the solicitor's office. Many young females of such a tender age would be inclined to drop a tear or two for old acquaintances they would be leaving behind. Jessica said her good-byes to the housekeeper and Cook, the vicar and his wife, and those few acquaintances whom she knew wished her well, and she prepared to go without a backward glance.

Still, though she appeared to be quite coolly taking leave of all she had known, there were two that she was deserting whom she was prepared to shed a tear for. And only one that she would admit to. The morning of her departure found Jessica on her knees in the garden with her arms about her dearest friend.

"Ralph, my love," she sighed, burying her head in the great dog's massive shoulder, "it wouldn't do. I cannot take you with me. But Mrs. Dane shall watch over you, and when I return, I'll take you with me wherever I go, I promise."

The huge animal burrowed his muzzle into her armpit, almost overbalancing her as he did so. He affected an air of high tragedy, for not only was he sensitive to his mistress's every mood, he was also well aware that she had readied the traveling chaise and he was not to go with her. Her father had given the beast to her when she and it had both been tiny, and he had been her constant companion ever since. Although most in the district often said they thought Ralph a cross between a hound and a barn, Red Jack had claimed the animal had Swiss ancestry more finely documented than his own pedigree. He had dubbed the struggling bundle of fur "Ralph" that long-ago day, so that, he told his little daughter, he could grow to be the only dog that could speak his own name.

The memory made Jessica chuckle weakly as she knelt upon the dusty flagstones, causing Ralph's great tail to thump happily in response. "Ralph," she whispered brokenly, "how I shall miss you."

"And no wonder," a laughing voice intruded, "for I have always thought he was your one true love. Now, I could never hope to receive such a fond farewell."

Jessica rocked back on her heels and saw the new arrival slip easily from his horse and stride toward her. She accepted the proffered hand and was drawn smoothly to a stand.

"Tom," she said in embarrassment, brushing dust from her skirt, "I didn't see you there."

"How could you," the young man laughed, "while you and Ralph were lost in each other's embrace? But it's too bad of you, Jessica, to waste such passions on old Ralph while I did not even get a note of good-bye."

Jessica felt her face flush, for she had wondered how to take her leave of him, and having hit upon no scheme that would appear to be casual enough, she had decided to let the matter go and leave with no notice. Thomas Preston had been, after all, her father's favorite; there had never been any defined relationship between herself and him, though she had always admired him. He had been a soldier, and a gallant one, her father had often said. But he had sold out after receiving a wound while in the peninsula and elected not to rejoin when he had mended, despite all Red Jack's encouragement. Though his father was minor gentry, as a fourth son, Tom had opted for the military. And while reducing the number of mouths to feed might assist his brothers and sisters, he had joked when Red Jack and Jessica had come to cheer his recuperation, he did not think his immediate future lay in the churchyard, so he needed a space to consider some new, less hazardous occupation.

"Fine lad," Red Jack had approved as they had left him. "See if he doesn't turn about and re-up after all." But he hadn't. He worked as a factor now, helping Lord Cuthbert run his huge estate. He was indeed a fine lad, Jess thought, looking up at him, and so the other females in the district thought as well. He was slender and tall, with a quantity of straight, bright primrose-yellow hair. His eyes were light blue, his face long and hollow-cheeked. His strong white teeth were thrust slightly forward, but that only served to save his appearance from mere prettiness. For without his ready smile his was a dangerous countenance.

He wore that disarming smile now.

"Now, Jess, confess it all. You would have been off to London without so much as a nod in my direction if I hadn't taken the time to come and see you today."

"I didn't know," she said honestly, "how to take leave of you without causing comment."

He looked puzzled and she went on earnestly, "After all, Tom, how would it have looked if I just announced myself at your lodgings? Tongues would have wagged and Cousin Cribb would have known it moments after you did."

He seemed startled for a moment and then peered closely at her. "What? You worried about gossip? Madcap little Jess? When we've known each other forever? But there's something in what you say," he mused, looking at her as she colored. "How old are you now, Jess? Can't be more than . . . Lord, you're eighteen, aren't you?"

He stood and silently assessed her. He had never thought of her as a woman or even as a female. She had always been Red Jack's little shadow, almost a lad, not quite a girl-child. Now, he saw her face had changed, although he could only guess at the form beneath her loose and ill-fitting gray traveling dress. But as he was something of an authority on the subject of her gender, he smiled again.

"Why, then, you're right, of course. But it's hard of you, Jess, not to think of some way in which to bid an old friend a proper good-bye. Come now, Jess, I traveled all this way to see you off, you can at least afford me the same courtesy that you did that mountain of a dog."

Without another word he pulled her close and, on an amused chuckle, bent to kiss her soundly. He was surprised immediately by a number of things: her warm lips, the hint of a full figure pressed up against him, and her sudden and convulsive jerk away from him. She stood flushed and confused as he gazed down at her with dawning realization.

The idea that the chit held a tendre for him greatly pleased him, though he would forget it by evening. His eyes glinted in the sunlight and he laughed as he brushed her heated cheek with one finger.

"Why, Jess, here's a predicament for me. I'm such a slow top I never knew you'd grown up until now. And now you're about to make a splash in London. Well, keep a kind thought for me and let me know the moment you return."

She was both angry and ashamed that he could read a response from one brief embrace. And even more dismayed to discover such feelings existed within herself, waiting to be released by only a chance touch of his lips.

"Lud, Tom," she answered in her father's best style, "if you've the need to improve your fortunes, I'm never the girl for you. There's Squire's daughter for a guaranteed five thousand a year, and Lord Cuthbert's niece is a good for triple that."

"If a fellow's of a mind to get shackled." He grinned.

"And if a fellow's not, there's Polly from the tavern and Mrs. White from the town, isn't there?" she answered in what she hoped were casual accents.

"Awake on every suit, just like your papa!" he chortled. "But I hear he's left you a fortune too."

Jess turned and began to walk toward the house with Ralph at her heels. The sun was getting high and she would have to leave soon. She could not leave him thinking she was angling for his future attentions.

"As to that," she said lightly, "Cousin Cribb is of the

opinion that it's all a fantasy. I confess I have my own doubts. Could you envision my father sitting atop a fortune for long?"

"Lord, no," he agreed, "for I never met a fellow who could go through money faster. Still, you never know. It's good to be sure. I wish you luck in London, Jess. Lord knows you deserve it," he added, for though he would forget her existence by the next morning and had, indeed, only remembered her leaving for her father's sake, he did wish her well.

As the sun climbed higher, Miss Jessica Eastwood, accompanied by Amy, her uncle's laundry maid, the only servant anxious to see London, waved good-bye to the sole two beings she was reluctant to leave behind. One was already turning his thoughts to his night's sport and wondering in which bed he would awake the next morning; the other would wait patiently and sleep at the foot of her empty bed each night.

When Miss Eastwood arrived in London, she discovered that her own bed would be in a great house rather than in a hotel. For Sir Selby had insisted, to the point of growing quite agitated, that no young woman of his acquaintance would sojourn in a hotel like a homeless waif. Instead, she would be the house guest of his dearest friend, Lady Grantham.

"For she's rattling around in that great house all alone since William died and her two girl's got hitched. Her companion's home on a mending lease and she's delighted at the idea of company," he had insisted as they rode from the coach station through the clamorous, confusing streets of London.

Jessica agreed, both to save dear Ollie's feelings and to forestall an apoplectic fit on his part. For he had grown both stouter and more red-faced since he had come into his honors. Her father would have been appalled at how out of shape his boon companion had grown.

Against all her better judgment, she had agreed. Now, she thought, laying aside her brush and plaiting her hair up neatly again, that she had been right in the first place. For, she nodded at her reflection as she twisted her hair savagely, Lady Grantham had not appeared to go into transports of delight when she had appeared that morning only a few weeks past. That tall, dignified dame had only stared at her new guest and blown out her cheeks in a sigh. She had looked over Jess's head and nodded sharply at Sir Selby. "Yes," she said simply, "you were quite right, Ollie."

Jessica remembered with great self-justification as she blew out her candles that she had been right in all her plans. She had insisted on going to see her father's solicitor at once, but Lady Grantham had argued long and vehemently about her needing new clothes to perform such a simple task in. It was not only her own determination that dissuaded her hostess, Jessica thought as she settled into her bed, it was the clear truth that without being in actual possession of Red Jack's secret legacy, which Mr. Jeffers was still making inquiries about, it would be folly to waste her carefully hoarded funds on such fripperies as clothes. She had made it, she thought righteously, perfectly clear that she would not consider taking money from Ollie for such nonsense. A great deal of wrangling had gone on before her two benefactors had exchanged defeated looks and sighs and agreed with her.

All she had ever wanted was to grow to be her father's companion, to keep house for him in his dotage, to be finally of some use and aid to him. Now she had to discover some new aim to suit her new life. The social whirl of London that her hostess provided did not seem to answer that question.

This ball, for instance, the indomitable Miss Eastwood thought before she traded her confusion for sleep, had not been her idea of a night's pleasures. She had suffered the thing only to please dear Ollie and Lady Grantham, and now they were angry with her for being only what she had told them she was. No matter, she decided, turning to her side, she would be gone in the morning and doubtless they would be as she would be then, deeply relieved and vastly content.

Miss Eastwood gave herself to sleep and dreamed sometime during the night of a vast ballroom where a hundred sheep did an intricate quadrille. And when she laughed at them, a tall gentleman frowned and asked her to join the dance. Before she could answer, she found herself being led into a polka by her father, who changed into Tom Preston before her eyes. So Miss Eastwood, who had spent her night sitting dumbly at Lord and Lady Swanson's great ball, spent the hours till dawn dancing and laughing with sheer joy.

3

The sensation of touch is the first to return to those who have been drowned in sleep, so the first thing that Lord Leith was aware of when he opened his eyes to the shallow light of the morning was the cool breeze that flowed over him. Then he saw the white curtains at his windows billowing out like miniature sails and he lay back upon his bed in contentment. It was a chill wind, but he made no move toward the windows to close them. He always cracked his casements ajar before retiring, no matter what the weather, no matter what protests from any companion who chanced to share his sheets, just so that he might feel the constant reassuring English breeze when he awoke. In that way he was sure to be reminded each morning of his life that no matter where he was, he was at least, at last, no longer in India.

It was the freshening wind that he had missed the most during his seven years in India. In the southern parts where he had spent his time, the air could never have been said to be salubrious. At best, when it was fanned by servants, it could have been said to have been moved, but no more than that. Only once since he had returned home had he let a single little clinging female winsomely coax him into closing the shutters tight. He had woken in the morning suffocated and alarmed, in some still-sleeping part of his mind convinced he was back in Bombay. Since then, the light ladies who wished to spend their nights with Lord Leith had to brave the night's breezes or do without his company. However much they distrusted the evil miasmas said to lurk in the night air, most felt it a fair trade-off and reckoned the gentleman's reassuringly large frame sufficient to protect them from drafts.

This morning the tall gentleman found himself in his own bed and quite alone. His mouth felt fresh, he had no pounding at his temples, nor did he experience dizziness when he swung

33

his legs to the floor and stood upright. So he wondered why he should feel less than perfectly at east upon awakening. He strode to a chair and picked up a dressing gown and covered himself. Sleeping without any bodily coverings was another strange un-English habit he had acquired abroad, though it must be said that few of his night's companions had ever protested against that peculiarity, however alien it might appear to be to them.

When his valet scratched lightly upon the door and entered with a tray and pot of coffee, Lord Leith had already performed his morning's abolutions and was just completing the chore of shaving himself. His valet clucked beneath his breath. Of all the heathen habits the gentleman had come home with, this, in the eyes of his man, was the worst. No matter that the master explained patiently that since he had seen what had happened to an acquaintance of his in Calcutta, whose native servant had gone amok and removed a large part of his master's throat along with his stubble, he preferred to shave himself, it was lowering not to be allowed to perform that task for one's gentleman. Still, the long-suffering valet sighed, on balance he was an excellent master, and no man could have everything.

"Good morning, my Lord," he said as he placed his tray upon a table. "And might I inquire as to whether you had a good evening? As you requested, I did not wait up for you past midnight, but I heard you arrive shortly thereafter."

"Damn," said his master, sitting upright as though stung, "that was it!" Seeing his valet's curious look, Lord Leith permitted himself a smile. "No, nothing you said. It's just that you reminded me of something I had rather have forgotten. Ah, well, best to get it over with. Lay out some courtesy clothes, Taunton, for I've a polite visit to pay before the morning's out."

As his valet hurried to put out fresh neckclothes and silently dithered over a choice between buff breeches or the new blue ones he admired, Lord Leith sat back and frowned.

It had been badly done, he admitted. He had promised Ollie he would do the pretty with his young protégée, but then after one petty insult, he had turned tail and gone off in high dudgeon. It hardly mattered if the chit had the manners of a boor or even if she had possessed the face of a baboon, for he had given his word. Not that he had seen her face, he recalled; he hadn't even given himself time to do that properly before he marched off. Then he had been forced to amuse Prinny upon his entrance and stay with him for the brief moments he decided to honor the ball with. Only then, on the heels of his Regent's departure, could he take his own leave. But not before, he remembered sourly, he had heard that Ollie, his aunt, and the farouche young female they had dragged along with them had themselves departed.

There were extenuating circumstances, Lord Leith tried to tell himself as Taunton helped him into his tightly fitting brown jacket. It had been stultifyingly hot, more crowded than a thieves' den, and both noise and temperature had been a dismaying contrast to the soft London night he had come in from. The cooing and outsized admiration he had been subjected to by the ladies in attendance had been especially annoying in contrast to the reception he had gotten at the last ball he had attended at the Swanson home.

That, Lord Leith thought as he nodded in satisfaction at the fall of his cravat, could hardly have been Ollie's fault. If anything, the memory of that ancient shame should have made him doubly anxious to assist the old fellow. For it had been a decade ago almost to the night when as a stripling youth of nineteen, he had been subjected to far worse insult in that very room.

It had been their eldest daughter the Swansons had been feting then. He had been standing close to the dining room, anxiously awaiting the call to dinner, when he had overheard the chance remark that had changed the course of his life. A potted fern had obscured the speakers, but not their carefully enunciated, cultivated voices.

"Yes," the female whisper had come clear to his ears, "he is extraordinary-looking. Very dashing, quite beautiful, in fact. But, Georgette, my dear, quite ineligible."

"But, Melissa," the other lady, whom he had only just done standing up with, complained, "he is so elegant."

"Elegant, yes," the other had replied, "but far too expensive for you, my love. He hasn't a farthing, my dear. His brother's got it all and Leith has naught but the clothes he stands up in. In fact, I do believe he's come for the dinner as much as he's come to have sheep's eyes made at him. It's

likely that there's more food on that table than he's had to
dine on for weeks."

"Poor fellow, then I'll ask him to dinner," said the other,
pouting.

"Do, and Mama will have your ears, sweet," the unseen
adviser countered before the music struck up to drown out
their laughter.

He had left immediately that night as well, but with his
ears burning and his stomach rumbling. He had felt ill, but
that had nothing to do with the loss of an anticipated dinner,
though, in fact, he had been just as hungry as the observant
female had thought. Now he could smile back ruefully at the
incident, for he had long since learned in more difficult ways
that a full stomach is worth any embarassment. But if it was
youthful folly that had sent him hungry into that lost night,
Lord Leith decided as he dismissed his valet, his leavetaking
last night had been just as callow and foolish a gesture.

It was never Ollie's fault that the country bumpkin he
sponsored had so neatly recalled the other incident to mind
by offering him rejection. Nor would any other excuse do for
it. He had broken his word, whatever the spur, and now he
must make reparations.

Lord Leith waved away any suggestion that his phaeton be
brought around. It was a fine spring morning and the walk to
his aunt's house was not so far that he required to ride. He
would, he decided, send for his equipage later, after he made
his apologies. Then he would take Ollie's young miss for a ride
around the park. He would, he swore as he strode along, go
round and round the damned park until she was dizzy and
every member of the Ton saw what a pretty couple they
made. It would be the least he could do to make amends for
the consequences of his touchy pride. He would ride with the
chit, he vowed, even if she resembled a gorgon and had the
conversational skills of a gnat.

The tall gentleman in buff breeches, brown jacket, shining
Hessians, and snowy neckcloth had to stop every few paces
and greet some of his many acquaintances that were on the
strut. He was now more than merely eligible. He had friends
among the Corinthian set, for he was said to be a sportsman
and a bruising rider. He had acquaintances among the dandies,
who swore by his way of arranging a neckcloth and envied his

taste in waistcoats. He was admired by the intellectuals, as they claimed he could appreciate a sonnet as well as any man and had a rare eye for art, while a few famous rakes called him friend and thought more of his eye for an ankle. In truth, while he was welcomed by all, he belonged to no one set, and no man could claim to know him entirely, though not from want of trying.

It was acknowledged that Leith was a closemouthed fellow who kept his own counsel. His elders approved that not all the admiration of his fellow man or woman seemed to turn his head. For while no sane man could fail to be touched by such constant acclaim and appreciation, still Leith, it was generally agreed, had his two feet on the ground. But it was not so much that as it was that he kept one foot firmly in the past. Not all the sighs, nor all the invitations could erase the fact that he had possessed the same face, form, and wit a decade before, without receiving any such approval. It was only his pockets that had undergone any great change. They, and not he, he often thought, smiling, had grown deeper.

He had gone to Ollie on a long-past morning in search of advice. For he had known that he had nothing, nor any expectations, since his older brother had gone through all his patrimony. But when he asked Ollie which regiment he ought to link up with, his old family friend had sighed. He had said, sadly, that while the army would lose a capital fellow by what he was about to say, in all conscience he must say it. There was precious little lucre to be earned in the service of one's country, and if it was fortune a fellow was seeking, a meeting would have to be arranged with a friend in the East India Company. The army was for glory, Ollie counseled, but the Company was for gold.

Alexander had met with the gentleman from the Company. Ollie's crony eyed him up and down, and said that if he were to be an industrious, clever, and scrupulous young gentleman, he would become a well-to-do young spring in the service of the Company. But if he were to be industrious, clever, and a little less scrupulous, he might become a nabob. For three years Alexander had labored in India. At the end of that time he longed for home and, adding up his accounts, realized that he was well-to-do by anyone's standards. But it was not till four years later that he went home at last, and then he was a nabob.

Now as he strolled the streets of London, he knew he had everything he wanted, almost to excess. He had funds, fame, and acceptability. He had no lady, for he had many ladies. No one friend, but a host of those who would call themselves such. All this amused him greatly. And amusement was the only thing he still sought. After all those years of privation, amusement was the one thing he believed he had earned—and the only thing left that he desired.

Ollie had advised him well and steered him to his destiny. He could do no less than to try to repay his old friend by doing the one favor he had ever asked. *En garde*, Miss Eastwood, Lord Leith thought as he strolled the fashionable street with a wry smile that sent a passing female's hopes careering off in the wrong direction, I shall bring you into fashion, like it or no.

"Take a seat, Alex. I'll ring for tea. Or sherry, or whatever you will," Lady Grantham greeted him distractedly as he entered her small salon and took her hand. "It's good of you to come today, but I, for one, would not have held it against you if you had not. Indeed, Selby left not just two minutes past—I wonder you did not fall over him on your way here—and he was of the opinion that he was in your bad graces. I shouldn't wonder if he's not calling at your house now to apologize to you. Excuse my going on like this, Alex, but I've had such a morning, I cannot think straight."

Lord Leith seated himself, crossed his long legs, and smiled at his aunt.

She was a slender woman past her middle years, tall, as all the family were, with gray hair and a haughty demeanor that was more a matter of childhood training than personal bent.

"Best of Aunts, I don't care how you rattle on," he said soothingly, "I'm just grateful that you didn't decide to part my hair with a table leg when you saw me. It was wrong of me to leave you in the lurch last night and I've come to offer up myself and beg forgiveness."

"It won't do, Alex," Lady Grantham said weakly, sinking back on the chaise.

"Bad as that? Then I'll order up burnt offerings. You're

not going to turn your back on me after an acquaintance of nine and twenty years, are you? Not to mention blood ties and ancestral obligations,'' he went on, rising and going to sit beside her.

"Oh, it's not you, Alex," the lady said, taking his hand and looking at him with fond approval. "You'd have to do a great deal to put me off; in fact, you have, and I've never lost my affection for you. It's that girl of Ollie's. She's driven me to distraction."

"Ollie's girl?" Lord Leith frowned.

"He acts as though she were," his aunt said in agitation. "I suppose it comes from his never having any children of his own, no matter that he says it's due to his respect for her father's memory. But in any case, both he and I have spent the morning trying to put things right. For she was going to leave this morning, she was all packed and ready to call a hackney. I knew Ollie would fly up into the boughs if she did, so I forestalled her whilst I sent him a message. And when he arrived, it took the two of us the better part of an hour convincing her to stay on here. Which she agreed to only on sufferance, for it looked as though Ollie were going to have a seizure. I shot her a look she could not miss, and she at last agreed to stay on. Ollie is a dear friend, Alex. I almost wed him, you know, centuries ago when we were young. But it's as well I didn't, for we have become the best of friends, and that, as you know, would scarcely have happened had we married."

Lady Grantham looked thoughtful, as though somewhere in her spate of words she had said something she ought not to, and her nephew repressed his smiles and said quickly, "Then I've come at a good time. I'll settle matters with Ollie's little filly, butter her up to her ears, and she'll settle down comfortably with you again."

"That she won't," Lady Grantham said dispiritedly, "for it isn't just what happened last night, you know. She refuses to be compliant on all things. She won't dress properly or attend social dos or even accept the fact that she is a young woman. She acts as though she were that wretched Red Jack's son rather than his daughter."

"Red Jack?" Lord Leith asked, and then answered himself, "Ah, yes, the famous father."

"Infamous is more the word." Lady Grantham sniffed. "I speak ill of the dead, Alex, though it pains me to. For I met him many times through dear Ollie. And he was a feckless, reckless dashing fellow who never appeared to wish to grow up. Ollie may lionize him, his daughter may light candles to him, but so far as I could see, he hadn't any more sense than a boy, all his life. After his wife went, he left his daughter there alone in the wilds of Yorkshire, and see how she turned out."

"Then why not simply let her collect her fortune and return to the wilds?" her nephew asked dryly.

"There isn't any fortune, Alex. Ollie is sure of it, and who would know better than he? For the fellow ran through money as fast as he ran away from obligations. The girl's only hope is to marry—if not well, at least securely. But we don't dare mention the word 'marriage' to her. Ollie tried the once, and she almost bit his head off. A wedding don't figure in her plans at all. She'd sooner run off to sea than even contemplate running off with a man. But if she attracted attention, she might change her mind. It's not impossible for even such an unnatural girl to have her head turned by some clever fellow. She has birth, and some wit, I'll be bound, and she might look well enough if we could dress her up a bit. But on that head, as on any other that runs contrary to her belief, she is obstinate."

"Then why not simply wait until she is told the truth," Lord Leith asked reasonably.

"I should be pleased to do so," Lady Grantham complained. "But Ollie is convinced she'll dash back to her home and live wretchedly, for she's too proud to take a cent from him."

"You know, my dear Auntie," Lord Leith said with a melting smile that made the lady feel as though she were at least a decade younger, "I wonder that you believed my asking her to dance would do a thing. For it wouldn't, you know. Not the Beau, nor even the Prince could have turned the trick. You can't bring a half-wild colt to market and expect to sell it as a gentleman's mount."

"Inelegantly put," Lady Grantham declared, making a displeased face at her nephew, "but true, we were desperate.

Don't sneer, Alex, it puts years on you. I suppose you could have come up with a better scheme?"

"I do. And I have," Lord Leith said, rising to his feet. "Now you must go abovestairs and have a nap or a fainting spell, or whatever it is you have to when you wish to escape company, and send the young woman to me. I think I know just the thing to put things right. At least temporarily. You hesitate. Don't you trust me alone in a room with your tempting little visitor?"

"I shouldn't trust you alone with a young female anywhere on the face of this earth," Lady Grantham declared fervently. "But in this case I should feel no qualms at leaving her alone with you in your bath. It's not your seducing her I fear, it's the likelihood of your slaying her. You do have the family temper and she is enough to try the patience of a saint."

"Which I am," her nephew replied, easing the tension in her aspect and causing his aunt to laugh merrily as she rose to pat his cheek.

"Do you remember that, Saint Alex," she cautioned as she swept from the room, her spirits much restored.

Lord Leith wandered about the salon as he waited. He gazed out the window, picked up a figurine, and idly flipped through pages of a volume of poetry that lay upon the table. After several moments he heard the door open. The new arrival entered and stood staring at him as though he carried a writ for her immediate arrest in his hands. He bowed and then smiled at her to put her at ease.

She was, he thought as he took the time to study her in the clear light of day, a very small parcel to have caused such a large hubbub. Not diminutive, he amended, for she was of average height, but there was that about her which suggested vulnerability. Her face, he noted with surprise, was not at all bad. She was, of course, nothing in the style of the females that were the highest style of the day. Those fortunate ladies were imposing creatures, bold, deep-bosomed females with long straight noses, full lips, and great slumberous eyes. This nose was an insignificent member, nothing to take seriously at all. The mouth was not voluptuous, only dusky-rose and well shaped, and the complexion at least milky-white. It was the eyes, beneath the winged uptilted brows, that were the finest feature. For they were large, well-spaced, and of a rich brown that held a hint of fox color in their depths. On the whole, it was a light-boned delicate countenance.

Of the form and hair, Lord Leith was forced to suspend judgment. For the one was concealed very effectively beneath a shapeless lavender garment and the other was pulled back and hidden under some large hideous lace concoction. He thought he detected an echoing fox pelt gleam beneath the cap, but before he could refine longer upon her hair, or rather the curious absence of it, the face he had been surveying took on a mutinous expression and the mouth opened to speak.

"Lord Leith," she said in a foggy but sure voice, "Lady Grantham told me you wished conversation with me, but before you say a word, I beg you accept my apologies. I did not mean to seem discourteous last night and can only plead the lateness of the hour and my own lack of tact. It was not my intention to snub you, please believe that to be the truth."

It was a valorous little speech, the gentleman thought, just what one would expect of any well-brought-up young man. Since its execution dovetailed so neatly with what he had been thinking, Lord Leith smiled again and put up his hand to forestall any further comment.

"Miss Eastwood, please say no more," he said with such sincerity that any close acquaintance of his would have looked at him sharply, "for it is I who should be apologizing to you. I never have understood," he said smoothly, "why it is that Society places the burden of being eternally obliging upon females alone. For if a fellow doesn't wish to dance, he has merely to refrain from asking anyone to stand up with him and he is safe. Whereas a lady has to think of a dozen plausible excuses if she does not care to. Then, if a gentleman is refused, he thinks himself ill-used, unless the poor lady has a splint upon her leg, yet if she is not asked to dance, it is felt that in some curious way she has failed. So you see, I do understand and you must allow me to beg your pardon for being churlish enough to leave immediately upon your refusal."

Miss Eastwood looked up at him with a look of deep, albeit startled, gratification.

He went on lightly, "In my case, it was the heat and a fit of ill-temper which had nothing to do at all with your response. Accept my apologies, then, for I fear I gave you and my aunt the wrong impression."

Miss Eastwood hesitated, for it had not been her aim to accept his apology; rather, she had come to make amends to him. But since he stood there patiently awaiting her reply, she smiled up at him and then put out her hand. "Done," she said simply. After a moment's surprised pause, the gentleman took her hand in his large clasp and they shook hands solemnly.

Lord Leith averted his head for a moment, as though looking for a place to sit, and when he turned back to her, there was not a vestige of a smile remaining on his lips. He asked her straightly enough if she cared to sit and chat awhile, and Miss Eastwood graciously settled herself in a chair opposite him.

They spoke for a while about London and then idly pursued the list of places the gentleman considered vital for a visitor to London to inspect. It was only when he touched upon the subject of the duration of her stay that she interrupted the easy, inconsequential flow of chatter.

"I don't know," she said with a worried frown beginning to mar her white forehead, "for I've only come to see my father's solicitor and collect the legacy he wrote to me about. But now the fellow says that he has to make further inquiries and pursue several leads in his investigation. It begins to appear, he says, that my father left that which he wished to leave to me with friends somewhere upon the continent. Well," she said defensively, although Lord Leith had not uttered a word of censure, "it does stand to reason, since he spent so much of his life in foreign parts, that whatever it was that he put aside for me would not be here in London. But the worrisome thing is that he doesn't know how long it will take to locate this friend, or friends. The whole of Europe is in such upheaval, you know, since Boney's been shackled on Elba. It makes no sense for me to go haring back to Yorkshire when I might get a note asking me to return at any moment. And I cannot say that my presence here is making anyone comfortable.

"You needn't deny it," she said quickly as he began to speak. "I'm not like London misses, you see. I'm a sad disappointment to old Ollie—that is, Sir Selby—and I know I'm driving your aunt to distraction," she added.

"I won't attempt to deny it," Lord Leith replied as her eyes flew wide. "You are.

"But," he said, rising and pacing as he spoke, as though he were speaking to himself, "it would be a bad idea to fly off home, as you said. It would cause Ollie to feel he had failed you if you took up residence in a hotel, as I hear you had planned to do. For both Ollie and my dear aunt are conventional souls, and it is decidedly not conventional for a young female to stay in lodgings when she has either family or friends in town. It is their conventionality that is the clue," he mused aloud.

"I cannot pretend to be what their conventional souls expect of me," Miss Eastwood cried in agitation. "Indeed, I can't understand it either. Perhaps I can in your aunt, but Ollie's known me since I was in leading strings and he never disapproved of me before."

"Yorkshire is not London," Lord Leith said softly, "and you were never grown up before. You are all of nineteen years now, aren't you?"

"Next month," Miss Eastwood said glumly.

"Ah, well, and I expect that Ollie's grown very staid now that he's a titled gentleman," Lord Leith commented.

"Indeed not," she defended quickly. "He's still the best of fellows and I am sorry to trouble him so."

"As I am," Lord Leith said, standing over her and looking down solemnly, "Because he's a dear friend of mine as well. And when he's upset, so is my aunt. So I'm going to poke my nose in where you may feel I should not. But I'd like to offer some advice."

"Please do," Miss Eastwood said, looking up at him anxiously.

The tall gentleman hesitated, then seemed to come to a decision. He pulled a chair up beside the young woman and spoke to her in confidential tones.

"I think the best course for you would be to capitulate.

No, don't grow angry. I don't mean that you must change yourself or your ideals. But much of what they object to is only surface anyway. For neither of them has spoken ill of your manners, or your speech, or even your future plans, have they? I thought not. But they are two old dears, and have grown, as I said, very conventional. All you have to do is seem to comply with their wishes. There is nothing deceitful in that, either to them or to yourself."

He gazed into her eyes and went on, "While you await word of your legacy it can do no harm to put on a few of the frocks my aunt thinks suitable, can it? And how can it harm you to attend a few parties, stand up with a few gentlemen, and seem to enjoy the diversions that they urge you to? It would be only sound tactics. I'm sure your father told you what good fighters the Red Indians were. It was their practice to blend in with their surroundings, to appear to be one with the forest they sprang from. Our poor chaps stood out a mile in their scarlet and were thus easy targets. All you need do, Miss Eastwood, is to put off your scarlet coat, so to speak, and blend in with this London you find yourself in. It cannot change you and it can only please two people who care very much for your welfare."

Lord Leith finished speaking and watched Miss Eastwood carefully. She seemed much struck by his words, and when she looked up at him again, she was pink-cheeked and contrite.

"How very foolish of me not to have thought of it. You are right, my Lord. And I have been quite blind. It is an excellent suggestion. For it wouldn't be for long and it wouldn't be actually deceptive, as you say. Father often said that the best-cut uniform does not make the best sort of fighting man. And while gowns won't make me what they truly wish me to be, at least it will set their minds at ease. Thank you, my Lord, for some really excellent advice."

"If you like, I'll give you even more," he said, rising as she did. "I'll accompany you to the dressmakers and donate my opinions as to the suitability of the garments. Aunt is rather antique in her opinions on the matter of many things, and we want you to do her proud."

"It would be very good of you," she said as he took her hand.

"And very good for you as well," he declared, sensing her

unease and shaking her hand once again, instead of raising it to his lips as he had planned. "Agreed, Miss Eastwood?" he asked.

"Agreed, my Lord," she answered, almost gaily, withdrawing her hand quickly and thinking him the first really helpful fellow she had encountered since she had arrived in London. "And as we are on such good terms, you should really call me Jess, as all my friends do."

"Jess?" he said thoughtfully. "Yes, much better than Miss Eastwood, but I think for our purpose I shall call you Jessica. That will ring much sweeter to conventional ears."

"Yes, my Lord," she answered promptly.

"Yes, Alex." He smiled.

She looked up at the tall straight figure before her and noticed the broad shoulders, the well-shaped head with its aristocratic features softened by careless curling brown hair. An excellent fellow, she thought, who would have made a fine soldier—officer material, in fact.

Gazing down at her piquant face, he thought whimsically that she would have been far better suited if he had offered to buy her a set of colors, rather than a ballgown. Resisting an impulse to clap her on the shoulder as he would any agreeable young man he had just come to terms with, he instead rang for a footman to roust up his aunt so that they could be off to the dressmakers. It would be, he thought momentarily, an amusing expedition, a vastly amusing diversion, this getting an officer and a gentleman into proper petticoats.

4

Lady Grantham, a lady noted for her voluble speech, nevertheless sat quietly as a clam as the coach drove through London. Instead of voicing her firm opinions on all that transpired before her, as was her usual wont, she instead listened to her two companion's animated conversation and kept just as still and unobtrusive as did her lady's maid. For her nephew was a wonder, she thought gleefully, noting how he had her difficult guest entranced by his words. The boy must have learned a thing or two from the snake charmers he had told her he encountered while he was in India, she thought contentedly.

For here they sat, on the way to a fashionable modiste, the very place where she had urged the chit to go for these past weeks; and here the girl sat, complacent and biddable, as though mesmerized by his speech. True, Lady Grantham thought fairly, the girl was doing a great deal of talking as well in response to him, but there was never a refusal, not even one little peep of protest, even though every inch brought them closer to the very place she had formerly refused to even contemplate entering.

Their conversation had to do with naught but politics and horses—which was highly irregular, of course—but for the moment, the girl was agreeable and that was enough.

It was true that Miss Eastwood was prepared to ignore Alex's hand and spring down from the coach unaided, but as he quickly grasped her arm and smoothly assisted her anyway, even that small gaffe was overlooked by Lady Grantham as she stood beaming, waiting to enter the shop. While it was also true that the young woman checked and seemed to shrink within herself as she stepped across Madame Celeste's portals, it was again Lord Leith who smoothed the way by

47

prodding her gently into the room and continuing to chat lightly with her.

It was a well-decorated anteroom, more like a private salon with its oriental carpets, small tables, and gilt chairs tastefully arranged about it, than like a shop. The proprietress herself looked more of a society woman than a tradesperson, but that was what made her reputation among the highest of the Ton, just as much as her creations did. For one never felt as though one were dealing in trade when patronizing this establishment, so much as paying a pleasant afternoon call.

Lady Grantham explained her errand while Lord Leith kept Miss Eastwood in conversation. That, however, he found, was getting to be more difficult, as Miss Eastwood's eyes kept wandering about the room and her hands began to clutch her reticule more tightly. She began to resemble a startled colt and there was an almost imperceptible leap of her person when the stout, little dark-eyed Madame Celeste was introduced to her.

"Ah, yes, charming," Madame Celeste purred. "And if you will come with me, *chérie*, we will proceed to do the measuring and some preliminary fitting."

Madame Celeste swept her hand forward to indicate the way Miss Eastwood should go, but the young woman simply stood as though rooted to the spot and said simply, "Is that really necessary? Could I not just give you one of my old frocks? You could get the size from that, I'm sure."

Lady Grantham froze and Madame Celeste appeared puzzled. But Lord Leith said lightly, "Yes, that would appear to be simpler, I grant you, Jessica. But even though it is time-consuming and rather a bore—(forgive me, Madame Celeste, but although we all admire your creations, the construction of them is a mystery to us)—even I Jessica, have to donate some of my time to my tailor. A proper fit is essential in tailoring, my dear, so you needs must accompany the good woman to ensure one."

Although this speech seemed extraordinary to all the other females present, it seemed to strike the right note to the one it was addressed to.

"Yes," Miss Eastwood said finally, "I can see that."

Without another demurral, Miss Eastwood, raising her chin and gripping her reticule again, marched off toward the back room with much the same determination of a young lady steeling herself to have a tooth drawn, rather than to have a gown fitted.

When she had disappeared into the back of the shop with an eager Madame Celeste in pursuit, Lady Grantham sank to a chair. "Alex," she breathed, "however did you accomplish that? I have explained and importuned, but the chit would have none of it. She is a most unnatural female. Yet you breezed her in here and into Madame Celeste's fitting rooms without a murmur. I have underestimated you, Alex. No wonder you haven't wed," she added in chagrin, "when you can most likely talk any female into anything you choose."

"Would that were so, dear Aunt." The gentleman laughed, settling his long frame into a chair by her side. "I am not so gifted, I fear. But your mistake is to consider Miss Eastwood an unnatural female."

Seeing his aunt's puzzled look, he leaned and whispered, "When she is obviously a quite natural young fellow." He laughed softly as he saw his aunt growing more perplexed, and then he settled back, looking quite pleased with himself.

His expression did not remain so for long, however. Within a short time Madame Celeste erupted from the back rooms in a very agitated condition.

"It is not possible," she said without preamble. "There is no way I can fashion a wardrobe in the dark."

At that Lord Leith smiled even more hugely, envisioning his aunt's protégée's excessive modesty and he asked, "Has she blown out all the lamps, then?"

"No, no," Madame Celeste said in annoyance. "It is not that. I have the form, the size, and the length, but I cannot create a wardrobe without color."

Seeing her patrons incomprehension, she said in exasperation, appealing to Lady Grantham, "But how shall I say green, when it might overpower brown? Or how can I cut that lovely buttercup velvet when it might clash with blond? And the exquisite watered silk I have just received, how can I dare suggest it, when it is so light a cream that it would be disaster, a disaster, nothing less, for mouse color? It is impossible, impossible," Madame Celeste quavered, so upset that she forgot to color her own words with the light French accent she usually affected.

Lord Leith appeared at sea, but Lady Grantham understood at once. "She won't take off that ridiculous cap even for you?" she asked knowingly.

"She won't even consider it," Madame Celeste replied, adding belatedly, "*Dommage,* but my hands are tied."

Lord Leith chuckled. "Tell Miss Eastwood I wish to speak with her. It will be the work of a moment. Send her to me, all will be well then, I assure you," he said airily.

Although she was infinitely grateful to her nephew, Lady Grantham stiffened at his tone. She looked at his amused face and for a brief moment wished to see him less pleased. It was unseemly, she thought, for any male to be so sure of himself. But then she was amazed to see his smile slip and a look of deep surprise pass over his countenance. She turned to look at the apparition that had fulfilled her unspoken desire.

Miss Eastwood came creeping out of the back room. There was no other way to describe her entrance. She walked as one might who was on surface of ice for the first time in their life. But when she saw Lord Leith, she straightened and came forth more boldly. In a moment Lady Grantham saw Leith had his countenance back again, but still his eyes were opened wider than usual.

Miss Eastwood's face was the usual pale oval, perhaps a shade more pale than usual, Lord Leith noticed, but that at least was unchanged. But from that face down, there had been an enormous change wrought in the girl. She wore a blue frock pinned to her lithe figure. And it was lithe, he realized, and far more than he had imagined. For now that she was not shrouded in folds of material, he could see that she was possessed of a lavish figure. Her breasts were high and full, her waist slender, and her slightly rounded hips led to long supple lower limbs. The fashion of the day, which was to seem as though one were only a lightly draped Grecian statue, suited her to perfection. She might have only just, he thought, arisen so from the foam. Except he noted, narrowing his eyes, for the gray concoction of a cap that she still wore upon her head.

Seeing his notice fixed upon the top of her head, Miss Eastwood raised her hands to it. That action caused Lord Leith to drop his gaze a bit lower again, but she was too overwrought to notice.

"I accept that this is not a fashionable cap," she said defiantly, "but surely some more appropriate item can be made up in a material to match the rest?"

"Such as a turban?" Lord Leith asked languidly, in command of his reactions again.

"Nonsense!" Lady Grantham cried. "Even I do not affect one as yet. I am not in my dotage. And only such females wear turbans, child. And you are far too young for a spinster's cap. The very idea is ridiculous."

Watching Miss Eastwood carefully, Lord Leith added wryly, "Of course, Jessica, if you wish to attract attention, to create a stir and cause all eyes to be upon you, we can swathe your head in some material to match each gown you wear. It will cause a sensation. But I did not think you wished to cut such a figure. But, if you insist . . . Madame, do you think you could do it?"

Madame Celeste could not disguise the calculating gleam that came into her eye and said pensively, "But it might become all the rage. I never thought of it, but if mademoiselle wishes to be in the forefront of fashion, I could fashion such—"

"No," Miss Eastwood said abruptly, and then her lower lip began to tremble a bit and she said softly, "I don't want to create a stir, but I should if I uncovered my hair."

Lord Leith cursed himself silently and rose swiftly to his feet. It had not occurred to him before, but of course, the child might have some deformity she sought to keep from prying eyes. Perhaps a scar or some unsightly condition, he thought; he had been a fool not to think of it.

"Madame," he asked quickly, "is there a room to which I can take mademoiselle so that I may speak to her privately? I do not think I can come into your fitting rooms and not overstep propriety."

Madame Celeste led them to her private office. After ushering Lord Leith, Lady Grantham, and the shaken young woman into that sanctum, she closed the door behind them. As she composed herself to greet the new custom that had just entered her shop, she allowed herself to hope that the trio might solve the problem between themselves. They'd come down handsomely for a complete wardrobe, she thought, and s'truth, with such a shape the chit would be a good advertisement for her skills, even if she were as bald as an egg.

"Now, Jessica," Lord Leith said softly as he led her toward the window, "we are all friends. Surely you can show us why you refuse to doff that cap of yours? Lady Grantham and I cannot be counted as strangers and we are only trying to help. And," he whispered too low for Lady Grantham to hear as she seated herself beside the modiste's large desk and tried to read some dunning letters that had been left out upon it, "now that we've got you into fashionable gear, that cap looks most unusual. Just imagine a cavalryman wearing a flowered bonnet and you'll get the general impression. It just doesn't suit," he added, delighted to see a small wavering smile appear upon her lips.

"No, I suppose it doesn't," she agreed sadly.

"No matter what the problem," he urged, "it cannot give us a disgust of you. I've seen a great many things in my travels, and Lady Grantham isn't the sort of female to swoon."

Jessica looked at him curiously, as he went on. "So please believe whatever lies beneath is not about to overcome us. Whatever it is, it will be better if we can see and judge for ourselves what's to be done."

Jessica looked up at his earnest face, read sincerity and deep concern in the now-warm gray eyes, and slowly comprehension came to her.

"Lud," she breathed, "I haven't got horns." She reached up to her cap, removed it, and then began to unplait the tight braids that she had woven. "And I've got hair, if that's what you're thinking. It's only that I know what I've got isn't the thing at all. Cook even said so, she always said it was a pity I hadn't been blessed with conventional locks, and Papa always laughed at it," she went on desperately, never taking her eyes from the tall gentleman's face as he stared incredulously at what she was unloosing.

"Cousin Cribb said that I had the badge of a courtesan. There," she said finally, combing her fingers through the last of the plaits, "you see, it isn't the thing at all."

It was not at all the thing for a demure young miss, he thought as he stared at her in the full light of the window. A whole spectrum of shades of hair were acceptable. Despite the fact that brunettes were in fashion this year, blondes were classic English beauties, and raven-haired lovelies were envied, there was yet enough latitude so that light-brown hair inspired poets. Even so, Jessica's hair was not in style. For as he stood and looked at her, he saw masses of bright deep-red hair falling to her shoulders. Where shadows touched it, it was a dark living auburn; where sun struck it, it sparked blazing fire. It was neither carroty nor a ginger color; rather it was a true and startlingly distinct red.

Cousin Cribb, whoever that gentleman was, Lord Leith thought, had been right. It was the hallmark of a courtesan or an actress. To have such blatantly colored tresses was undeniably exceptional. To even be a redheaded person was thought in some way to be either sinister or strange, as if one were left-handed. There were still some rural places where to encounter a redhead was considered good luck; in others it was deemed bad fortune. Nowhere was it ignored. And, yes, he thought, nowhere was it fashionable.

Yet to see her standing there, wreathed around with that startling mass of hair, was to be enchanted. For the color gave life to her face and brought the hidden fox fire in her eyes to blazing light. Even Lady Grantham was affected. She left off reading a most satisfactory missive addressed to Lady Franklin, requesting overdue bills be paid, to gape at Jessica.

Lord Leith gave up his own reflections, to put up a hand to stop Jessica from braiding it up again. "No, leave it. It is lovely," he said, unthinking.

Jessica seemed to shrink back at his words and at what she caught a glimpse of in his unguarded face.

"It is," he said, recovering his bland, amused expression, "certainly unusual, and yes, you are right, not quite fashionable. But don't say you are suddenly concerned with being at the peak of fashion, and only after being in one of Madame Celeste's frocks for the space of minutes?"

"But I don't want to appear frivolous," she said, looking at him with trust again, "or spectacular, or as one who is trying to attract attention to myself."

Or delicious, he thought, though he said calmly, "Of course not. But to hide it only calls more attention to it. The best tactic, I think," he said reasonably, "is to simply live with it. For what you cannot hide, you must accept. After all, I cannot say that being tall as a treetop is the most comfortable way to go through life, but if I were to slouch or creep, I would look very strange indeed.''

Jessica laughed a little at the thought of this imperious gentleman crouching, and he said bracingly, ''Come, we'll let the good Madame Celeste design some clothes that will suit, and perhaps Aunt's maid can style your hair in some unobtrusive fashion, and we can forget the whole of it.''

''Forget?'' Lady Grantham said, startled into speech. ''Are your wits begging, Nephew? Why, she'll be a sensation.''

''No,'' he said, giving his aunt a look of such force that she shrank backward. ''Not at all. She will only look unexceptional.''

Understanding came to his aunt and she only nodded.

''You see,'' Jessica said, ''I don't wish to be sensational. In fact''—she laughed a little shakenly—''I recall when I was fourteen I concocted a brew that the apothecary book promised would turn my hair dark. And so it did. I was delighted. But each morning my pillow was a bit blacker, and after I combed it, little bits of soot kept falling. After a week, Cook said I looked like a tortoiseshell cat. And so I did. There is no way that the color could stay, you see,'' she confided in her husky voice.

''Well I know it,'' Lady Grantham said ruefully, remembering the results of one experiment when her tresses first began to gray; she had had to keep indoors for a month.

''But your father,'' Lord Leith said as he turned to open the door and began to shoo his aunt away from another promising letter upon the desk, ''as a fellow named Red Jack, he had to have such a mop as well.''

''He did,'' Miss Eastwood said sadly, ''but not so bright as mine. And,'' she added, looking up at him, ''he was a man.''

''Ah, yes,'' was all he could reply, reading the infinite sadness in her eyes.

''A good day's work, Alex,'' Lady Grantham said to Lord Leith as he took his leave of her. ''A dozen frocks on order, and two already in hand. And even now, my own little Nellie is fashioning her a suitable style for that mane of hers. Ollie will be pleased as Punch. You've done well and I thank you. But mind, you're not free yet; you've promised to take her for a ride in the park when her clothes arrive and there's the theater next week.''

"I hear and obey," he said, taking his aunt's hand and touching his lips to it.

"Shan't be surprised if we get her popped off yet. She's well enough in her own fashion," his aunt mused. "Now if you can work your magic to the point of getting her to speak as a young lady should, we'll be at the winning post."

"Is that how a proper lady should speak?" he asked, grinning.

"I'm too old to be proper," she said airily, "and she's too young to be improper. So, if you'll leave off talking of horse-flesh and politics with her for a bit, we may wean her from it."

"And if I do," he said quietly, "she won't speak to me at all."

"That remains to be seen," Lady Grantham said reflectively. "Now be off about your nefarious ways, Alex, I've got to oversee Nellie so there's not a slip. I shouldn't wonder if that little amazon don't stab her with the scissors if she doesn't care for the cut."

The tall gentleman bowed again and took himself off into long shadows of the afternoon.

He returned to his town house, where he relaxed and read through the newspaper and then perused a small heap of cards of invitation that his man had left for him. He dined alone. When he was done, he went to his rooms and changed to more formal evening wear. Pocketing a few cards, he told his man not to wait up for him and went quietly out into the night.

He strolled the streets alone, ranging far in deep abstracted thought, and did not even bother to peer into the shadows at alleyways of the quiet streets, as though he knew that his large form gave sufficient pause to any footpads. Then he straightened and made his way with more resolve back to the fashionable section of town.

Lord Leith, it was reported in some tattle the next day, ornamented Baron Oakes levee for the space of an hour, had a run of luck at Argyles, and then had a greater success at a less-reputable hell a few city blocks away. He advised young Percy Swithin on the purchase of a nag, accepted some unasked-for advice on matrimony from a bibulous Viscount

Travis, gently repulsed the attentions of Lady Travis, and shared a few jests with an old school friend. It was at an advanced hour of the night, when the lights in respectable establishments began to dim, that he made his way to the imposing, dignified white stone house.

A stolid butler showed him in and, taking his cloak, suggested that, as he was expected, he go upstairs. After taking the flight of steps, he paused and knocked upon the door, although he knew he could have walked straight in, since he was at the moment providing funds for the house, the butler, and the person who waited within. Still, he thought wryly, life was made bearable by the inclusion of such grace notes.

The female who greeted him did not seem to agree.

"Alex," she said with delight, opening the door, "why do you stand upon such ceremony? Especially when I have been waiting here for you so many hours?"

"You expected me, then?" he asked entering the bedroom. It was a tastefully furnished chamber; the only feature of it that was not perhaps in the highest reach of respectability was the coloring, which was composed of blatant red and scarlet hues, extending even to the coverings of the huge bed that dominated the room. That, he reminded himself with a smile, and the mirror that was placed in the ceiling above it.

"I always await your pleasure, Alex," the woman said, slipping up to him and reaching on tiptoe to link her hands behind his neck.

He bent to kiss her slowly, and when he reached to enfold her more closely, she skipped out of his arms.

"Do take off your jacket, my dear," she said, laughing, "and do sit and speak with me awhile, it has been ages."

"I have spent an evening in talk, my dear. Is that all you offer me after this 'age' of a week?" he asked, standing quite still and watching her.

She laughed again and came close to bend her head submissively. As she spoke, she began to undo the buttons of his waistcoat.

"We can talk later, then," she said softly, ever compliant, ever obliging, ever accommodating.

It was only later, as he was staring up at the red curtain that concealed the mirror over the bed—for he always insisted she cover it, saying lightly that such sport was for more vain men than he—that he at last did speak to her. She lay relaxed beside him, her dark hair tangled, her plump white body a soft gleaming shape in the dim light. She was not a beauty, he thought idly, looking over toward her. Her hips were too wide, her nose too long, her eyes too close set. For all that she was famous and expensive, she was not an exquisite. Such women seldom were. It was her wit, her cleverness, and her talent that had brought her to the top of an overcrowded profession. The men who sought her out did not seek only beauty, for that was a cheap-enough commodity, but rather the more erotic temptations of making love with a female who might be an intellectual equal. He had met her at Harriet Wilson's and he had gladly become her protector for a while, for such women had only transitory protectors. Neither did he have to rent rooms to house her, for she had her own establishment. He had only to pay a large sum while she was under his protection, and should he shear off from her, there was a long line of others who would be pleased to take his place. In all, theirs was an easy, undemanding relationship.

Her dark hair and complexion reminded him of his long-term mistress, whom he had reluctantly left in India, and her wit amused him. She valued him for his fame, which could only help her reputation as a woman of discretion, and for himself, since it was not often that she had the advantages of having both a keen mind and a comely person embodied in one patron.

He gazed at the bed hangings and thought now only of red. The color seemed to be haunting him today, he realized. To dispel the thought, he turned his head to her and stroked one large hand over her soft stomach.

"Have you ever wished to be a man?" he asked at length.

She laughed again, and rising to one elbow, she looked down at him. In one easy motion, she then swung her body atop his.

This time he laughed till she frowned down at him. Then he gently toppled her over and, propped on his elbows, looked down into her confused face.

"No, no. Not for that mode. I meant it truly. Have you ever wished to be a man?" he asked gently.

She thought for a moment, not quite hiding the calculation in her eyes. Then she answered the false answer that she thought would please him, for she was incapable of any other sort of reply.

"Of course," she said, "so that then I could make love to myself and discover what it is that most pleases men."

He gave the subject up. Clearly, she would always sacrifice honesty for the sake of amusing and arousing him.

"Then," he said softly, "there is no need to trouble. For I shall tell you that which you wish to know."

Then, successful, she gave herself up to his embrace, and unsuccessful, he soon forgot the question.

5

Jessica had not thought much of the idea of a mere amble about a city park; yet, when Lady Grantham had urged her to get into her new riding habit, one that Jessica privately thought a deal too dashing, she had obediently done so. Though a tame canter through the park was not her idea of high adventure, there had been little else to do that offered even that much diversion.

She had sat and read and stood and gazed out the window, or sat impatiently listening for any arrival at the door for three days. Lady Grantham had been pleased enough to see her so docile, thinking her eagerly waiting for her new wardrobe to arrive. Jessica did not think to inform her that it was news from her father's solicitor that she was on fire to receive. Still, when Lord Leith arrived with two fine mounts in tow, Jessica had been happy enough to rush up the stairs and scramble into the green riding habit that Lady Grantham had rhapsodized over. She had done up her hair, pleasing her hostess by agreeing to simply draw it up and allow it to fall naturally in back, and pleased herself by being able to set a comfortably concealing hat atop the whole creation.

Still, the hat was necessary for the costume—and roguish as well, Lady Grantham allowed, for her hair could be glimpsed beneath it. And when the two ladies, for once in charity with each other, descended, Lord Leith expressed himself overwhelmed by how well Jessica looked. Much she cared, she thought as she eyed with delight the roan mare he had fetched for her, for even if she were forced to don a spangled ballgown for the excursion, it would be worth it to be able to exercise on so fine a creature.

She approved of her companion as well, for aside from that one unsettling moment when he had gazed at her and complimented her, he was the best of companions as they led their mounts toward Hyde Park. Amused and cool, he set her at her ease, until the moment when he told her in an offhand, yet determined way that however foolish it seemed, they could do no more than gently canter or walk their horses through the park.

"But why?" Jessica protested. "When it's clear that they would like to fly on such a beautiful day."

"Because," the gentleman said firmly, "the fur would fly when you got back if Lady Grantham heard you were abandoned enough to gallop on the paths. It simply isn't done. One rides in the park to chat, to be seen, and to catch up on gossip; never, I fear, simply to ride."

The park was bright with new spring green. The trees were tender-tipped with new leaf, the shrubbery was putting forth first flowers, and the air was as delightfully mild as a tepid bath. Jessica was toying with the idea of urging her mount to more speed, despite her companion's warning, but two things dissuaded her. One was the knowing look in Lord Leith's eye as he saw her hands tighten on her reins; the other was the simple fact that if she had chosen to race, the only direction her mount could have taken would have been straight upward. For the paths were thronged with riders. Although they rode through verdant open spaces, the area was as crowded as the Swansons' ballroom had been.

There were many mounted on horses as she herself was. But there was also a dizzying array of wheeled conveyances inching along the lanes as well. There were high-sprung phaetons in all colors, simple carriages, and vehicles of every devising, with every sort of crest blazoned on their sides. Masses of people were strolling the pedestrian paths. There was such a profusion of ladies' parasols that they seemed to be some giant sort of radiant spring blooms covering the park, quite dwarfing the beds of actual blossoms. Prides of old persons were arrayed upon the benches in great numbers, and there were even clutches of young children skipping alongside their governesses and nannies.

"You see," Lord Leith said pleasantly, "I was safe in cautioning you. Unless you're of a mind to commit murder, you'll have to be sedate. Terribly sorry about that," he added in an extremely unsorrowful tone.

Jessica laughed despite herself. "I'm not such a madcap as

that. No, I'll go quietly, I assure you, Alex. Only, where's the sense in it? One could get more exercise taking the stairs, I think."

He eyed her quizzically. The well-cut green of her costume complimented her neat figure; the hat, with its ridiculous afterthought of a plume, pointed out the dazzling contrast between her white skin and her outrageous hair. The bright sunlit day seemed to have been tailored exactly to her style. Already, he could see several gentlemen of his acquaintance urging their mounts in her direction. There's the sense to it, he thought, watching one young lordling neatly cut off another in his haste to reach her first. But he only said languidly, "They are taking the air, but that is exactly all they are willing to do with it."

Jessica laughed again and was about to retort to his sally with one of her own when a fresh-faced young gentleman scarcely older than herself angled his mount close and cried, "Leith, I haven't seen you in days, how are you, sir?"

Soon Jessica found herself forced to hold her mount to a stand as one and another and yet another gentleman hailed them. All were duly introduced to her. While some seemed content to chat with her escort, though all the while darting looks at her, she found herself replying to the queries of others. But hardly any sense could have been made of what she said, for no sooner did she begin to respond to one when she had in all politeness to answer another.

Seeing the clot in traffic that they had become and noting Jessica's growing unease, Lord Leith soon put an end to the impromptu meeting by declaring to all, "Come, fellows, Miss Eastwood's mount is still fresh and we have to have some exercise. We must be off, if only to save our necks, for we're obstructing the road. I give you good day, gentlemen."

"But who is she, Leith?" one round-faced gentleman implored in a loud whisper as the others began to drift away. "And what is her direction?"

"Good morning, Turner," Lord Leith said decisively as he turned his horse and beckoned Jessica to follow. He smiled at the young man's disappointment. The fellow would find out soon enough, he thought, and there was nothing like a little mystery to spur an interest.

No sooner had they ridden their horses on a few feet, and

Jessica was about to begin the first of many questions that had occurred to her, than they were hailed by a couple in a light barouche. When they had done with the civilities there, another regal-looking pair caught their attention as they rode past a stationary high-wheeled phaeton. Each time they parted from one group, they were accosted by another.

It was when the sun was high in the sky, and when Jessica thought she would burst with impatience, that her escort cast a knowing eye over her overheated countenance. He motioned her to follow him and they rode on farther and then off to a side trail. Now, when they were hailed, he paused more briefly, begging an impending engagement. As they went on, Jessica noted that they encountered fewer and fewer people. It was not long before she saw to her relief and surprise that they rode quite alone and through a leafy narrow trail. Only the groom that had accompanied them from the house yet followed, at his respectful distance.

"That was neatly done," she breathed.

"Long experience," he answered briefly, and then turning in his saddle, grinned down at her and asked casually, "Should you like to see how well that roan can travel?"

"You know I should," she said angrily, "but I've no doubt you'd have my head if I dared to let her out."

"Ah, but that was in the park proper." He smiled. "And now that you've shown you can be a good little girl, you may have a little gallop. But only so far as the end of the meadow," he added, pointing to a distant line of trees. "I know this is a seldom-frequented lane, yet beyond this secret stretch lies another twist to the fashionables' trail."

But at the words "good little girl," Jessica had given her horse the spur, and they went flying down the trail. It was lovely, she thought, to feel the wind and the air and the movement of the animal beneath her, and it was with regret that she finally pulled up beside Lord Leith. His great black horse had been the faster, and he was already halted and motioning for her to stop when she reached the trees.

She was buoyed up by the pleasure of the exercise. Her hat was askew, her color high, and a vagrant switch of hair had tumbled down across one flushed cheek. He looked down at her sparkling eyes and glowing hair as she laughed up at him and cried out, "Oh, that was capital, Alex."

There was nothing of the coquette and yet everything of the siren in her excited abandon, and without pausing to wonder why, he felt random anger with her in that moment.

"Come," he said so abruptly as to make her wonder if he regretted their lapse of propriety because they had been seen by someone else. But looking about, all she could see was their groom, making his way toward them.

"We have to return," her escort said, regaining his easy smile, "or else my dear aunt will think I have sold you to the gypsies."

"Do you know," she confided as they rode sedately back through the park, "I have always wanted to see how they lived."

"Somehow, I felt sure of that," he replied wrily.

He was about to leave her at the entry to his aunt's house when he caught a look of such sudden sorrow in her eyes that he impulsively gave both horses to the care of the groom and accompanied her inside. She led him into the blue salon. It had been such a shining sunny day that the inner house seemed dark as a tomb by contrast, even though he had always admired the light touch his aunt had with the furnishings of her home.

"Your aunt must be taking a nap; she always does so before lunch," Jessica said as she seated herself in a chair close to the window. "Do you care to wait for her?"

"Of course I shall," he answered, seating himself, even though he had had little intention of doing so a moment past.

"What are you plans for the afternoon, Jessica?" he asked absently, and noting the sadness returning, he realized that he had hit upon her problem, for she sat up and looked at him with approval.

"That's just it, Alex," she said at once. "I have none."

He had great difficulty in repressing a smile. She could not know that most young misses of her age and station would have cut out their tongues before uttering such a phrase to a gentleman. But then, he remembered, so exactly would a young man speak if he were angling to accompany an older fellow upon his rounds.

"What?" he asked with a show of incredulity. "No reading to catch up on, no letters to write, no knitting or stitchery to unravel, no watercolors to paint, or instrument to play?''

"Oh, bother," she said in exasperation, "I've read till my eyes crossed, there's no one to write to since Ollie lives so close, I cannot knit or stitch, and," she said with a sneer, "such ladylike pursuits as painting and playing at music are of no interest to me.''

"Ladylike pursuits?" he asked with interest. "Really?"

He rose and bowed to her, while she watched him with her head to one side in confusion, wondering what she could have said to insult him now. But, she noted with relief, he wasn't leaving, he only walked over to the pianoforte in the corner of the room. He seated himself at the bench and she smiled, anticipating some great fun. For he seemed to be about to act out a charade of a demure young miss at the piano. In truth, before he began, she thought, he had already made his point, for he looked quite out of place seated at the delicate inlaid instrument, with its gilt side panels illustrating nymphs and shepherds at play. He was too large for the picture he entered, his long masculine figure, his riding clothes, and his high boots made a parody of his very pose.

Then nodding toward her, he placed his long fingers upon the keys and began to play. Her smile slid off into nothingness. The music that issued forth filled the room. It was exquisite—by turns, tentative, then tender, then strangely stirring, almost angry, and then at last tapering off into a hushed oblique regret. At least Jessica felt regret when the room was still once more. She had no idea of how long he had played, she had been so intent upon the music. Only when he had stopped did she wonder at his mastery. But now he rose and executed the mock curtsy that she had expected in the first instance. Now, however, she did not smile at his clowning.

"Wasn't it ladylike enough for you?" he asked, noting her stillness.

"I'm sorry," she stammered, "I didn't know. That is to say, Red Jack had no use for such things as music. No, that's not true, he often said there was no sound more valiant than that of bagpipes. But I thought— Oh, dash it all, Alex, I never heard such sounds. And it wasn't ladylike in the least.

Why, I should give all my father's fortune if I could create such music," she said honestly.

"But what would be amiss with it if it were ladylike, Jessica?" he asked, returning to her side. "For I played a somber composition by the German Herr Van Beethoven, but had I played a light one by Haydn or Mozart, I suppose one might say it sounded delicate and fragile and mannered. Is that what you mean by ladylike? For if it is, then where's the harm? Would playing such music make me less the man? And why should manly be so much superior to ladylike?"

Jessica rose and paced a step or two, then wheeled about and faced him. "I haven't said it correctly," she began, her color rising as she mounted her favorite hobbyhorse and rode off in conversation in much the same way as she had galloped across the meadow earlier. "In music, there's no harm. But in life, why, yes, there is. Just think of this morning, my Lord. Why you could have ridden across the park for hours by yourself, but I could not have. And you could have done without a groom as well. And you can take yourself off this afternoon and do whatever pleases you, from riding, to visiting, to gaming. While I, if I am to be ladylike, must sit and sketch or sew and read."

"But, Jessica," he interrupted, "you could visit, or ride, or even game, if you so wished."

"Not without an escort," she said, plunging ahead. "And just think of the advantages you have grown used to, without even considering them as such. Do you have to lay cucumber slices upon your eyes to make them bright?"

She was glowering at him now, and he was so taken aback by what she said that it took a moment for him to begin to laugh.

"Seldom, I grant you," he said, sobering at the fierce look in her eye. "But you don't have to, surely, do you?"

"No," she said with satisfaction. "For when I told Nellie I wouldn't, Lady Grantham did not press me further. But all I am supposed to concern myself with is my face and my hair and my form. Nellie suggests barley water, lemon juices, and milk baths. I vow, my Lord, sometimes I believe that to be a lady is to be prepared for dinner. Yes, laugh," she said bitterly, "but you do not have to undergo such torments daily."

"No, no," he managed to put in while attempting to regain his equilibrium. "But, my dear, I cannot slip into company as easily as a raw egg, either. Just think, Jessica," he said, aping her affect as he rose to face her, "do you have to shave daily, or have your hair snipped so frequently as to feel like an overgrown garden weed? You see that last I refuse as vigorously as you shun cucumbers. And do you have to worry about whether you have a shapely leg? Not at all, for as a female you've always got them covered up nicely enough, while a gentleman's limbs are much remarked upon and always on view."

"There's that," Jessica said consideringly, "for Father used to tell me that in his day a spindly gentleman often had to pad out his leg with sawdust. But surely you don't concern yourself about that, do you?" she asked with disbelief.

"Not at all." He smiled. "I was merely trying to show you that attention to personal appearances is not solely the province of females."

"You don't understand," she said angrily, "or you do and you are just playing with me. I have no freedom. None. I am my father's only child, yet I had to stand and watch a stranger come to take over my home and lands when he died. But had I been born a male, I should even now be master of Oak Hill."

Lord Leith sobered quickly. He placed his hands upon her shoulders and looked into her glistening eyes.

"No. That, I agree, is too bad," he said, knowing, perhaps for the first time, that it was.

"But that is in order to carry on the family name," he began to explain.

She dashed away in incipient tear and broke in, "I know, I understand, but my life is ringed around with such. You have the freedom of all of London, but I cannot even go out and consult with my solicitor, who is an ancient fellow, without an escort. Do they think me such a wanton, abandoned creature that I cannot be trusted with a male, even decades older than myself?"

"No, no, Jessica," he said, looking down at her. "There's right in what you say, but you have it the wrong way around. It is you that could be endangered, not he."

"I should not be endangered," she said stubbornly, resisting now the tenderness she saw in his gray eyes.

"But you are beautiful, Jessica," he said softly, "and as such, you would be at risk."

"Bah, beauty," she said, raging again, her eyes sparkling and her chin high. "That is no excuse and no danger."

He made no reply this time, but only placed one large hand aside her face and buried the other hand in her bright hair on the other side. Then he lowered his head and, holding her lightly, kissed her gently. Her lips were warm and yielding, and soon what was meant to be sweet consolation became a great deal more. She did not pull away, and it was he who finally drew his mouth away from hers, slightly shaken by what he had discovered there.

She stood still for a moment, with her eyes closed, quite silently. He searched for words of apology, since she did not stir, and his hands dropped to his sides. But before he could draw breath, her eyes snapped open and she stepped back a pace and spoke in an unsteady voice.

"There," she said in a broken whisper. "You see? A gentleman can do that, but a female cannot so impose upon—"

"No," he said gravely. "No, Jessica, a gentleman cannot. And I apologize for overstepping the bounds. Please forgive me, but perhaps now you understand what I meant about the danger of beauty. And it is unfair, yes, that your freedoms should be decided by the limits of your physical strength."

"I understand the lesson," she said, turning her head away from him, "and why you gave it. But not why the chance that I might leave myself open for insult should so restrict my life."

"It was no insult," he said, but she raced on, overriding him, "Or why a mere happenstance of birth should allow you to live so free while I am so pent up."

"Jessica," Lord Leith spoke with carefully controlled anger, turning her to face him, "I don't know what conditions prevail in Yorkshire, but even here in London, we know that mere happenstance of birth means primarily that I cannot give birth. It is because you can that you are so protected."

She stared at him as though he had slapped her, while he was startled at himself for what he had said. Even though he knew that there was no other answer he could have given her, he could have phrased it differently, put it better, he realized suddenly.

"And that, of course, puts me in my place firmly," she said bitterly, and then lapsed into silence, although her eyes hinted at all that was hovering on her tongue.

Good heavens, what could she have said now? Lady Grantham thought as she came through the door to see her guest and her nephew standing silently staring at each other. But she was nothing if not socially adept, and so she only asked them if they were to lunch with her. And was not at all surprised at either refusal.

The man behind the huge desk looked up with satisfaction as his visitor entered the dim-lit room. Then, without preamble, he said abruptly, "Took you long enough to come around to see me."

The fair-haired young man did not seem to be discomposed. Even though he had no invitation, he sat down in an available chair, inclined his head for courtesy to the massive woman who sat silently beside the desk, and then addressed himself to the man who had first spoken.

"I had other matters to see to, Mr. Cribb. I'm not at leisure to come and go as I please. I have a position to fulfill."

"And it pays you enough to put into a flea's ear. That's why I summoned you," Mr. Cribb replied.

"You have a position to offer me?" the younger man asked with a fair amount of disbelief tinging his voice. "I was not aware you needed help in running Oak Hill. Is it such a prosperous holding now? I am surprised, between Jess and Red Jack, and I thought the place had been run into the ground."

"Don't come over clever with me," the older man said, motioning his visitor to remain seated. "I've not called you here to exchange compliments. I've a job for you, one that will pay well. Of course, if you're rolling in clover, be gone. For what I say won't interest you."

Since the younger man settled back in his seat again, Mr. Cribb nodded knowingly.

"Thought not. Good family, but no prospects. I may not

be the most-well-liked fellow in the district, but you won't find a more knowing one, eh, Tilda?''

At the enormous woman's laughter, he went on, "And I've blunt. Plenty of it, don't let that worry you. It's true Oak Hill ain't a patch on your lordly employer's place, but I've plenty of silver put aside. I didn't cut such a fine figure in a uniform as my dear cousin did, but I worked hard and dealt sharp all my life, so I'm no pauper. But more's better, eh? That's always been my motto, why just look at Tilda here.''

The young gentleman tried not to, and tapped his foot impatiently.

''Right, lad,'' the older man said approvingly. ''All business, down to tacks, then. You're a gentleman born, Thomas Preston, but your trouble is that there was three gentlemen born before you. You've no expectations. I know it.''

''I don't deny it,'' the fair-haired young man replied.

''Couldn't,'' Mr. Cribb said bluntly, and then he opened a drawer and withdrew a leather purse. He flung it upon the desktop, where it landed with a thud.

''There's coin in there, Tom Preston; not enough to set you up for life, but enough to pay for six months of your wages. And if you do a simple task for me, you'll get another such purse. And if the task is completed to my satisfaction, yet another. A fair wage, eh, lad?''

''Fair enough,'' was the cool, noncommittal answer. ''Who do you want me to murder?''

The older gentleman allowed himself to be consumed with mirth. The enormous woman rocked with laughter. But a moment later the room was still again.

''No. I'm not such a fool,'' Mr. Cribb said, all traces of laughter gone. ''You know my dear little cousin, Jess, don't you?''

''Your ward, yes,'' the young man answered, still coldly.

''Not my ward anymore, there's the point.'' The older man became agitated enough to half-rise from his seat. ''For I've a document from a fine London lawyer says that Red Jack left his daughter to the guardianship of his dear old friend Sir Selby. That's naught,'' he said, sinking down, as though speaking to himself. ''I can get my man of law on that, if need be. But I said to Tilda, 'What's this?' First she's off to collect some fortune her dear pa's left her, and then I get such a letter. Something's in the wind. I can smell money, Tom Preston, and such doings tell me, mad as it sounds, that Red Jack left more than this old house and debts. Something fine someone's trying to diddle poor old Cribb out of. There's where you come in, lad. I want you to go to London and sniff it out. I've eyes. The girl's half-boy, but the half that's female notices Tom Preston, don't it?''

The young man did not bother to deny this. He only sat, his head half-inclined, listening.

"So you are the lad to discover all. I want you to go to London, she'll greet you warmly enough," the older man said as his wife chuckled, "and discover what's toward. There's your first purse. If she's coming into something, I want you to tell me, and there's your second purse. If it's a fortune, there's your third purse. What do you say?''

"I say," said the lean young man, rising swiftly, "that if Jess is to inherit something, it is about time. And as I knew Red Jack and called him friend, I won't spy on poor Jess for you. Good day, Mr. Cribb.''

"Fine talk," his host called after him, "but you'll be back. I'll only give you till tomorrow, and then I'll find another way. So it makes no difference to me. But you'll be back, for you're a likely lad.''

It was shortly before midday, the next day, when the doors to the study swung open and Tom Preston walked in. This time he strode in and did not take a seat. The two facing him seemed not to have stirred since the last inverview. They must, he thought, eat and sleep and, heaven help us, even make love, but they did not appear to have moved a pace since he had last seen them. He wasted no time in conversation and avoided his new employer's eye as he reached for the purse that still lay upon the desk where it had been flung the previous day.

"I'll leave tomorrow at dawn," he said calmly. "You need only to give me her direction.''

The older man did not show surprise, nor did he gloat, he simply handed a piece of paper over the desk and said abruptly, "I knew my man. As soon as you get the facts of it, come back to me. If it takes a long time, send me a letter each week. You don't have to sign it. But find out what treasure it is that Red Jack left. And then let me worry about how to get hold of it.''

"Done," said the fair-haired young man, and without a farewell he strode out of the study, out of the house, and out into another clear spring day.

6

Jessica sat in the salon, awaiting her morning caller. She sat demurely, with a small volume of poems upon her lap, and her feet were placed carefully beneath her chair, toe to toe, heel to heel, neither crossed at the ankles nor tapping with impatience. Her hair was neatly brushed and tied at the back so that the careful fall of locks cascaded against the nape of her neck, their radiant hue a picturesque contrast to the quiet blue of her frock. She seemed all that was correct and seemly. No one could know that she was quaking inwardly like a raw recruit, she berated herself, on the eve of battle.

Her hostess, who sat silently flipping through the pages of a fashion magazine, was well-pleased, if a bit surprised by her difficult guest's new affect. She could not have known how many long and midnight hours had accounted for it. For Jessica had vowed to spend what little remained of her sojourn in London in as quiet a manner as possible. She had finally concluded that in order to do that, she must leave off trying to actually communicate with the persons she was forced to have daily communion with. If she were thereby to be deprived of friendship and honest dealings with her fellow creatures by these efforts, then that was the price she must pay.

Her encounter with Lord Leith had badly shaken her. For she had thought she had found a friend, been sure she had discovered someone in this great metropolis who at least understood her. He had seemed to have taken her just as she had come. But then, just two days past, he had betrayed and insulted her by an embrace and a kiss.

Now, as she awaited his arrival, she felt only anger. But the anger was not directed so much toward the tall gentleman she had thought to call friend, as it was toward herself.

She was even angrier because for the first time she did not fully understand herself.

She had flown off to London to collect her fortune. From that moment onward, events had conspired to put her thoroughly at sea. Now, for the first time, she was forced to realize that she had no idea of what her future was to be even when she got her hands on the legacy her father had left her. She had thought neither of marriage nor of any sort of useful employment for her later life. She was simply unprepared for the future. For all that she had wished to be a boy when Red Jack had been alive, so that she could win his complete approval and go adventuring with him, she found now that she had no desire to be anything but what she was. But what precisely that was, was now the question.

She had hoped at least that she could go on being just Jess Eastwood as she had done all these years. But Jess Eastwood herself had turned traitor to her.

When Tom Preston had kissed her good-bye, she had been shocked by the force of the emotions that the simple pressure of another creature's lips upon her own could cause. Those brief seconds of unexpected response had cracked her image of herself as a sensible young person. Lord Leith's embrace had completed the destruction of the image, for his kiss had shattered the picture completely. At first, she had been coolly observant, wondering at how such a large, strong gentleman's mouth could be so soft, velvet, and gentle. But then, just seconds later, she had forgotten her role of observer and had felt only a strange and giddy welling of her senses till he had left off. She had lashed out at him, thinking his kiss a low unfair ploy to silence her logic and point out to her what an inferior creature she was. Only later, when she was alone, did she realize that, whatever his aims, she had frightened herself far more than he had.

Jessica chanced a glance over at her hostess. Then she repressed a sigh. She would have dearly loved to be able to discuss the matter with another, older female. But Lady Grantham was the tall gentleman's aunt. Ollie would be embarrassed at the very thought of such a conversation, and however much she loved him, somehow she knew that even if her father were still alive, it would not have been a subject she could have spoken of with him. Somehow, she felt sure he would have been disappointed in her. Curiously, the one person she felt would have been best able to advise her was the one person she could never even broach the matter to. And he was expected momentarily.

Thus, when Lord Leith was announced, Jessica hardly knew where to look as he strode into the salon. While he was making his bow to his aunt, she tried to get her countenance under control. At last she ventured to lift an impassive face and greet him so coolly that she was surprised and delighted at her own sangfroid.

"Good morning, Jessica," he said affably enough, with a smile playing upon those well-remembered lips. "Are you ready for our excursion? It's been decided to show you some of the sights you've had to miss while you've waited for Madame Celeste to complete her labors. We've got the marbles Elgin toted back from Greece at the top of the list, then the museum and the Tower, and then just some general sightseeing to round out the day."

"Quite ready," Jessica replied so tersely that Lady Grantham wondered whether the girl thought she was to be dragged to the Tower to be incarcerated there for life. But her nephew gave each lady an arm and they strolled out to his carriage.

It was another mild, sweet spring day, one of a string of days that seemed to have been given to the populace as if in apology for the cruel winter they had survived. The fine weather, the happy mood of the city, and Lord Leith's oblivious attitude soon put Jessica into a better frame of mind. By the time they were perambulating the halls of the museum she was beginning to both forget and enjoy herself.

While Lady Grantham halted to chat with a large elderly female in a violet turban, which Jessica winced to see, remembering that she had requested just such a one not too long since, Lord Leith urged her to accompany him to see a remarkable work at the end of the corridor. Once far from her hostess, Jessica found herself facing a very ordinary landscape, one, moreover, that was to her countrygirl's eye singularly unrealistic, since it showed one lone sheep moodily grazing over a burnt-umber meadow. She gazed up at her escort with a frown of confusion.

"Yes," he said ruefully, "admittedly an inferior work. The

poor animal would starve in a week if he were forced to consume such unhealthy-looking fodder. But it's not the picture I wanted to speak to you about, its only merit lies in the fact that, at the moment, it is deservedly far from any human eye or ear. Look, Jess," he said quickly, surprising her by using the name he had said was not seemly, "I don't wish to spend half our time together apologizing to you. Let's have done with it. I do regret my actions the other day. I misjudged you and I do promise that it will never happen again. Unless," he said jokingly, "you request it of me, of course. But quite seriously, Jess, let us be true friends and have done with apologies. Lord," he said, looking past her shoulder, "I thought Old Rigby would be good for an hour's gossip. Worse luck, they've done already. What say you, Jess? Friends, then, and all past misunderstandings forgotten? For I've your best interests in mind, believe me. Be a good fellow and accept my surrender."

Jessica smiled and quickly breathed, "Of course." Then, when his aunt came abreast of them, Lord Leith took their arms and strolled the halls with them in tandem.

He had confused her yet again, Jessica had one moment to think. For she found herself both vastly relieved at his apology and eager to be his friend again, and yet there was something in his words and new comradely manner that strangely vexed her. But she had no time to brood over her admixture of feelings, for he was an excellent, diverting guide. He kept both ladies in high good humor, being both knowledgeable and amusing. He transformed antique works that were being reverentially and quietly contemplated by others, to exhibits that had them laughing and chuckling together.

Lady Grantham was pleased to see that all was going well again with the two junior members of her party. Once the girl relaxed, she was a charming, genial companion. Though Jessica had never traveled, nor had been properly educated, she had obviously read a great deal and had a quick wit. It was almost, the elder lady reflected, as though she were touring with two merry young blades, there was so much gentle joshing and good fellowship going forth.

They were greeted by a host of acquaintances as they walked, for all wanted speech with the trio that seemed to be having such an immoderately good time by simply viewing the art treasures of the realm. Lord Leith noted with wry amusement that the gentlemen who stopped to chat with him seemed to be in general agreement about what was one of the greatest new art treasures on view. She did look lovely, he thought, with her animated face, supple form, and unusual hair. But when he called her attention to a redhaired female painted by Titian and idly remarked that she ought to consider wearing such garments, she dismissed the gauzy-clad voluptuous figure by saying lightly, "Lud, Alex, I have no doubt Madame Celeste would comply, but that gear looks a bit drafty for an English spring."

Lady Grantham muttered something about "Indian manners" and led them off to the Roman rooms. It was when they were leaving the gallery of statuary that his aunt commented disapprovingly that it was a mean exhibition of sculpture, for there wasn't a one among them that wasn't maimed in some fashion. Since Jessica was at that moment gazing at a woman's figure that not only lacked an arm and two legs, but had also dropped off a nose somewhere in its travels through the ages, she could not suppress a giggle when Lord Leith answered airily that the ancient Romans were notoriously fond of multilating their womenfolk.

"Their men, as well." Jessica laughed, pointing toward a marble depiction of an athlete who lacked sufficient limbs to run the race he was clearly preparing for. "It's no wonder Rome fell when so many of the men lacked the necessary appendages."

"Why, Jess," he drawled slowly, "that's a subject well-bred young persons are supposed to ignore. It does account, however," he said, looking over to the statue she indicated, "for the fact that they were eventually outnumbered here in Britain. Our fellows were not so deprived."

Jessica did not know what he was referring to and was surprised when Lady Grantham slapped at her nephew and said haughtily, "Naughty fellow. If you don't stop talking so warm, I shall toss you out and hire a proper guide." Seeing Jessica's confusion, the lady explained, "Alex would notice, of course, that the poor fellow lacks a fig leaf."

While her two companions laughed and strolled on, Jessica looked back and at last realized that the statue was missing yet another part. Only then did she feel the warm blood rising to her cheeks. Her escorts, noticing how late realization had come to her, exchanged conspiratorial grins.

Amazing, Lord Leith thought as he watched his aunt and her young guest halt to greet a couple of acquaintances and saw how greedily the gentleman eyed Jessica and how oblivious she was to him. It is truly amazing both how little she knows of men, though she apes them in manner, and how much less she cares about her own impact upon them. She probably does believe that all that benighted Roman fellow is missing is his fig leaf. It is rather a shame, he thought, rather as if someone had given a rare Stradivarius to a tone-deaf man. All that beauty and appeal are completely wasted upon her.

It was lucky for him, in a way, he mused, that she was not up to all the feminine rigs, for had she been, his action of the other day might well have resulted in his speedy engagement to be married. Had she set up a screech when he had kissed her, in all honor he would have been committed to her. One simply did not attempt to embrace a respectable young female in her own parlor. But it turned out her reaction spoke more of incipient murder than of wedlock. As for her immediate response, that he had lost in contemplation of his own jolt of surprise. He had not kissed her just because she had looked so tempting. In all honesty, he had, he suspected, been somewhat startled by her railing against the privileges of his gender, and he had used the embrace as a sort of object lesson in the obvious difference between them. So be it, he thought. London is filled with women who do welcome a man's attentions. He refused to contemplate the matter further, and was only glad that he had smoothed over the incident.

Still, he thought, watching Jessica as she spoke happily about the sights she had seen to young John Percy, and that budding rake half-listened to her words and eyed her up and down, if she wants no lover it is apparent that she stands in need of a friend. And that, Lord Leith vowed as he came forward to engage the young man in conversation before his aunt caught the direction of Percy's wandering eyes and gave him a sharp set-down, it is easy enough for me to be.

They spent the bright morning wandering marble halls, causing those cold corridors to ring with their muted laughter. Jessica felt comfortable with her escort once again, but now and again, as she looked up at his unguarded face while he delivered himself of some impossibly amusing commentary, she felt a distinct thrill of unease. But she did not spend too much time puzzling at how someone who was fast becoming a close friend could also be someone she could not entirely trust. For the moment it was enough for her that it was the best day she had yet passed in town. That was, she amended silently, if one did not count the other day in the park. So, even though she had never considered herself a great art lover, she was distinctly regretful when they at last left the museum and stepped forth into a rare spring day.

It was so fine a day that the young man unpacked his bags with haste, not wishing to spend any more time than was absolutely necessary settling himself into his new digs. Since he was accustomed to traveling lightly, it did not take him long to empty his bags into the wardrobe of his small bedroom. He had, he thought as he stowed the last of his garments, paid far too much for so mean an accommodation. But since he wished to present a respectable face to the world, he had to take rooms in a decent hotel, even though being an ex-army man, he would have been content to camp out in any lodgings where there was room to lay his head. It was a lot of blunt to expend, he frowned, but then he did not expect his mission to take long to accomplish.

It took far longer for him to adjust his person to his satisfaction than it did for him to secure his belongings. It was, after all, important to look well, for he knew that his appearance was to be an important tool for his new endeavor. Not that Jess would notice, or care, for she already approved of him, thanks to her half-daft father's influence. His face, form, or attire would not mean a thing to her, any more than they would to any other young lad who recognized an old companion from home. But he could not look rustic in comparison with other gentlemen in London, for she had eyes, even if they were not precisely looking for the same things other females were. There were doubtless relatives or protectors other than Sir Ollie whom he must impress.

Thomas Preston gazed at his reflection with satisfaction. His neckcloth was dazzlingly clean and his jacket fitted well.

His boots, of course, were spotless, for certain habits the army had ingrained were never lost. He did not look at his face at all. That, he knew without conceit, was more than acceptable. It was perhaps, he thought wryly, his greatest asset. And with it, he must make his gamble for his fortune.

There was no other way open to him, he thought, resting his hands upon the dressing table and searching beyond the looking glass he faced. He had stormed out from Jeremiah Cribb's gloomy study furious with the man for thinking he could be bought. Yet even then he had not insulted him or burned his bridges. For even while he fed his rage, a small part of his mind had been working on possibilities. Once he had achieved the room in Lord Cuthbert's great house where he went over his employers' accounts, he had buried himself in work.

But he had not accomplished much when his employer came in and greeted him in the usual hearty, boisterous voice he used with all his employees.

"Still at work, Tom?" he had boomed. "Take a rest, lad, it's noon and even the housemaids are relaxing. Actually, I've come to tell you that you'll have a few days off soon. Lady Mary and I are off to the Midlands for a celebration. That's right," he said as Tom's head came up. "M'niece has bagged herself a husband. Little minx has got Cumberland fast in her net. Quite a catch, eh? You shouldn't be surprised, I recall she even had you in a dither when she visited us here."

"Cumberland?" was all that Tom could answer, thinking the only man he knew by that name was an aged nobleman, at least thirty years senior to the vivacious, giddy young woman he had known, the young woman he had kissed tenderly in secret, the young woman who for all her light-headedness had a fortune as dowry and who had hinted that she would have him as husband as soon as she could convince her parents of her earnest intent.

"Aye, Cumberland," his employer had said with satisfaction. "She's a clever little puss, for he's worth a fortune. No one thought he'd marry again, for he's already got himself heirs. But she sent him mad with jealousy, Mary says, and he finally took the bit in his teeth. It'll be quite a wedding," he mused.

"But he's old enough to be her father," was the only answer Tom could blurt out.

"What's that to say to anything?" Lord Cuthbert had said angrily, annoyed at having his niece's coup denigrated, and assuming the role of employer again, he said abruptly, "He's a belted Earl, and swimming in lard. So, Tom, take off a few days. Don't worry, I'll pay the usual," he added diffidently, to pay Tom back for his presumption.

That evening Tom Preston had gone around to the Oak and Crown and waited for Polly to finish her chores there. He had brooded as he drank and fretted as he chatted with the farmers, laborers, and minor landowners who frequented the place. Much later, as he lay in Polly's bed and she slept soundly, worn out by her labors, both in the taproom and in his arms, he had thought long and silently. At dawn, he had risen and placed some sovereigns by her pillow. That was the way of the world, highborn or lowbred, he thought as he drew his clothes on. He could see no difference between Polly's way of earning extra funds and Lord Cuthbert's niece's mode of ensuring her future. If anything, he thought, Polly was the more honest of the two. And while doubtless the honorable Miss Cuthbert did not have such grimy feet, nor would her sheets be as gritty, she would soon be performing the same services for pay as well.

But he would not, he constantly assured himself as he took his first salary from Jeremiah Cribb and made his preparations to leave. He would not sell himself or his services, he reminded himself as he bade his family farewell and told Lord Cuthbert of the urgent family business he had to attend to in London. Though Jess's cousin thought he was in his snare, he would not be so caught.

He felt better about what he was about to do, he mused all the while he rode the pike toward the great city, than he had about attempting to woo and win his treacherous heiress. For he would be doing Jess a service, while neatly outwitting Cribb. No, he thought now, locking his light-blue gaze onto his own eyes in the glass, Cribb, you do not know your man, not at all. You'll be caught in a trap of your own devising. There's a possibility you've overlooked in your greed. For though I shall locate Jess's treasure, it won't be for you. I shall have it and the blessings of our dear departed Red Jack as well. For I shall marry Jess and you shall have nothing but the taste of ashes in your mouth.

Rather than selling myself, he thought as he straightened and prepared to pay a call on Sir Selby, I shall be doing a sort of missionary work. I won't be a preferred suitor, for I haven't a penny piece. But doubtless there's not a man in London willing to wed such a half-woman, and more to the question, there's not a man Jess would be willing to wed. I've had Red Jack's approval in the past and I've Jess's admiration now, and with all her lack of feminity, I've tasted her lips and they are woman enough for me. And if not, he shrugged as he paused in his doorway, her legacy will buy compensation enough. And what else is there for the poor chit if I don't, he decided as he strolled out, besides a lifetime squabbling with Cribb and the tender affections of a great hound? Then he laughed aloud at his next thought, startling a servant who was polishing the staircase railings. At least, he concluded, I shall be a comrade who shan't give her fleas.

Sir Selby was delighted. Any passerby could see that. He walked alongside his younger companion, his face wreathed in smiles.

"But Jess will be tickled," he said for the third time since he had set out from his house, "she will be beyond everything excited. Not that she hasn't been having a merry old time since she got here, but having both you and I with her will be just like old times, and perhaps she'll leave off grieving for Red Jack now. Not that she's solemn, understand, but I've always felt she hasn't quite gotten over his loss. Seeing us together will remind her of the good times. "Y'know," he said confidentially, "I always agreed with him that you oughtn't to have sold out, but now I see that there's a reason for everything."

"Ah, but I shan't stay here forever," the slender blond young man replied. "I'm only down for a brief visit."

"Any time that you spend here you'll be welcome," Sir Selby said happily. "Put her more at ease."

"How long is she to remain with your friend?" the younger man asked carelessly.

"No telling," Sir Selby said, a slight cloud passing over his face. "That damned lawyer fellow keeps talking about the inquiries he's making and letters he's expecting."

"And," Tom Preston asked carefully, "then she'll have her fortune?"

"No saying," the older gentleman replied. "At first I thought it was all a hoax, but now . . . Still," he went on, shaking his head. "I wish I could believe it. You know what a wild man Red Jack was with money. He couldn't let two coins keep company in his pocket above an hour. No, the best thing for Jess would be for her to get hitched up with some well-breeched fellow."

"I agree," Tom Preston said on a laugh, "but does Jess?"

"There's the rub," his companion said ruefully. "But just wait till you see the wonders Lady Grantham has done with her. And with her nevy, Alex, my old friend, to see her into Society, and with you here now to drop a word or two into her ear, we may yet see her safely off into marriage before she knows what she's about. Would you be willing to talk to her about it?" he added anxiously.

"Of course," the younger gentleman said pensively. "But even if between us all we can get her to see the advantages of that leap, it won't be that easy for an undowered female to make a catch on the marriage mart. For if Red Jack's legacy proves to be a bubble, Jess will hardly be sought after for her fortune."

"Oh, as to that," Sir Selby said dismissively, "I've quite a bit put aside for her, but she's not to know of it, don't you know. All I have for family are a parcel of nephews waiting for my breath to cool before they pounce on my estate. I'd be a poor specimen if I didn't provide for my best friend's daughter. She'll be well-dowered, even if all that mad rogue left her was a button. So you'll have a word with her, will you, my boy? Because for all she looks a female now, I've a suspicion she still thinks like a lad."

"Certainly," Tom Preston said at length, "I promise to make every effort to see her wed."

The two gentlemen paused in the street. The elder espied a carriage that was drawing up to the curbside.

"What fun," Sir Selby said, all abeam again, "for here they come now. Just wait till she sees your face, lad. That will be a rare treat."

The carriage halted and a young boy swung off the driver's platform and raced to let down the steps. Sir Selby ignored the footman that had come from the house to assist the occupants to alight, and gave his hand to a tall elderly dame who greeted him with a pleased, "Hallo, Ollie, you're just in time for tea."

Tom looked beyond the modishly attired young woman who alighted next in an effort to catch a glimpse of the expression on Jess's face as she first saw him. But then, when all he saw was a very tall aristocratic gentleman emerge, he swung his gaze back to the young woman, who was standing stock-still on the pavement, gaping at him.

They stood thus, the slim young man with bright-yellow hair and the fashionable young woman with a blazing crown of lustrous red hair visible beneath her bonnet, simply staring at each other for a moment. Then, with a cry of pure joy, the young woman launched herself into his arms. She embraced him impulsively, then stood back and seemed suddenly abashed at her temerity. A slow flush suffused her face. He, oblivious to the raised eyebrow of the tall gentleman who stood watching them, and to the bemused expression on the elderly female's face, slowly took in the young woman's appearance. She wore a draped walking dress of white with sprigs of green, and her face was radiant, her form so exquisite he was momentarily speechless.

"Lord, Jess," he then breathed, unwittingly repeating words she had heard so long ago and had never forgotten, "you've changed."

And she, as though reliving another scene on another day, looked down at herself and said in a low, hurt voice. "Never say you don't know me, Tom."

"I'd know you, Jess, whatever your getup," he answered with that slow dangerous smile lighting up his lean countenance, and his words neatly overlapping another's so as to obscure and heal them forever. "How could I not? But give me a moment to get my breath back, for I think I'm imagining things. Lord, Jess, you look just as I always thought you should when you grew up. It's a pity Red Jack isn't here. He would be proud of you, you do him honor."

"But I don't know the young man, Jessica," another cool voice cut in, breaking into the intimate conversation.

Jessica turned swiftly and said happily, "Oh, Alex, this is Thomas Preston, a very dear old friend. And Thomas, this is Alexander, Lord Leith, Lady Grantham's nephew and a new friend of mine. I'm sure you two will take to each other. Oh, this is lovely. Now you're here, we'll have the best times together."

The two men stood and appraised each other. Cool gray eyes exchanged looks with cold blue orbs. Each man bowed and each murmured the proper greetings. Neither took their gaze from the other until Lady Grantham, sensing something in the air that was not in concert with the fine spring day, said hastily, "And since Selby here is beaming so much, he's forgotten my name. I am Lady Grantham. And I would like my tea, I'm quite worn out with enlightening myself. Should you care to join us, Mr. Preston?"

"Of course he will," Sir Selby said immediately, "won't you, my boy?"

"Of course," Tom Preston replied sweetly, "with the greatest pleasure."

They mounted the steps to the town house. Sir Selby assisted Lady Grantham and Jessica, who had been prepared to skip happily between the two younger men, found herself at once with her hand taken by Tom Preston and placed lightly upon his arm. As they began to go up the stairs together, she asked at once, "And how is Ralph?"

But Lord Leith, who still stood for a moment on the sidewalk watching the pair, did not hear the low, murmured answer, only her delighted laughter drifting back toward him.

7

Lady Grantham poured the tea for the impromptu party, even though in ordinary circumstances she would have delegated that simple ceremony to her younger female guest. But since she had observed that young woman attempting to do the task on a previous day, she very wisely filled the teacups herself and only suggested that Jessica hand them about to the company. It was simply amazing, the elder woman thought fleetingly as she filled the last of the delicate cups, that a girl with such slender graceful hands should have held the handle of the pot as though it were red-hot, and managed to slop most of the liquid upon her own lap. The thought that such a skill had to be acquired by a young lady, instead of being bone-bred, was one that had never occurred to her until she had seen Jessica leave the simple afternoon tea with skirts asop and face almost as flaming red as her hair. That father, Lady Grantham growled to herself, had much to answer for, wherever he now was, although she thought she could hazard a guess as to his present whereabouts.

They had politely discussed the weather. Tom Preston had been gently but thoroughly catechized about his family and prospects by his hostess. Sir Selby had just begun to explain sadly that he could not lend Tom a mount for his stay in London, as he had given up his stables due to his advancing age, when that young man had put a light note into the general conversation.

"Red Jack, though, I should imagine he would have ridden well into his dotage, Ollie. I used to wonder when I was a lad if he took his horse to bed with him, since I never saw him when he was not astride some magnificent animal or other."

"Oh, he was a rare terror on a horse," Sir Selby said happily as Jessica laughed and assured Tom that her father never even thought of taking his horse into the parlor, much less the bedroom.

"And a lucky thing too," Tom Preston said, grinning at Jessica, "for if he'd gotten that idea into his head, there would have been a rare scene if you had objected."

"He never was one to have his will crossed," Sir Selby reminisced. "Did he ever tell you about the time we ran out of fresh meat in Seville, Jess?"

"Lud, yes," Jessica crowed, clapping her hands together in delight. "I wish I could have been there!"

Seeing her face alight with joy and her eagerness to tell the tale to someone new, Lord Leith leaned forward and encouraged her gently to tell the story.

But it was Sir Selby who told it. He had interrupted so often to correct minor details that soon Jessica gave up and sat back happily to listen to him relate it.

When Sir Selby's memory flagged, either Jessica or Tom would prompt him. So the incident, which had to do with a great deal of confusion on the part of ranking officers, and skulduggery on the part of Red Jack in procuring a stolen chicken from villagers, was spun out for everyone.

Lady Grantham was heartily bored by it, and even Lord Leith wore a polite but strained smile. For, as is so often the case with a well-beloved story that people have shared in their common past about a personage best known to themselves, it was dull and pointless to those who had never heard it before.

When Jessica, Tom, and Sir Selby had recovered themselves, only occasionally wiping their eyes or letting out little fond chuckles, Lord Leith turned to the fair-haired young man who sat beside him and said offhandedly, "Since Selby has given his nags to pasture, I'd be pleased to offer you one of my mounts. I keep a fair-sized stable here in town, and I've a bay that would suit you well, I think."

While Tom bowed his head in pleased acquiescence and began a suitable thanks, Sir Selby cried, "Handsomely done, Alex. He knows his horseflesh, Tom. And you needn't worry, Alex, for Preston here has velvet hands."

Lord Leith was just beginning to disclaim any reservations about the fate of his bay gelding when Tom put in with a little crooked grin and a sidewise glance at Jessica, "Not at all like the time Red Jack gave me the use of his new phaeton, eh, Jess?''

Before another word could be said, Jessica was laughing heartily, while Sir Selby crowed in delight. And once again, the company was treated to another tale of the idiosyncrasies of Red Jack Eastwood, this time told lovingly by the blond young gentleman. Again, Lady Grantham sat with a polite smile pasted upon her face and Lord Leith lounged silently, watching the company.

Another pot of tea was rung for, another plate of small cakes and tea sandwiches was absently devoured, while another and yet another exploit of mad Red Jack was recounted and greatly appreciated by his daughter, his boon companion, and the young gentleman who had lived nearby. Lady Grantham spent the time tapping her toes beneath her chair and thinking of what she would wear that evening. Lord Leith sat quietly, saying not a word, almost as a shadow guest at the party. But he often glanced toward Jessica as she both listened or spoke of her late father. Her face was alight with intelligence and eagerness, her affect was natural and free, and though she used the cant expressions of a young blade, there was nothing either masculine or underbred about her behavior.

It was true, the tall gentleman mused, that she did not simper or giggle, rather she laughed aloud. But there was that naturalness and gaiety in her laughter that took the curse of boisterousness from it. Neither did she bat her lashes, nor dangle a little white hand from a lowered wrist when something personal was addressed to her as a young woman of her years might be expected to do. Instead she grinned boyishly or clapped her hands together. No, Lord Leith corrected himself, not so much the boy, after all, but rather an ingenuous child.

The afternoon was advanced and his aunt appeared bored to oblivion when Lord Leith realized he had scarcely said a word for an hour. Whenever he had attempted to broach a fresh subject or introduce a new concept, the subject of Red Jack had come up again. When he had brought up the topic of Tom doing some sightseeing in town, the answer had to do with Red Jack's tale of his day at Tattersall's purchasing new mounts. When he spoke of Tom's lodgings and asked if they were suitable, the reply contained a reference to Captain Eastwood's accommodations in some provincial French town, a tale that Sir Selby had quickly fastened upon. There seemed to have been, Lord Leith perceived, no conversational gambit that Tom Preston did not link up with Jessica's absent father. And all the while, Jessica herself had been oblivious to all else but the teller of such tales.

At last, when shadows began to lengthen and his aunt seemed in almost a trancelike state, Lord Leith took advantage of a lapse in the conversation. He bowed slightly, and, smiling, said, "Although it has been delightful, I really must be off now. Don't forget, ladies, we have an engagement at the theater tonight. It's time to show off your new finery, Jessica, as promised."

As he turned to leave, he added as almost a thrown-away suggestion, "Oh, Preston, should you care to accompany us?"

"I'm sure it would be difficult to get tickets at this late hour," the blond gentleman demurred quietly as he too rose, "but I thank you for the offer."

"But Alex has a box," Sir Selby said heartily. "Come along, Tom."

"Oh, do," Jessica put in quickly. "It will be great fun. You must come, Tom."

"Why, then, I must," he said, shrugging helplessly, "or Jess will commandeer me, as her father used to. Remember the time I did not care to go fishing, Jess?"

Under cover of the laughter the remark sparked in both Jessica and Sir Selby, Lord Leith took his leave. While the other three sat down again to continue the tale, Lady Grantham accompanied her nephew to the door.

"Lord," she sighed, and then asked in an under voice, "What's being presented tonight, Alex?"

"*Othello*, and then a farce, I think," he answered absently, looking past her to where Jessica was gasping with laughter, never noting his absence at all.

"Fine," his aunt said, rolling her eyes in the jubilant trio's direction. "I only pray that Jack Eastwood never chanced to see it anywhere in his travels, or else we shan't hear a word that's being said on the stage all night."

Her nephew laughed and then took his leave. Interesting,

he thought as he strolled toward his town house, thinking about the odd tea party and the newly come loquacious chronicler of the late Captain Eastwood. Interesting, he thought as he remembered Jessica's brown eyes lit with laughter and her gaze fastened on Tom Preston's lips as he spun out every word. Interesting, but no, not amusing.

The frock was sea green and the soft kid slippers were dyed to match the exact shade. Lady Grantham had given Jessica a jade pendant to wear as well as a pair of ornately carved jade ear bobs. Now Jessica sat and twisted her head this way and that, as if in silent negation. But as she sat alone in the downstairs salon, awaiting her hostess's entrance, there was no one she could have been arguing with.

Rather she was testing the effect of the unaccustomed weight of the stones upon her earlobes, and soon she was indeed shaking her head in a determined negative gesture. Her ears felt leaden and she scowled fiercely. Thus the first sight that Lord Leith had of Jessica as he was announced and shown into the salon, was that of her angry frown.

"But I haven't said a word as yet." He laughed lightly. "Is it that you disapprove of my waistcoat?"

"Oh, no," she said, bringing her head up with a guilty start and staring at him. "Indeed you look fine." Then after she stared at his closely fitting black jacket, white neckcloth, black evening trousers, and muted gold waistcoat, she added, "Very fine, indeed, in fact. But it is these ear bobs your aunt has lent to me. She says," Jessica said, rising and coming close to him so that her whisper could not be overheard, "that for a lady to go out of an evening with her ears bare is for a lady to go underdressed. But I cannot like it, Alex, I cannot. A small pearl or a tiny gold ring might be unexceptional. After all, when I was very little a governess saw to the alterations of my ears so that I might wear such, before Papa came home and gave her marching orders. But these huge pendants! It feels as if I had great weights hanging from each ear, and when I turn my head, they swing against my cheek. It's very foolish, now I think on it, to have to wear such ornaments at all. It's rather like wearing a bone through one's nose. We had a book at home with pictures of savages and they wore bits of jewelry in the most remarkable places. I cannot think it is quite civilized to hang gems from one's head, can you?'' she asked quizzically and with such a solemn face that he could not ascertain whether she was serious or not.

"But it looks very attractive," he said. Seeing how his words seemed to displease her, he added, "Still, if it is not in in your style, I'm sure she would understand if you return them to her."

"That she would not," Jessica said sadly, "for I tried to tell her, but she only said I'd get used to them in time. I won't, you know," she said wretchedly, turning from him. "But you are so used to seeing females hung with fripperies, I doubt you'd understand."

"But I do"—he smiled, watching her as she shook her head slightly and frowned again—"for I am sure that I should dislike wearing them. But it is your century to do so, you see."

She ceased shaking her head and turned a questioning face toward him.

"Why, yes, I should have to had worn them a few hundred years ago. Cavaliers did, as a matter of course. Then you females took up the fashion, so we had to give them up."

Jessica glanced up at the aristocratic visage above her and thought for a startled moment that he was right, and further that it was a pity that it was so, for such ornaments would suit him very well. There was that of the courtier in his bearing and in his refined features. She recognized suddenly that there was, in fact, an aura of elegance about him that must have been from some more graceful, antique age. It was a subtle insubstantial thing, ranging from the clean, faint, delightful essence of sandalwood that emanated from him, to the cool dignity of his bearing. She could almost envision him with ruffles at his throat and a great gleaming barbaric jewel depending from one ear to balance the civilized cast of his face. The thought disturbed her and she shook her head as though to clear it.

He took the gesture to be a denial of what he had said and so added idly, reaching out to gently finger one trembling jade pendant, "You are right, though. I'll admit that I don't repine because I cannot bring them back into fashion. But don't look so stricken, Jessica. Just ease one off during intermission and I'll say that there's something amiss with the clasps. I'll wear them for you for the rest of the night. In my pocket, of course," he added as she understood and laughed.

"You don't plan to divest yourself of any other adornments, do you?" he asked hopefully, raising one brow wickedly.

She stiffened, then relaxed and giggled. "And if I did, there would still be room in your pocket and to spare," she said merrily. "I know this frock cost the world, but there is so little of it, it seems a waste of money."

He threw back his head and laughed as she turned a pirouette for him. It was true that the gown was cut low and was of simple design. But, he thought, she needed no bows or ruffles or tucks to compliment her supple form. He was admiring the way her red tresses fell in long coils against the nape of her neck when she stopped her spin and said sincerely, "I want to thank you, Alex, for you were quite right. I seem to have made both Ollie and your aunt sublimely happy simply by allowing myself to be tricked out in fashionable togs. And it's really not so bad at all. Just a trifle chilly." She grinned conspiratorially.

They were laughing together when Lady Grantham, clad majestically in hues of silver, came into the room. She nodded approvingly at the way they seemed to be getting on but overrode her nephew's compliments as she told them to stir themselves so they could get to the theater when the curtain rose. "For I cannot tolerate latecomers," she confided to Jessica as they settled in the carriage, "since they arrive late only to attract attention, and it always galls me that they succeed, since there is no way to see the stage without seeming to stare at them as they walk past your line of vision." As she went on about the inequities of being a captive audience to fops and dandies, her nephew sat across from Jessica and grinned at her. Jessica, wrapped tightly in her lush cream velvet cape, looked out the window at the sights of a busy London evening. She frankly gawked at the procession of coaches that stood in line, pulling up to the theater.

For one moment Jessica felt unease well within her. London by day no longer frightened her, but this glittering gaslit, torchlit night with all the fashionables congregating, dismayed her. She drew in her breath when she alighted from the coach, and almost clung to Lord Leith's sleeve. But then she saw Sir Selby and Tom waiting in the press of people, and greeting them and hearing their familiar voices above the babble, she felt her breath go out again.

Tom looked very different, she thought as they came forward to greet her. She had never seen him looking so fine back at home in Yorkshire. His black evening clothes were almost spectacularly set off by his buttercup hair, and when he laughed, his strong white teeth shone in contrast to his outdoorsman tan. Jessica saw several young ladies casting surreptitious glances toward their party, and thought that if the young females at home could but see Tom now, they would never have let him go past the outskirts of town. Sir Selby was correctly dressed, but now so portly and distinguished that she could scarcely recognize the wild Jolly Ollie that she knew from her childhood. Still, they were her friends, even if they were done up in their new finery. Just as she was still Jess, although masquerading as Miss Eastwood. She relaxed as they ranged around her. As she entered the theater with them, she recalled her father had always said that no matter what the circumstances, wherever one's friends were, one was always at home.

Thus she did not mind when she was ogled as she mounted the broad staircase to Lord Leith's box. Nor did she tremble when fashionable gentlemen raised their quizzing glasses not only to better see, but to better salute the new beauty in their midst. She did not turn a hair when several gentlemen rose to get a better glimpse of her as she settled herself in her plush chair in the box, and she did not stammer when several young blades presented themselves to be introduced to her even before the theater darkened. For Ollie was there, his voice bringing back memories; and Tom was there, again telling her how proud her father would have been to see her; and curiously, the silent presence at her side of the tall gentleman she had only recently met was reassuring to her. She was among friends, she thought as the lights dimmed so that only the footlights flared and danced in the darkened hall, and she was safe and secure as she had not been in years.

After the featured vocalist's presentation and at the first intermission, Lady Grantham suggested that Jessica accompany her to the ladies' withdrawing room. Jessica did not see the broad hint of a gesture her hostess gave to her nephew as he rose to see them from the seats. She did see, however, the press of persons that seemed to be awaiting them on the broad balcony as they walked from their curtained box. Withdrawing seemed to be the furthest thing from Lady Grantham's mind as she greeted dozens of acquaintances and as her nephew performed endless introductions. It seemed that Jessica had met an even dozen Lord Thises and curtsied to a score of Sir Thats before Lady Grantham finally decided to act in earnest to achieve the private precincts of the ladies' withdrawing room.

Lady Grantham seemed strangely pleased as they settled in their seats once again. But the only comment she made, and that only when Lord Leith bent over to whisper, "Note the golden ear bob on the fellow, aren't you all over envy?" to Jessica as Othello strode out upon the stage, was "Hush, I can hear you speaking any old time, Alex, but I can hear this fellow Kean only at the theater."

As soon as the second intermission came, Sir Selby, upon receiving an urgent stare from Lady Grantham, rose to escort the two women for "a stroll to stretch the legs."

As the three left, Thomas Preston arose and made as if to follow. He was about to leave the box when he was forestalled by a touch upon his sleeve. Lord Leith smiled and motioned for him to reseat himself.

"A word," the tall gentleman requested softly.

Lord Leith sat back and contemplated Thomas Preston. They had had no chance at private speech since they had met in the lobby of the theater, and now Lord Leith asked idly as the blond young man took his seat again, "How long shall your business keep you in town, Mr. Preston?"

After a pause the fair-haired gentleman smiled and answered sweetly, "I expect until it is finished with."

Lord Leith's eyes narrowed, yet he went on in the same light, bored tones, "I imagine you were staggered to see the change in Jessica."

"No," the other man answered, looking directly at him, "Not really. It is only a change in her attire. Jess is the same as she always was. I have no doubt that once her business is finished, she'll return home and put off these London airs and graces."

"But surely you know," Lord Leith replied, "the plans Ollie and my aunt have for her?"

"I have known Jess since the days when she was only a shadow of her father. I doubt those plans will mean much to her," Tom Preston replied, not looking at his host but rather letting his gaze idly rake the crowd below.

"I thought," Lord Leith said, "that you had agreed with Ollie that marriage was the only answer for her future."

"Oh," the gentleman said, letting his cool blue eyes wander to the other's face now, "but I do. Still, my Lord, you must agree that she would never make a conformable, contented helpmeet for such fellows as you all are throwing in her path?"

"No," Lord Leith answered, "I don't agree at all."

At that Tom Preston threw his head back and laughed. "Lord," he gasped, "Then you cannot know her very well. She strode before she could walk. She never played with dolls but at tin soldiers. The villagers used to say that when the midwife raised her by her ankles at birth, Red Jack asked, 'Is it a boy?' and when the answer came 'No,' he sighed and said, 'Well, we'll make do.' I'm not saying," he went on pensively, "that she was by nature a boy, but her father filled her head with tales of how perfidious females were, using her mother as example. Now, I can recall from my infancy what a beauty that one was. But the fighting that went on between the two of them made the Captain's battles with Napoleon pale by contrast. No, Red Jack made sure that Jess would not follow in those little footsteps. How you got Jess into such fashionable attire, I do not know. But I do know that it is only surface. Good Lord, she cannot sew, or spin, or, more to the point, even flirt or dally with a man, nor does she want to."

Lord Leith only sat and watched Tom Preston as he laughed again and went on, "She'll only bat her eyes if she's got a cinder in them, and all she's looking for in a man is good fellowship."

The tall gentleman did not share in the laughter; he only waited till his guest had done speaking and asked quietly, "so then you think she can never wed?"

Laughter fled from the light-blue eyes, and Tom said with a slight smile that did not signify amusement, "Now, I never said that. I only said that Jess would never suit a chap who was looking for the usual. And these young lordlings you're casting in her way will never do. She needs to be married, yes, for her own protection, because it's clear she's not fly to the time of day. Still, she's neither a female nor a male. She needs a husband who will protect her but who is willing to let certain female duties go by the board.''

"Duties that can be performed by others for her husband elsewhere, if necessary?" Lord Leith asked mildly.

"Perhaps," the blond gentleman said, now looking levelly into his inquisitor's eyes, "for, as I see it, you've Jess in a shop window, like a manikin on display. Oh, she's lovely all right. Very tempting, in fact. Yet, even if by some magic you get her acquiescence and if you persuaded some besotted fool into wedlock with her, that's all he'd find in his marriage bed . . . a manikin. Now, that's hardly fair, either to Jess or to the fellow you hope to catch, is it?"

"But some fellows wouldn't mind, you think?" Lord Leith asked quietly.

And just as quietly, Tom Preston replied, "No."

The tall gentleman stirred and then lounged back in his chair and asked carefully, "Because of charitable instincts, or in the cause of good fellowship, or"—and here he paused and then added pointedly—"because of other compensations? Such as her father's legacy?"

The other gentleman stiffened in insult and rose to his feet as if to conclude the discussion.

"I think I understand you well enough," Lord Leith said dismissively, rising to his full length as well. "even though I must tell you I don't agree, and," he added with emphasis, looking directly at the other man, "I don't approve."

"But, my Lord," Tom Preston asked coolly, although his face was rigid with suppressed anger as he looked insolently over the other's tall form, "why should you protest? You are only participating in this ruse with Jess as a favor to your aunt and to old Ollie, who, if truth be told, only wants to rid himself of the responsibility of her future. You don't want her; the case is that no one ever did, or will, once they see beyond the facade. And as you have put her up on the market, I cannot see why you cavil when you find yourself with a buyer."

"Is 'buyer' the right word?" the other gentleman asked musingly. "Now, I had thought of this transaction you suggest more in terms of a donation."

"So it's that I don't have a feather to fly with," the blond young man said angrily. "I am candid about it. Why should you care? You stand in no obvious need of compensation. And as for females, you already have the pick of the town. But as to Jess, I can see to her welfare, and I will at least treat her well."

"And with loving affection," Lord Leith said sweetly.

"Ah, love," Tom Preston said with a sneer. "What a sentimental fellow you are, my Lord. How many men marry for love? Or women, for that matter? I did not think you a man to dwell on fairy tales. Affection is more than most marriages have."

"Yes," Lord Leith acknowledged, "I see your point, Preston, but still such an arrangement as you suggest would be sort of a half-life, would it not?"

"No more than for half the population," the blond gentleman said dismissively. "And if it is affection that is missing in the 'arrangement' you are so discreet as to hint at, why, that would be subject to change in time, wouldn't it? Upon demand, of course," he added with a mocking smile.

"But whose demand?" the taller gentleman asked quietly.

The only answer he received was a slow smile, which turned broader as Jessica reentered the box with Lady Grantham and Sir Selby.

"Lud," Jessica said as she dropped into her chair, "what a press of people! And whatever am I to do with all the invitations I have been given? Now, carriage rides through the park might be good sport, and if someone wants to pay a morning call, I can see that might be pleasant too, but afternoon teas? And sewing circles? And, Lud, that little Miss Protherow invited me to go shopping with her! 'For bonnets and gloves,' she said." Jessica gave out a little laugh. "And when I suggested we have a look around at the new bits of blood at Tattersall's instead, I thought she'd drop. Although," Jessica added more soberly, daring a glance over toward Lady Grantham's wrathful countenance, "I truly did not know females were not admitted there, my Lady, until Ollie told me so. And though the thought sunk me, I agreed to go to the Pantheon bazaar with her to purchase fans and ribbons, someday,'' she concluded on a grin.

Thomas Preston laughed with Jessica and shot one triumphant look toward Lord Leith. But that gentleman only took his seat quietly. Just before the lights dimmed for the farce, Sir Selby noted Jessica casually passing something into Alex's hand. What he could not see was how, throughout the last of the evening, while the audience was laughing, Lord Leith absently fondled the small objects in his waistcoat pocket. Nor could Lady Grantham know that her antique jade ear bobs lay cool and hard against his breast.

The gentlemen politely refused refreshments as they saw Lady Grantham and Jessica safely home again. Then each of the party bade the others farewell with a show of amicable good feeling.

Lady Grantham gave her guest good-night and went off to solace herself with a Minerva Press novel about evil noblemen and endangered young women chasing each other about drafty castles. Sir Selby went home to sink into a steaming hip bath and brood about whether the purchase of a discreet corset might not now, finally, be in order. Thomas Preston tarried for a while at an establishment known as The Coal Hole and after several hot rum punches took himself to another establishment that had no name or sign blazoned over its portals. The young female he tarried with there bore no name either, or at least none that he could recollect in the morning, though he did recall her proportions and her skill with a particularly unique configuration, with a fond smile.

Lord Leith went directly to Crockfords, where he played lightly and thus did not lose too heavily before he became bored with his turn of luck. Then he strolled to the white town house he so generously supported and soon found himself surrounded by familiar red curtains and furnishings again. It was as much to evade that color as anything else, he later thought, that at an interesting moment he idly requested the red draperies that covered the ceiling mirror be finally drawn back. But it was much as he had suspected. The effect took more from his performance than it aided, since what it inspired in him was, much to his lady's annoyance, more laughter than lust. And thus it was not long before he was home again, immersed in a hot bath as sedately as his mentor Sir Selby was, but with never a thought to corsets at all.

Jessica found herself as wakeful as any of the gentlemen, but with no place to go except the length of her room. Had she been home, she would have gone to the kitchens in search of a chicken leg or a biscuit. But being an obedient guest, she dismissed her maid and prepared for bed in her usual fashion. Only in one thing did she deviate from her custom. For a moment, after she had divested herself of her gauzy chemise, she turned and stared steadily at her unclad form in the looking glass. Almost, she began to linger there, but she laughed lightly, threw on her night rail, and shook her head at her own foolishness. Still, somehow, here in London, in Lady Grantham's stylish chamber, the curving figure that Jessica so briefly reencountered in the glass was not such a stranger. Rather, she thought aimlessly, as she courted sleep with pleasant thoughts of treats that might be in store for her before she went home again, there was a certain sneaking pride in knowing that one could look just as one ought. If one wanted to, that is, she amended.

And then she thought of Tom and Ollie and the good times they would share, and thinking of that, she began to slip easily into sleep. It was the thought of Alexander, Lord Leith, that caused her eyes to snap open again. It was the fact that he still held Lady Grantham's precious ear bobs, of course, that brought his pale face as clearly to her as the face of the full moon that peered through her window. It was that which made her squirm in disquiet at the memory of him, she reasoned, and that which banished sleep for her until the swollen moon had soared up and over her window to sit upon the highest towers of the town.

8

The sky was solidly gray and there was a dank, humid feel to the air in Lady Grantham's salon, but even so Lord Leith said as he took his chair, "It cannot rain forever, three days seems sufficient for any deities' purpose. Doubtless tomorrow will dawn fine and clear. So don't fret, Jessica, for your face is cloudier than the day."

"Oh, it's not just the rain, although I admit it lowers me to be so pent up, it's that I'm anxious for Mr. Jeffers to arrive and to hear what he has to say. I know," she said on a sudden smile, "it's very childish to be so excited, but when we got his message yesterday, I knew I would not be easy till I had spoken with him. Do you think he finally has all the information, Alex? For if he does, I can be on my way again."

If he does, Lord Leith thought, looking at the anxious face before him, Ollie will have a spasm, for nothing's been decided for the chit yet and there'll be the devil to pay if she decides to just up and leave here. But all he actually said, in a languid tone, was, "We'll know soon enough. He and Ollie will be here straightaway, and as soon as my esteemed aunt feels she's dressed correctly, we'll hear all. Although," he added, "that may take another week, for Aunt's ideas of dressing for an occasion, even an occasion as mundane as receiving a visit from a solicitor, are very baroque."

Seeing her apparent nervousness as she rose to peer out the window again, he said softly, "There's no hurrying a thing by worrying, Jessica. Come sit and tell me how you've been occupying yourself these past days. I can't believe that a mere spot of bad weather would stop the redoubtable Miss Eastwood from completing her rounds."

Jessica sank down into her chair again and at last laughed. "No, not in the usual way, it wouldn't. But there's nothing to do for ladies in London when the weather's off-key. Oh," she said quickly, "there are visits to pay and visits to endure, but you know, that's a dead bore."

"A dead bore?" he mimicked. "When Ollie tells me your sitting room's been clogged with all manner of fellows anxious to make your acquaintance? Why, I hear this chamber's been graced with the likes of Jeremy Tutton, and Lord Greyville, and even dashing Harry Fabian and his bosom beau Charlie Bryant. Why, I understand the house has been a thicket of young sprigs of fashion, all paying homage to you."

"Homage?" she complained. "All they do is sit and goggle, or prate on about all sorts of nonsense. Jeremy Tutton was no wit, Charlie Bryant no chin, and Tom says that Harry Fabian's in the basket and looking for a wife with a fortune, and Lord Greyville's in the market for matrimony only because his uncle insists."

Lord Leith concealed his distaste and asked offhandedly, "Tom Preston says so? Have you seen much of your old playmate, then?"

He caught the quick flush that came to her cheek and watched closely as she turned her head aside and answered quickly, "Why, yes. But we had all sorts of other plans, for riding and for sport, but the rain's put an end to that."

She looked very well today, he thought inconsequentially, in a demure white muslin frock, with her hair combed back neatly, almost as an obedient young girl just out of the schoolroom, not at all like the siren her dramatic evening dresses made her appear to be. But there was a certain sadness about her, an air of a lost child that clung to her.

To lighten her spirits, he asked quietly, "Are you homesick, then, Jessica? For it wouldn't be extraordinary if you were. This is, after all, your first trip away from home."

She looked up at him with a start and then said slowly, "Why, yes, I suppose I am, at that. But not homesick for home precisely." She laughed in embarrassment and then added, "For there's no one there to miss, save Ralph, and he's only a great hound that I've had since I was a girl, and it would be foolishness itself to pine for a dog."

"Not at all," he said sincerely, "for when I was first shipped off to school, I found I missed my spaniel Flanders far more than I missed my mama and papa."

Jessica turned her full attention to him. It never had occurred to her that this complete, aloof, fully grown fellow had ever been a child capable of devotion to a dog. So there in the rain-dimmed salon she questioned him about his home, and his youth, and his absurd spaniel Flanders. And in return she heard about his late bookish father, his deceased invalid mother, his spendthrift elder brother, and even about his terrier Beaux, who had replaced the lost Flanders.

The time went by quickly and she was sorry to hear him say finally, in his soft deep voice, "So you see, Jessica, there's nothing new in feeling the lack of a beloved dog. Although I do agree, Ralph seems rather too large for my aunt's salon. And I daresay he would find her bed far less a welcome refuge than he would expect."

She giggled at the thought of Ralph nesting down on Lady Grantham's great gilt canopied bed, and at the same time felt gratified at how he understood that Ralph would in all truth probably attempt to do just that. But then, realizing how ungrateful she must sound toward her hostess, who was after all, his own aunt, she added, "But there is a great deal here that is very nice, indeed." And surprised herself by listing all the inconsequential childish pleasures she had discovered in London, everything from the ease in taking frequent hot baths accompanied by sinfully lavish transparent amber slips of scented soap, to the pleasure of being able to merely stroll to a booksellers, to the ridiculous wonder of discovering gas lights in the streets.

But he laughed at nothing she mentioned, only shook his head sagely in agreement with her and won her over completely by saying, when she had done, "Still, none of those things quite makes up for the loss of freedom or for the inconvenience of not knowing quite how to go on, do they?"

"Just so!" she breathed in concurrence and was about to embroider upon that theme when a great bustling at the door signaled that Sir Selby and the solicitor had at last arrived. Jessica went to greet him and for a fleeting moment surprised herself even further by momentarily regretting the arrival she had been awaiting so eagerly, chiefly because it had interrupted so pleasant a conversation.

They all settled down in the salon again to await Lady Grantham. They made polite desultory conversation and

Jessica restrained her impatience, although she eyed the solicitor's bulging briefcase in much the same way that Ralph might eye a juicy leg of lamb.

Another fifteen minutes passed before Lady Grantham, at last attired in garb she thought suitable for the occasion, entered the room. After an exchange of nervous pleasantries, Mr. Jeffers, finding every eye upon him and every pleasantry passed, cleared his throat and placed his briefcase upon an end table he had drawn up before him.

He was a small rotund gray man with a bassetlike wrinkled face and drooping eyes, and he cleared his throat and then asked Jessica, "I take it you have no objection, my dear, to my divulging what I have discovered before your friends? I know Sir Selby is your legal guardian, and though I know Lord Leith and Lady Grantham's reputation and discretion, I want to make sure you feel they have your confidence."

Jessica's bosom swelled with self-importance and her spirits rose. She nodded acquiescence immediately, for she found her throat too dry to speak.

Mr. Jeffers extracted a great many papers from his case and perused them quickly while Jessica's heart thumped so loudly she feared everyone could hear its heavy beat. Lord Leith sighed and thought that the fellow would have been far better suited for a life upon the stage than within law offices. At last Mr. Jeffers put down the papers and spoke to them all.

"There's something there," he said portentously. "I confess I originally had thought not. But I sent out letters of inquiry and received some interesting answers. The sum of it is," he went on as Lord Leith restrained an impulse to leap up and throttle an answer out of him and Jessica did the same, "that your late father did leave you a legacy, my dear. And one that he makes clear can in no way be considered part of the entail. You see, it must be proven that anything a man leaves to his heirs must be a thing that he has not himself inherited, if he wishes to leave it away from the main estate. Thus your father made it plain that he came into some funds whilst in the service of his country, invested those sums in an object of great virtue, and left it specifically to his daughter."

Jessica let out her breath in a sigh so great it was audible.

Mr. Jeffers looked up at her again and then said, "But, my dear, there is one catch to it."

Even Kean, Lord Leith thought, had never had so rapt an audience as those in the salon who waited upon Mr. Jeffer's next words.

"Perhaps out of fear of his legacy being considered part of the entail, perhaps because his life was so untimely cut off, or perhaps because he did not trust his next of kin to do the right thing by his daughter's legacy, Captain Eastwood left this object in the care of friends . . . upon the Continent."

Mr. Jeffers sat back after his deliverance with a smug smile upon his face.

"What is it?" cried Sir Selby while Lady Grantham asked, "Where is it?" and Jessica sat mute as a mouse.

"As to what it is, I cannot say, as I have not yet seen it," Mr. Jeffers said slowly. He was about to expound upon this when he caught Lord Leith's eye. There was so much incipient murder in that cold gray gaze that he hastened to say, "But I do know that it is in safekeeping in the hands of one Corporal MacKenzie, late of His Majesty's service and now dwelling in Brussels. I shall go there, present the proper papers, collect it, and follow up on certain other inquiries that I have made. And," he added, now that Lord Leith had withdrawn his intent surveillance and seemed to be totally self-absorbed, "I do have other business to attend to on the Continent for some other clients, so that I can set out within a few days."

Jessica at last broke the silence. She sat forward upon her chair, with her hands clasped together and blurted eagerly, "What day, sir? For I shall be ready to leave whenever you say."

For the first time, Mr. Jeffers seemed discomposed. He gave Jessica a shocked look and said hastily, "You misunderstood, my dear. There is no need for you to disturb yourself. I have said that I shall leave and see to the acquisition of your legacy almost at once."

Jessica's face assumed a mutinous expression and she said clearly and loudly, "But it is my legacy, and my father who has left it. I can save a great deal of time and effort by accompanying you and collecting it."

"All you have to do, my dear," Mr. Jeffers said in bewilderment at her militant tone, "is to sign a paper giving me that right, as your man at law. It is not necessary for a young girl to travel upon the Continent at this dangerous time. I am here," he said with a broad satisfied smile, "expressly for that purpose."

"But I shall go," Jessica said coldly. "It makes sense for me to go. For Red Jack surely distrusted anyone else. Oh, Ollie, can't you see the sense it makes?" she cried, looking beseechingly at Sir Selby.

Mr. Jeffers began to go on about how difficult it would be for a lady to travel in the places that he must frequent, while Lady Grantham drowned out his protests by speaking loudly to the general company about how foolish it would be for a young chit to go haring off to the Continent in search of a mare's nest. She was in full spate about the danger of Bonaparte leaving his island kingdom for another go at the English and painting vivid word pictures of murderous Frenchies and sneaking Spaniards when she paused to hear her old friend, Sir Selby, say in reply to Jessica's heated plaints, "Oh, well, Jess, I suppose you have the right of it. And Red Jack wouldn't want you to be a pudding heart. But I would have to go with you, for I wouldn't forgive myself if anything befell you. And you're right, I do know the turf, as a matter of fact. I even know old MacKenzie, fine fellow he is, too. But you'd have to give me time to get my affairs in order."

"But I'm ready to set out within the week," Mr. Jeffers protested, aghast at a possible delay and possible complications on his journeys.

Lady Grantham arose quietly and walked to her nephew's side. She noted that he was already white about the lips. But still she bent and whispered briefly in his ear. He rose and nodded; then, with icy aplomb, she interrupted the argument between Jessica and Mr. Jeffers.

"Mr. Jeffers," she said loudly, "Selby, would you both come with me for a moment? I believe my nephew desires some private converse with Miss Eastwood. Jessica," Lady Grantham said with a tinge of warning in her voice, "I suggest you hear what Alex has to say before you say another word. We shall await you in the rose salon."

Without a further syllable, Lady Grantham, by the sheer force of her personality, commanded the startled Mr. Jeffers and the surprised Sir Selby from the room with her. Jessica stood in confusion, looking at the papers Mr. Jeffers had left strewn upon the table in his haste to obey his imperious hostess. It was suddenly silent in the room and she looked up to find herself the object of as direct and pitiless an angry gaze as she had ever encountered. Instead of quailing, her natural courage and her anger at having been so summarily ordered to attention caused her to glare angrily back at the tall gentleman standing before her.

"That," Lord Leith said frigidly, letting each word fall and drop and echo before he added another, "was as selfish a piece of business as I have ever seen."

"Indeed it was," Jessica said, relieved at finding him in agreement with her. "Can you imagine that the fellow wished to leave me out of the entire business, as if I were a witless calf?"

"Indeed?" Lord Leith said in a dangerous low voice. "I had thought that only a witless calf, as you so succinctly and correctly put it, would force an old fellow like Selby out of his deserved retirement and ease and send him jaunting about Europe like a fellow half his years. And send him to that folly by playing on his insane commitment to an old comrade-in-arms. Have your wits gone begging, girl?" he thundered, now rounding upon her as she shrank back from the blazing fury in his eyes. "Do you think he quit himself of his career only because he came into a title? Why, the fellow is old enough to be your father's father. Did you never see how junior a partner your father was to him, or that your father himself was no mere lad? He himself should have sold out years before the wars put paid to his career."

Jessica had been at first genuinely shocked at his accusation, and then momentarily shamed at the truth he spoke, which she had never perceived. But then she had heard words of disapproval directed at her father, and all reason fled. She wheeled upon her attacker and cried, "He was a soldier! And a soldier never quits when there is need of him. And if Ollie wants to come with me, if Ollie thinks he can, why are you so ready to bundle him into an old man's slippers? So that your aunt may have an escort to all her London frolics? Because they are so much more important than my future?"

The tall gentleman stared at the wild creature before him.

She was shaking with rage and her eyes glistened with unshed tears of fury. Her intensity stirred him to step toward her. But then, he recollected himself and began rather more calmly, "See here, Jessica. I meant no disrespect to your father. I only meant to say that Selby is too old for such larks, and it's unfair of you to ask him to accompany you—one, when there is someone your father already entrusted with the task, and two, when you know that Ollie's sense of duty must make him agree, even though it might be uncomfortable or even dangerous for him to do so."

Jessica rapidly acknowledged the truth in his words, but only to herself. For, like so many people, she did not enjoy being told that she was in the wrong, and being Jessica, she could not easily back down from the heights her rage had sent her towering off to.

"Then," she said, quickly raising her chin, "he need not go with me. I can go by myself. With Mr. Jeffers, by myself, I mean."

"And what," Lord Leith asked sarcastically, "do you think your dear Ollie will say to that?"

"Aha," cried Jessica, quite unfairly, even to her own ears. "Then you fear he will ask you to go in his stead and you don't wish to inconvenience yourself."

As this thought had not occurred to the gentleman, but as it was quite logically just what Sir Selby would expect of him, Lord Leith felt defensive and so roared back, "There is no need for a young female to go jaunting off to the Continent on such a sheer pretense. And no sane one would expect to do so."

"There!" Jessica said with grim satisfaction, tears of anger brimming her eyes. "There we have it! For if I were a young man, it would not be at all out of the way for me to accompany my man of law to secure my own fortune."

"But you are not, however much you may pretend to be so, a young man," Lord Leith shouted.

"And how I wish I were, so that I could show you a thing or two," Jessica countered in an attempt to startle the tall implacable figure before her and only succeeding in losing all her control. She grew even angrier at the tear that coursed out of hiding from the corner of her eye.

Lord Leith was transfixed to immobility by guilt and by

the conflicting desires to either tenderly brush away that tear with hand or lips, or cause her to shed several more; he knew what would happen if he dared to even gently touch that flushed cheek. But he only sneered and said with a touch of spite that shocked him to the core as he uttered it.

"And how I wish you could as well. But you are safe enough from me in your woman's skirts, even though you are hardly fit to wear them."

"Forget my skirts," Jessica challenged him.

"And if I did," he said angrily, goaded beyond discretion, "I think you might learn at last how pleasurable it is to be a woman."

Lady Grantham, Sir Selby, and Mr. Jeffers, seated uneasily in the rose salon, had long since given up any attempt at concealing their interest in the muted sounds of battle that came from the direction of the small salon. Thus it was that they greeted Thomas Preston when the butler announced him, with an absent, distracted air. And soon there were four persons craning their ears to hear the far-off deep masculine rumbles and the occasional high shrill of a woman's voice.

"The young people," Mr. Jeffers said at length in an attempt to state the unstatable, "are having a disagreement."

That remark caused all present to turn and stare at him until he fell to contemplating his fingertips.

They were startled to some degree when the sounds of a fragile object shattering reached their ears. Lady Grantham only nodded knowledgeably, "I have only Limoges and Wedgwood in there. Nothing of any consequence."

After a longish silence, the door to the small salon opened. Jessica walked calmly across the hall to where the others waited. She was ashen and her eyes were red-rimmed, but she held her head high, and simply said, "I have decided that it makes no sense for me to accompany you, Mr. Jeffers. Please advise me as soon as you discover anything. I have a bit of the headache, ma'am, and desire to go to my room. Godspeed, Mr. Jeffers, and good luck. Oh, hello, Tom, I'll speak with you later, I hope."

And having delivered herself of this message, she curtsied and, head held regally, ascended the staircase to her room.

As the assembled quartet recovered themselves and waited

for one of their number to find the presence of mind to utter something acceptably noncommittal, Lord Leith appeared in the doorway. A thundercloud sat upon his high brow and his gray gaze was shuttered. He spoke coldly, through clenched teeth.

"Good morning. I fear I have let the hours go by without noticing, but I have a pressing appointment the other side of town. I'll take my leave now. And, oh, Aunt, my regrets. In my haste to leave and in my clumsiness, I overset a vase on the mantel. I'll send a replacement."

"The Meissen vase," Lady Grantham said thoughtfully. "I'd forgotten that one."

"Just so," her nephew agreed. "Your servant, ma'am. Good day, Selby. Mr. Jeffers, good hunting. Hail and farewell, Mr. Preston."

"Well," Mr. Jeffers commented into the silence that came after Lord Leith's departure, "I think I shall take my leave now as well. I'll write, of course, as soon as I get word of what Captain Eastwood's legacy precisely constitutes. And," he added more feelingly to Lady Grantham, "I shall try to perform that task with all possible haste."

It was only a little while later, after Sir Selby and Tom Preston had strolled off together and Lady Grantham had sat motionless in deep thought in her sitting room, that she rang her bell and requested her maid to invite Miss Eastwood to take tea with her. It was shortly after that that the two sat quietly at a deal table in the same small salon that had echoed to so much wrath a while earlier. Now all was calm, every last shard of the ill-fated vase had been swept away.

Jessica was pale, but composed, and as she accepted her teacup from Lady Grantham, she said in a small voice, "In my excitement at hearing the news this morning I fear I overset a handsome vase of yours, my Lady. I shall be sure to purchase you another to replace it."

"No need," her hostess said airily, "for Alex has already confessed to oversetting it himself and he shall take care of it."

"Oh, shall he?" Jessica said with a heightened look in her eyes, but then she recollected herself and subsided meekly again.

"If I had known how heated your discussion would

become," Lady Grantham said mildly, "I should have put you in the ballroom. It's in disuse just now. Everything's in dustcovers and there's not a breakable object left in it."

"Oh, ma'am," Jessica said suddenly, putting down her teacup, much to her hostess's relief, for she had noticed how much that delicate object had trembled in her guest's hand, "I am so sorry. It was quite unconscionable. But I have never gotten so angry in all my life. No, I recall that the chandler's son took a sweet from me when I was eight and I shied a candlestick at him. But never since then, I swear it. I confess I seized up the vase, but then the enormity of my action struck me and I dropped it in horror. It would have been both cowardly and dishonorable to strike an unarmed man," Jessica concluded with only a trace of her usual spirit.

"But Alex could have availed himself of other bits of crockery to defend himself with," Lady Grantham said smoothly.

"It is very kind of you to jest, ma'am," Jessica grieved, "but it was undoubtedly bad of me to so lose control and I am heartily sorry for it."

"And Leith never loses his temper," Lady Grantham said obliviously. "It must have been the weather, so lowering to the spirits."

"No," Jessica said miserably, "it is my fault, and I apologize. And shall to him as well."

"It's not at all a bad thing," the elder lady mused as she picked up a strawberry tartlet. "Alex has been so serene since he returned. Too complacent. Swift water carries one over bumpy places, but it's time he left the shallows of his life."

She was so pleased by her poetical phrasing that she sat and munched her sweet and seemed not to notice how downcast her guest had become.

"You know," Lady Grantham ruminated, "it is very bad Ton to display unladylike anger. But then, I am not at all sure that to be completely human is very good Ton, so I, of course, forgive you." She smiled, her angular features taking on the elfin look that had so enchanted the departed William and the young Ollie all those years ago. "And then again," she added slyly, "one knows, of course, that those persons one cares the most deeply for incite the highest passions of every sort." But seeing no response to this daring suggestion, she went on more prosaically, finishing off the tart and picking up a sugared nut cake, "Then, too, I suspect you have a bit of your father's temper to contend with. You two must have been a sight when you set at each other."

"Oh, no," Jessica breathed. "Why, Father and I never disagreed."

"You didn't?" Lady Grantham asked in surprise. "Why, then, child, you must be a saint. For your father was the most provocative fellow."

"Oh, no." Jessica laughed weakly. "You musn't believe all the stories Ollie tells.'"

"It has nothing to do with those tales," Lady Grantham said placidly, attacking her nut cake with concentration. "Why, I confess, each time I met him, he seemed to deliberately try to set my back up. He thrived on altercation."

"You knew him?" Jessica asked in astonishment.

"Of course I did, my dear," Lady Grantham answered, puzzled at Jessica's surprise, "didn't you know? No? Well, of course I did. Each time he came to town he put up with Selby. The two of them would veer about the town, raising cain. I knew him, after a bit, almost as well as I knew Selby. But, I confess, we never did get on well. He had, you know, no use for women."

Jessica's thoughts tumbled about her. She said in dazed fashion, "But he never mentioned coming to London at all. I never guessed. I thought that he came home and then went straightaway back to his unit. How often," she asked suddenly, "Did you see him?"

"At least several weeks each year," Lady Grantham said lightly, and then chanced a look at Jessica's stricken face. "Oh, my dear, I am so sorry. I thought you knew. But then, a grown man would find little to keep him in the country long. Having no wife at home, I mean. And however much he disliked our gender, he did not live as a monk. He did not care for females, but he never gave them up. That is to say . . . How very difficult," Lady Grantham breathed to herself.

But her guest scarcely heard. She had only seen Red Jack at brief intervals, she had always thought of those stolen weeks as his only surcease from war, she had never guessed that he would have been in the country and would not have come to see her. Or that he would have left her, lost and longing for him, while he cavorted in London.

"It makes no matter," Jessica said brightly, although her hostess noted her lower lip trembling. "You are quite right, there was nothing at home but several thousand sheep and, of course, me."

"My dear," Lady Grantham said, putting down her cup and turning to Jessica, "such is the nature of men. Oh, dear, that is not at all what I wished to say. Not all men, of course. My own William was as constant as the Northern Star, and your father, of course, had no need to be constant, having no one to be constant to. Good Lord, I am making little sense. What I think," she said bracingly, "is that you should stay at home today and quite forget that little shopping expedition we had planned. I'll take your maid, Amy, with me, as she knows your requirements and sizes. And you just stay at home and rest. And then we'll have a nice long coze when you're more easy in your mind."

Jessica nodded her agreement, still lost in her own thoughts, but as her hostess began to rise, Jessica suddenly remembered and said, "But, ma'am, Thomas Preston said he would call again today."

"I should be back by then," Lady Grantham said imperturbably. "And if I am not, simply leave the door to the salon open and have our butler, Bartholomew, within calling distance. For propriety's sake, you know. Although I understand that Thomas is as family as you, still there are the conventions to attend to."

After Lady Grantham left, Jessica sank in thought, rising every so often to complete useless circuits of the room. So when, after only a little while, which seemed to have spun out into an eternity, Thomas Preston was announced, she flew to her feet to await him.

When she saw his face, not dangerous at all now, but dear and familiar and bearing a look of such concern, she quite forgot herself. She was no longer the grown-up Jessica Eastwood, but rather little Jess, Red Jack's shadow, seeing an old and trusted friend. She gave one sob and cast herself into his waiting arms.

He stroked her hair and hushed her incipient storm of tears. There was nothing of the lover about him, nothing of the vital attractive male she had half-feared at their good-bye at home. He was only Tom Preston now, her father's favorite, and now her father's stand-in.

"Why, Jess," he said softly, "whatever is the matter? Tell me, please. Whatever has overset you so?"

But as she did not fully know herself, she said nothing, and only stayed there, close in his arms, feeling that here at last, for the moment, was surcease from all her confusion.

And he held her close and smiled to himself as he rested his cheek against her glowing hair and inhaled the honeysuckle fragrance of it, and he soothed her and told her that all was well now, for he was there.

9

The door to the salon stood open so that the gentleman caller could be seen from any part of the hall by the omnipresent Bartholomew. The butler could then perceive if anything were to go amiss. It was not as though anyone truly expected a gentleman to go mad with lust and give way to beastly appetites if left alone with a young female. But since even that unlikely eventuality had to be forestalled, Society decreed that it was not proper for any man to remain in seclusion with any young lady of breeding if there were no responsible female in the house—unless, of course, they were related by blood, law, or marriage.

However, Miss Eastwood, without even having heard the butler's cautionary cough, after only moments of tearful indulgence upon Thomas Preston's shoulder, decided for herself that she should not remain so close to him. Not for reasons of propriety, but because of her sudden realization that she was behaving very missishly.

She soon eased herself away from him, returned his handkerchief, and sat and composed herself. Then she explained in disjointed phrases the cause of her tumultuous greeting. He listened quietly, his face and body still, though his mind ranged far.

At length, when he felt he had heard the whole of it, he sat across from her and asked, "So Leith forbade you going to Brussels to collect your legacy?"

"I suppose he did, in a way," Jessica answered, cocking her head to one side as the notion caused her to slow her jagged breathing. "Though not in so many words. But blast it, Tom, it is true that if I went, Ollie would feel bound to as well, and he is, after all, no longer a youth."

"Of course," the blond gentleman answered quickly, "but then, I suppose Ollie could have deputized me to accompany

113

you, and you know that I should have been glad to lend my aid.''

Jessica sat up straight. That thought had never occurred to her, and her face lit with enthusiasm, but after a moment's thought she drooped again. "Still, Alex is right, perhaps Mr. Jeffers can act more swiftly by himself. 'He travels fastest who travels alone,' you know. And it is true that the fact of my skirts would have meant that I could not be quite the easiest of traveling companions for Mr. Jeffers. He's such a stuffy, pompous fellow. Why, you know I'd be glad to bed down anywhere just like any hale campaigner, but he would doubtless want to slow his steps or book accommodations ahead just because of my sex.''

"There is that,'' Tom acknowledged, "but then I could have perhaps reassured him on that head. With two men as protection for you, he might not have felt so constrained.''

"But it's done,'' Jessica said miserably. "I cannot go back on my word now and I've told the fellow to get on with it.''

"Are you sure it is too late Jess?'' Tom asked quietly. "I can pack and be ready to go within the hour. You know, old soldiers travel light. And I'm sure you can as well. I don't think you're the sort to worry about whether you have enough matching gloves or whether your slippers need their buckles reshined.''

Jessica chuckled softly and he went on with a bit more enthusiasm, "You'd like the Continent, Jess. And it would be a good change for you. In fact,'' he said, watching her face brighten, "it would be far better for you than sitting here in London, worrying yourself to flinders. It's always better to go out and meet one's fortune than to sit by and let others do for you.''

Jessica held her breath and then let it out slowly. "It is too late. For there's the bother of convincing Ollie and Lady Grantham and Mr. Jeffers and, Lud, Tom, I'd have to have another go-round with Alex. No, I can't go back on my word in any case. But I wish you had spoken when you were here earlier, Tom, for it is a capital idea.''

"I, too,'' he said savagely. He rose, turned his back to her, and then wheeled around on his heel, a look of great frustration upon his face.

"Truthfully, Jess, I cannot like what has been going on

here. I know Ollie and Lady Grantham mean the best for you, but it has been hard for me to hold my tongue, seeing how they are misusing you.''

"Misusing me?" Jessica echoed in bewilderment. "Oh, Tom, no. It is just that they don't know me so well as you do. They mean it all for the best, I think.''

He began to speak and then let out his breath in an explosive sigh. "Jess, Jess," he finally said, shaking his head, "they have not been honest with you, and it pains me to have to sit back and only watch, having no right but the right of an old friend.''

"Well, I suppose it was thoughtless of Lady Grantham not to tell me that she knew Red Jack. But then, Tom, it wasn't quite right for him not to tell me he spent so much of his time in London, either. Even though I was only a child, and a girl, at that.'' Jessica brooded as she thought of her recent hurt.

"I don't mean that, Jess," Tom said, sitting again, but dragging his chair up close to her, lowering his voice and speaking earnestly. "Of course Red Jack didn't tell you. Nor did I. It is my thinking that he came to London so often because he was looking for another mother for you. Yes," he said quickly, watching her face as the thought penetrated and a gleam of hope appeared in her eye, "he must have felt that you needed a woman to look after you, and where was he to find a wife? At home in our tiny village? Or on the battlefield? It is my opinion that he was searching for a life's mate. But as you well know now that you've been here awhile, where was a fellow like your father to find the sort of caring responsible female for the job here among the gilded flowers of town? And could he have told you of his intentions, only to dash your hopes each time he failed? No, Jess, never believe Red Jack betrayed you.''

Jessica felt as though some crushing weight had been lifted from her spirit. She gave Tom a look of such pure enraptured gratitude that he felt silent, only watching her radiant face.

Then he spoke again, slowly and hesitantly, "But it wasn't that I was speaking of. Damn, Jess, you know I'm a bluff fellow and have no sweetened words like all the titled fops and popinjays you've been forced to consort with. But, Jess, I've got to tell you something.'' He paused and went on only after she laid one hand upon his own and urged him to speak.

He clasped her hand hard, looked her directly in the eye, and said bluntly, "Jess, they're trying to marry you off."

She withdrew her hand as though his were afire. "What?" she asked, disbelieving, her equanimity shattered again after it had so recently been so patiently restored.

"Oh, it's true," he said bitterly. "And the more villain I, for I knew of it from the first. They enlisted my aid in talking you into it as soon as I arrived. You see, they don't quite believe that Red Jack left you anything of import, even with Mr. Jeffer's evidence. And they feel that even if he did, a female ought to have a man to take charge of her affairs. That's why they togged you out so fine and that's why they've been throwing you at the head of every eligible fellow they've come across."

"But Alex said all they wanted to do was to see me behave as they think a female of my age ought. And that the dresses were for propriety, and the social whirl for something to do . . ." Her voice trailed off as she thought. She stared at the wall for a moment and then turned her rich brown eyes wide upon him. "Alex too?" she breathed.

"Alex first, you might say," he growled.

"But they can't . . . if I don't agree," she cried.

"As to that, I cannot say. They can't starve you or beat you, you know," he said. "This is the nineteenth century, after all. But, Jess, they've already changed you out of all recognition with sweet words and reasonings. They've played upon your sense of duty and honor. Why, they've gotten you to change your style and your mode of life. They've gotten you to stay and sit patiently whilst someone else tracks down your legacy. And that was never the Jess I knew. Or Red Jack neither. You are changed already. Who's to say what they can or cannot do with more time? Ollie is your legal guardian, you know."

Jessica rose and stood silently, taking in the truth of his words.

He stood as well, and took her by the shoulders. "Jess, you shall always be the same for me, no matter how they deck you out. I know you think of me only as an old friend, but you cannot have failed to see how highly I regard you. I am your friend. I could be more." He looked at her trembling mouth and began to draw her infinitesimally closer to himself, when the sound of a light cough in the corridor caused him to drop his hands and step back.

"I only mean to say that you need not feel alone in this. I *am* here now. And I will always be here to help you."

But she scarcely heeded him. She only nodded and said absently, "I know, Tom, and I thank you for your friendship."

Seeing how troubled he appeared to be and sensing his frustration, she added more calmly, "And if ever I need it, I will call upon that comradeship. But I need a bit of time to think. This really has been the most disturbing morning. But," she said with some spirit, "think on it I will, you can believe that. And you needn't worry," she said quickly, for he was about to speak, "I won't peach on you. I know who my true friends are and I shan't say a word."

"I confess that relieves me," he said, "for I should hate to break company with Ollie, for old times' sake." And he added, with a slow menacing smile that made mockery of his next words, "And I should hate Leith to call me out."

She laughed with assumed amusement. "Oh, don't quake, Tom, it don't suit you. Anyhow, I doubt I'm important enough to be a dueling matter for my Lord Leith."

They spoke for a few more moments, and then Tom, becoming aware that enough time had passed for a proper afternoon visit, judging by how often he could heard Bartholomew gently clearing his throat and treading back and forth in the hallway, prepared to take his leave. But before he left, he pressed a card into Jessica's hand.

"It is my present address," he whispered. "Just as a precaution, remember, Jess. Anytime, any day that you have need of me, you can contact me there." Then he bowed and left her standing bemused in the salon.

As he strode down the street toward his lodgings, he thought swiftly. It would have been better to have been alone with her longer. But he had returned as soon as he had seen Lady Grantham leave, and he had left only when the butler had made it apparent that overstaying his visit would have been overstepping his bounds.

He hummed to himself as he walked. So there was a legacy,

after all, as well as Ollie's promised settlement. He would have to add that tantalizing bit of news into his weekly report to his employer Cribb. He almost laughed aloud at the thought of the greedy anticipation the bit about the legacy would be received with.

Then he chanced to think upon the expression upon Jessica's face when he had absolved Red Jack of his wenching. And then he stopped humming. He thought that perhaps there might be more advantages to this plan of his than even he had anticipated. For her father had been wrong after all. There was a woman there, somewhere. Perhaps with patience she could someday even be brought to realize it. He grinned at the thought, and though it was only early afternoon, he went off for a celebratory pint for a good day's work done.

Jessica could not appreciate the fact that the sun had finally come to clear the morning dreariness, for it seemed to her that there was a red haze about everything that she perceived. If she thought that she had ever been angry before, it was as though she never knew the meaning of the word "rage."

As she refined upon all that she had been told, her anger grew. First it was directed at her hostess, and then at the perfidious Ollie, and then at the smooth-tongued, plausible Lord Leith. As she thought of him, her hands curled into claws, then fists. But then, being Jessica Eastwood, her anger turned back again at herself. And there she found the worst blame. Thomas Preston's consolations were washed away in thoughts of the others that had duped her, and of her own gullibility.

It was only when Bartholomew, growing uneasy at the sight of his mistress's young visitor standing stock-still in the center of the salon for so long, entered the room and asked if she might like some tea, that Jessica whirled around to face the exterior world. Her mind made up, her fury became a towering and awesome thing to see.

"No, thank you," she said with great care, such underlying force in her soft husky voice that the butler almost winced.

"I shall be going out," she said decisively, "as soon as I get my wrap."

"But, Miss Eastwood, your maid is with Lady Grantham," the old servitor protested. "Shall I fetch one of the undermaids to accompany you?"

"No, indeed," Jessica said rashly, thinking that she could bear the sight of no inhabitant from this den of liars, even though she knew full well that she ought not to go out by herself, since everyone had told her no lady walked unattended in the streets of London.

She ran to her room and flung a wrap about her shoulders, and while she hurried down the stairs, she tied her bonnet on with shaking fingers. She paused only once before she reached the door.

"Bartholomew," she asked so directly that he had not time to think of his answer, "what is a decent hotel for gentlemen? One where an army officer might stay?"

"Why, Stephen's Hotel, miss," Bartholomew answered automatically.

"And where is it located?" she demanded.

"Only a few streets down," he answered, "to the left. But Miss Eastwood," he protested, feeling like Pandora, who had let the Furies out by also simply flinging open a door, "what shall I tell Lady Grantham?"

So many vile answers came to Jessica as she fled the house that she had to bite her lips to keep from voicing any of them. "I shall send word," Miss Eastwood only paused to say over her shoulder before she reached the pavement and hurried down the street.

Jessica was so preoccupied by her seething thoughts that she did not notice the curious glances she received by passersby as she stalked along the fashionable streets. She looked quite magnificent, but also decidedly odd. For what the curious saw was a slender young female, dressed in a demure muslin with an ecru wrap, with strands of blazing hair peeking out from under her stylish bonnet, striding along unattended and muttering to herself. She was too well-attired to be a servant girl, too young to be an eccentric, and too modestly robed to be a fancy piece. Just what she was, no one quite knew, but she was worthy of being watched and commented upon. But this she did not respond to, being so intent upon reaching her destination.

Her first impulse had been to leave, and her second was to do it alone. Thomas Preston had been kindness itself, but she had no wish to encumber him. She would not stay with Lady Grantham a moment longer, neither would she trust Ollie a step farther. She must take matters into her own capable hands, she thought, and the first step would be to procure suitable lodgings. A hotel that would suit a military gent like her father would suit her as well. She would obtain rooms and then return only to collect her maid and belongings. Let Ollie rattle away, she swore to herself, once she was well-ensconced in private apartments, it would be difficult for him to prize her out again. Knowing Ollie, she reasoned, he would argue and protest, but in the end give way.

Marry me off, she thought, her thoughts blazing brighter than her hair, as if I were some simpering nodcock from the provinces, as if I were a Johnny Raw from the country, ready to fall into wedded bliss with some titled oaf who will take over my life and my fortune? She almost laughed aloud at the idiocy of their plan. And then she shivered at how well they had already lulled and cozened her into stepping along their well-plotted path.

By the time she saw the dignified entrance to Stephen's Hotel, she had worked herself into a rare state. So intent was she upon her thoughts that she did not heed the stir she caused as she marched across the carpeted lobby. For Bartholomew had spoken no less than the truth: Stephen's was a suitable hotel for a military gentleman, but only for officers and men-about-town. It was no place for a lady, not even for a less-exalted female. Few of her sex, except for chars, had even set foot within its portals, and never any unattended.

As she approached the desk, where a startled clerk watched her entrance in dazed fashion, several gentleman who had been lounging about or doing some desultory reading in their chairs, straightened and gaped after her. But in the tunnel vision of rage, Jessica saw none of this.

"Good afternoon," she said immediately upon reaching the clerk. "Have you any rooms available?" Impatient with his stupid, uncomprehending stare, she added, to clarify matters, "For this evening. Commencing this evening, I should say."

"For whom?" the young clerk managed to reply, hoping he might retrieve some sense from her bizarre entrance into these sacred masculine precincts.

"For myself, of course," Jessica stated, "and my maid, of course."

By this time, Jessica began to note that her request had quite discomposed the young man, and so she was relieved when he was shouldered aside by a dapper, thin older man, who was obviously the manager of the establishment.

That gentleman was a fastidious sort who loved his position well, and not the least of his reasons was that it brought him into contact with very few females. For they were of an order that he had never cared for. The sight of Jessica demanding rooms in his hotel made him bristle. Though she was well-dressed and well-spoken, he did not for a moment doubt that she was there to cut up his peace for nefarious purposes. Either she was a tart seeking business within his establishment, or some wild young creature acting on a dare from inebriated companions. In either case, he rose to battle. But since he waged warfare as he did all else, with innuendo and sarcasm, Jessica did not perceive his horrified anger at all.

"We have no rooms tonight for such as yourself, madam," he said with a sneer.

She thought him a very lofty and disagreeable fellow, but thought it reasonable, though regrettable, that so well-known an establishment would be solidly occupied. She shrugged off her disappointment and asked, "That is too bad. But perhaps you can recommend another hotel to me?"

The manager was staggered at the barefaced insolence of the baggage. He smiled what he felt was a terrible sardonic smile and leaned toward her. "Why, yes, my Lady," he sneered, "I should think there were several suitable hostelries for you and your maid in Tothill Fields or in Seven Dials."

He leaned back, well-pleased with his stunning rejoinder, and was shocked to hear the trollop ask in dulcet tones, "And what direction might that be in?"

Holding his temper as best he might, he answered—(as sweetly as a dove, as he later related to his breathless staff)— "To the east of here, my Lady. Just follow the river and you will end up just where you belong."

Then he watched in stunned stupefaction as she nodded, thanked him kindly, and took herself off again through the doors. Several of his clients whistled after her, and a few teased him about being so mean to them by forbidding such a pretty piece a roof for the night.

"Why, there are acres of room in my bed, sir," one portly gentleman said, guffawing, while another lamented that Stephen's should have thought of such amenities for its guests years before. But it was a seven-minute wonder and soon the room calmed down to the quiet, respectable place it was meant to be, with only the memory of the brazen light-skirts to remain and take its place with the other minutia of the hotel's long history.

Jessica walked on in the direction that the manager had indicated. She had gone a long way before the outer world began to intrude upon her consciousness again. She could never sustain anger for too long, her rages being like summer storms that created noise and light but then moved swiftly on, leaving the air cleansed behind them. Then, too, she had little experience with anger, having never had that much commerce with people she really cared about before. In fact, she mused as she slowed her pace, she had experienced more anger, more shock, and more disappointment this very day than she had in the whole of her previous life.

Now, and only now that she was free of the grip of her emotions, could she begin to take in what she had done and where she now was. Neither aspect was pleasing.

She seemed to have left the part of London that she knew far behind. She had gone east and followed the river, as the manager had specified, and the landscape about her had changed drastically. Here there were no sedate clean town houses or fashionable couples out for a stroll. She found herself on a mean street, walking past piles of rubbish and among crowds of rough-looking persons. While she had seen a few children in the care of nursemaids before, now she saw flocks of swooping, running, laughing urchins, winding in and out of the alleyways. Here the women wore no fashionable frocks and the gentlemen no beaver hats. The women wore tattered drab clothes and looked at her hard-eyed. And the men, she noted suddenly, were begrimed and eyed her with frank interest.

Suddenly aware that somewhere she had erred enormously, Jessica turned abruptly and tried to retrace her steps. But now she heard the muttered suggestions as she passed, and now she began to grow very much alarmed. For while she had been oblivious to her surroundings, she had been impervious of them. Once aware, it was as if her armor had been pierced and her very fright fueled further comment.

"Here, miss," one obese villainous-looking fellow uttered as she rushed past him, "you lookin' for something you forgot? I got just what you're wanting."

Another brushed against her as she tried to push through the crowd and asked, "Lost, little missy? Let old Joe give you a hand. Or two." He laughed as she gasped and evaded him.

No female came to her aid, for it was clear she was not of their sort and none of their business.

Trying to avoid the grasping hands and muttered invitations, Jessica began to run. Finding that attracted even more comment, she turned as she came to the head of a street, and walking down it, she saw a fistfight between two rowdies and turned aside again. Now, as she stood gasping on a quieter yet dilapidated side street, she realized that though she had successfully evaded pursuit, she was quite lost. The dreadful slum seemed to stretch on for miles.

She stood still for a moment, catching her breath, leaning against a half-fallen fence that had at one time been erected to protect grass, but now provided safety for only a bare patch of dirt and dust. Jessica stared about her at the sullen derelict houses, scented the noisome aromas of the district, and knew at last that she had been a fool. Now she recalled the exact expression upon the manager's face, and now she remembered the shock on all the peripheral faces that had been within the entry hall of Stephen's Hotel. Now she admitted the commotion when she had left, and she acknowledged what the reaction to her passage through the fashionable streets had been. For she had not been unconscious then, only totally self-absorbed.

But primarily now, Miss Jessica Eastwood did not feel indomitable. She was, at last, only very young and very confused. The worst of it was that as she stood and regulated her breathing she could visualize an elegant face and hear his words, "You are beautiful, Jessica, and as such, you would be at risk." It was not only her present risk that made her shudder, thinking of her rash actions.

She looked about her for some sign of a friendly or at least unthreatening face. But she saw only shabby houses, some one-eyed with broken windows and some with faded curtains stirring in the afternoon breeze. Jessica was about to go on, to attempt to find her way home again, when she perceived a small figure hurrying along the street. As it approached, she allowed hope to spring up, for it was a welcome sight.

The older woman who came toward her looked as though she might be as misplaced as Jessica herself. She was short, plump, and very gray, dressed cleanly and properly in a dress of light lavender color and expensive design. There was an amethyst necklet at her throat and she wore a turban of dove gray. She did not seem to notice Jessica and had come almost abreast of her, her eyes intent on the street, casting glances down at the pavement left and right, when Jessica thought to reach out and ask her assistance. But there was no need for her to utter a word, for as the woman passed her by a pace, she turned and looked back with a puzzled frown.

"Why, my dear," she said in deep cultured accents, "excuse me, but are you in any distress? You seem to be, I don't wish to presume, but you seem quite discomposed."

"Oh, ma'am," Jessica cried with relief, "you do not presume. You are quite right. I seem, to my folly, to have lost my way."

"I thought it," the older woman exclaimed. "Then some good can come from this dreadful day, after all! You see," she said, looking at Jessica forlornly, "I have lost my naughty little Sampson. He's only a foolish little dog, and when my coach stopped in traffic, he espied a cat or some such and leaped straight from my arms to the street.

"I have been searching everywhere for him. John, my coachman, would have it that I ought to go straight home and rest. But I said, and say it still, how shall I get my Sampson back if I don't call him myself? For he won't come to any other hand. So, despite all protests, I have left John to search another street and here I am. But how does such a child as yourself come to this place? For I must say you look quite out of place."

"I am, I am," Jessica said eagerly. "You see I was looking for lodgings and was directed this way, quite by mistake, I now see, and I became hopelessly lost and cannot find my way back home.''

The older woman nodded as though she knew the whole of the tangled tale Jessica was not quite sure how to tell. She looked appraisingly and said in more confidential tones, ''Lodgings? I see. But to where were you returning? I don't wish to presume, but where is home?''

''Why, Yorkshire, actually,'' Jessica said ruefully, ''but I wasn't returning there. I am staying with some friends in London presently.'' And here Jessica faltered, for she was not at all sure she wanted to bruit Lady Grantham's name about, feeling that she had done enough in one day to bring disgrace upon herself and her hostess. ''And I wanted to strike out on my own, you see.''

But as the older woman's expression became more thoughtful and Jessica realized she couldn't actually see anything from what she had been told, she went on to say quickly, ''But for now, all I want to do is to be reunited with my friends and find my way back to . . . Grosvenor Square,'' she invented quickly, knowing that to be a street nearby Lady Grantham's home.

''Oh, I do see.'' The older woman nodded, as if coming to some swift understanding. ''Why, then, my dear,'' she said, looking up at Jessica kindly and taking her arm and linking it in her own, ''I shall abandon my search for naughty Sampson and devote my energies to you. For the Bible says one must help the wayfaring stranger, and my little doggie will have to come home on his own. It's not the first time he's done it, so don't fret. But you look very exhausted, my dear. I think I shall take you home to tea and then, when you have recovered, I'll see you safely back to your friends. My name is Mrs. Carey, dearie. What's yours?''

The little woman began to urge Jessica forward, but Jessica hung back. She did not at all wish to divulge her own name, not knowing what sort of gossip this kind Mrs. Carey was. Neither did she wish to go to some strange female's home for tea; she was embarrassed enough at her situation and did not care to complicate matters further.

Mrs. Carey stopped in her tracks at Jessica's first sign of resistance. Before Jessica could utter a word of explanation, she nodded and exclaimed in a brittle voice, ''The more fool I!

I see, you are so tired, you cannot budge another step, and who shall blame you? Well, just you wait here, my dear, and I shall go and get John with the coach. We'll have you snug and secure in a shake of a lamb's tail. Just you wait here, my love, and all will be well.''

As Mrs. Carey began to bustle back along the street, Jessica protested that there was no need for such assistance, but the little woman was far more spry than she had thought. She was already disappearing up the street, calling back, ''Don't stir, love. There's a dear. Just you wait.''

Jessica stood alone again, as her benefactor vanished from view. The whole incident seemed to be an illusion brought about by exhaustion and she was shaking her head to clear it and about to start out again when she heard a woman's mocking laughter behind her.

''Oh, yes. 'Just you stay there, luv. Don't you stir.' We'll have you safe as houses, don't you fear. Aye, safe as burning houses, luv, you'll be with Mother Carey.''

Jessica spun around to see a face regarding her from a ground-floor window behind a fence. It was a raddled visage, the face of a female with carmined lips and rouged cheeks, the whole surmounted with a frizz of hennaed hair. As the woman spoke, Jessica noted that two of her none-too-white teeth were missing from the front of her mouth, a deficit that the creature sought to conceal by speaking with one grimy hand in front of her lips, causing her speech to sound oddly distorted.

''I beg your pardon?'' Jessica said, not knowing what else to say and feeling all the while that the whole of this day might only be some distorted fantastic dream.

''Don't beg me, luv,'' the woman answered. ''It's a higher person you will be begging if Old Mother Carey gets her claws into you. S'truth you're staying with friends in London? Or are you in the trade, after all?''

Jessica wanted very badly to move on and not reply to the strange female, but years of breeding could not be denied. She answered hesitantly, wishing Mrs. Carey would come back, for she'd sooner sit through six dishes of tea with that strange female than address two more words to this one.

''It is true. And I wished to find a decent hotel because I grew impatient with being so dependent upon them.''

"Thought so," the other woman said. "Now look sharp, missy. I'll say it the once, for who knows when the old harridan will come pelting back. She's no friend of yours or mine, for that matter, else I'd not be sticking my nose in where it ain't asked. Mark me well, missy. Mother Carey's in the trade. She's got a house full of chicks like you. She waits about posting houses, she's got agents at the inns. She gets young milkmaids from the country in town for the first time and she gets them to come to her house to work for her, all unawares. And once they start the work, they stay, mark me well. So if you think it's all soft and gravy, let me tell you she don't give them up till they don't attract the gents anymore. Then it's the streets for them."

Jessica had not sat at her father's knee and listened from quiet corners of the house while he entertained Ollie, Tom, and other local men for years, for nothing. She made more sense of this artless speech than many another girl of her years might have done, but still she could not believe her ears.

"But if I don't agree to go with her . . ." she began, but the other interrupted her by giving out a raucous laugh.

"And who's to stop John from flinging you into the coach, miss? All these helpful neighbors?" She indicated the empty street. "Besides, no one would interfere with Mother Carey and one of her chicks. You're far from home, alone, and as good-looking as you can hold together. You're her meal ticket, luv. She must have come running full tilt from her house when she got word that there was an innocent young smasher wandering lost through her streets. 'Naughty Sampson.' Oh, there's a laugh. Mother Carey don't give a free scrap to nothing that walks upon this earth."

"Then I'll go now," Jessica cried, staring up the street in fright. "And thank you."

"How far do you think you'll get?" The other woman laughed.

"Then what's to do?" Jessica whispered in real panic.

"Come on in. And be smart about it. She's bound to be back in a minute. I've only the one room, but I can see she don't come in. Well, what are you waiting for? Do you think I've got a grand and gaudy fancy house in here? Oh, yes, with dozens of pretties to choose from, lined up on my grand stair-case,'' the woman mocked.

"But,'' Jessica protested, even though she yearned to hide beneath any available bed, "why should you do this for me?''

There was a silence and she feared that she had so insulted her would-be helper that she had taken offense and gone from the window.

But in a moment the voice came back low and hard, "Because I owe her one back. Now are you coming in or not?''

Jessica paused. She weighed both women's words and aspects. She called on her highest reasonings, she called upon her greatest judgment. In the end, she called upon her feet to move. She turned, hesitated, then fled into the shabby house.

10

The room was not as seedy as Jessica had expected it to be. It was small, with mean furnishings, but it was, withall, clean and tidy. The narrow bed was made up with a colorful quilt, the few pieces of furniture were old but clutter-free, and there was even a dainty vase filled with flowers upon a table. The woman gave Jessica an ironic and knowing smile when she saw her surprise, and told her to stay well back from the window. Then, nodding as though satisfied, she picked up a light shawl, went with slow and unhurried step to the door, and stepped out into the tiny yard in front of the house.

Jessica hung back, close to the wall. From her vantage point she could peep through the curtains to see the street, and she could hear whatever transpired through the open window as if the persons were in the very room with her.

After what were only a few minutes, Jessica's breath caught in her throat as she saw Mrs. Carey arrive in a large old-fashioned gray coach. The horses stopped and Mrs. Carey hopped down as sprightly as a girl. She looked up and down the street, quite ignoring Jessica's unknown new friend, and then began to call out in a high sweet voice, "Oh, my dear, you can come out now. All is well. My coach is here. Oh, my dear, it's Mrs. Carey, do come along now. Oh, young woman. . . ."

After a few more tries, Mrs. Carey grew still. She muttered beneath her breath and finally turned to the woman who stood insolently leaning against the half-fallen fence. She asked abruptly, "Have you seen a young woman hereabouts, Maria?"

"I might have," the woman answered, yawning.

"Don't play with me, Maria," Mrs. Carey flashed back in anger. "Have you seen a young girl?"

"Seeing how I live right here, Mother," the woman

129

retorted idly, "I'd have to be deaf not to have heard your nattering outside my window."

"Well?" Mrs. Carey asked angrily, crossing her arms about her breast. "Are you going to enlighten me as to her whereabouts?"

"Begging your pardon, Mother," Maria answered, "but why should I, after all?"

"Oh, very well," the older woman complained, and fishing in her purse, she extracted some coins and passed them to Maria, who stood holding them in her open palm and gazing at them as though she had never seen coin of the realm before.

"There," said Mrs. Carey, adding a few more to the others, "now have done, Maria, I'm a busy woman and you shan't have a ha'penny more. Where is she?"

Maria slid the coins into a pocket of her skirts and laughed in such a friendly fashion that Jessica's heart sank and she looked wildly about the room for either a bolt hole or a weapon.

"Too slow off the mark, Mother," Maria said. "I saw it all. Didn't blame you in the least, either. She was a love all right. But as soon as you'd turned the corner, and I was wondering whether I ought to ask her in, just to make sure she was right and tight when you got back, a young blade comes tooling down the street in a curricle. He sees her and gives out a shout, 'Mary, my love!' He's at her side in a second and the two of them fall about each other like Romeo and Juliet. She's crying and he's telling her he never meant a word of it, and begging her forgiveness, and giving her such slop that it fair turned my stomach, Quick as you can stare, he's got her up on the seat with him, and they're driving off. Don't fret, though, Mother, for by the look of him, she was well connected and you'd have found her more trouble than she was worth."

Mrs. Carey stood seething. She finally gave Maria one long direct look and shook her head. "There's where you're out, Maria. For once I'd had the chit a day, her family would have been done with her forever."

Maria shrugged. "What's done, done. I told you all I know."

Mrs. Carey gave her one last long piercing look. "You'd

better have done, my dear. I pay well for service, but I pay back for a disservice twice as well.''

Maria drew herself up and gave back a haughty stare. ''Don't come heavy with me, Mother. I know what side my bread's buttered on. Just because you've lost a chick is no reason to eat me!''

Mrs. Carey paused for a moment before she reentered the coach. Then she said bitterly, ''Aye, sweet little Maria would never cross me. Still, you're right. The world's full of pretty young baggages. As you should well remember, my dear.''

Maria stood awhile lost in thought after the coach had driven off. Then she shrugged again and came back to the room where Jessica stood, still fearing to move a muscle.

''That's a debt paid, and in more ways than one,'' Maria said almost to herself as she took the coins out and recounted them. Then she gave Jessica a bright look and laughed. ''You can breathe again, 'Mary,' it's all over now.''

''Thank you,'' Jessica said rapidly. ''It was more than good of you to hide me and counsel me so well. I'll go now and I promise never to forget you for your kindness.''

''Oh, I wouldn't do that.'' Maria laughed. ''For the old cow didn't half-mistrust me. She'll keep an eye peeled for you a good while yet. No, you're safer to stay with me till evening. For that's when the trade picks up and she'll have to be back at her house, and she'll need her bully boys about her.''

''But even if they do lay hands on me,'' Jessica said bravely, ''I shall set up such a ruckus as they have never heard. And surely you could notify my friends if I left an address with you. Or I could convince them that I want no part of their plans.''

''You're so wet around the ears I wonder that you didn't swim up the street,'' Maria chortled. ''Set up a ruckus? But there's always some sort of to-do around here. And as for your reasoning with that lot, I tell you, missy, that it can't be done. No, they'll give you a nice cool drink, or some such, and before you know it, you'd be walking on the ceiling, doing anything they asked, never knowing what you were about. And when you did know, a few days later, it would be far too late to send for help. There'd be no help for it. No,

love, that's their way of business, and business is what
they're about.''

Jessica gave Maria such a look of consternation that the
older woman laughed again.

''Well, you do have a choice, sweet. You can either rest
here with me, or go and take your chances with Mother. It's
all the same to me.''

''You must think me very ungrateful,'' Jessica began,
embarrassed at how easily the other woman had read her discomfort with her surroundings.

''Oh, yes, to be sure,'' Maria mocked as she turned and lit
a fire in her small grate and began to assemble the makings of
small tea. ''I am shocked at how any young woman of breeding could possibly not wish to remain with such a fine lady as
myself. Give over, do, love. Why should you want to stay
here with me? But you may as well have a seat. I'll brew up
up a nice cuppa. ''

Jessica sat and wondered at the chameleonlike affect of her
hostess. One moment she seemed no more than a low slattern, but the next she could affect accents of high gentility.
Jessica was unsure of how to ask any questions without giving offense, and it was not until her benefactor sighed and
came to sit down at the table with a steaming pot of tea
that she spoke again.

''I owe that old witch a thing or two,'' Maria brooded as
she poured Jessica's tea into a simple white mug. ''For there
was a time when I was down on my luck and so muddled that I
even asked her if I could work in her house till I got on my feet
again.''

Jessica's tea splashed in her cup as she realized just what
her hostess's occupation was, but Maria didn't seem to
notice, she was so deep in recollection.

''And the old sow said as how I was too old and washed out
to work for her. I . . . too old and washed out! Ha,'' Maria
said, boiling with remembered resentment. ''I, Maria
Dunstable, who once was the toast of Covent Garden. Well,
it's a lucky thing that the old besom's eyes is as bad as her
business, or I'd have been for it. I got myself together again,
straight off, and I've been doing well on my lonesome ever
since. I daresay it won't be long before I'm back up on top
again.''

But chancing to glance at Jessica's white face, she misread the look of consternation and sighed again. "No, I suppose you've the right of it. Those glory days are gone forever. It's my teeth, I daresay. But as soon as I get some gold together, I'll take myself off to a surgeon in town who can make up some crockery to disguise what I've lost. Then, you'll see who rules the roost."

Jessica eyed the other woman. It was true that the two missing teeth disfigured her, but even if there had been no gaps in her smile, her lined face, bulky form, and strange over-dyed hair would have been enough to discourage compliments. Wisely, Jessica said nothing and only sipped at her tea.

The older woman made a slight face and then said defensively, "I was on top once, you know. That's a gospel truth. I danced at Covent Garden in the opera. Soon as you could stare, I was set up in my own apartments by a nob. But that wasn't the half of it. I trafficked with nothing but Quality for a while. Aye, I was in the keeping of a Duke! Jason Thomas, Duke of Torquay. He was a right one, all right, but fickle, you understand. We parted best of friends, we did. No sooner had he shown me his back when I was snapped up by the Marquis of Bessacarr, and then his friend, Lord Hoyland. I lived in style, my girl, and don't you forget it.

"But," Maria said in a diminished voice into the silence that had fallen when Jessica had no idea of what to reply, "I didn't play my cards right. That's the truth, too. You have to be as wily as a politician, that's what counts. And I let my heart rule my head. And here we are," she said broodingly.

After staring for a space, she looked up at her guest. "But here I am giving you my life's story and I don't even know your name or your game. Whatever brought you here, missy?"

Jessica cleared her throat and began to introduce herself. Before long, she had lost her shyness at finding herself in such a bizarre situation. Somehow there in the close room, with an interested listener—and one, moreover, who knew what sort of questions to ask and seemed to make no judgments— Jessica found herself unburdening her story. As the afternoon dwindled, she told Maria of her childhood, her father, her visit to London, and her present circumstances. She was careful, however, even in the thick of her narration, not to name names, for somehow she felt she should shelter Lady Grantham and Ollie and the others from random gossip.

When she had done, her hostess peered at her closely. "Go on," Maria breathed. "You call those problems? My Lord, I would give anything to have your sort of troubles, Jess."

"But they've none of them been honest with me," Jessica protested, dismayed that Maria should feel she was enormously privileged to be in such distress.

"Oh, get away with you." Maria laughed harshly. "You've got a fortune coming to you. You've got looks. You've got a parcel of Quality gents falling over each other to get to you. What else could you want from life?"

"I don't know," Jessica said somberly, "but surely, I do know that I don't want to marry. Or to be ordered about until I do know what to do. Can't you see that?"

"Don't fancy men?" Maria asked knowingly. "Well, there's a hurdle, all right. Got a girlfriend you want to set up as a life's mate, then? I can't see anything in that, myself, but it takes all kinds."

Jessica's cheeks flushed bright. "Oh, no," she exclaimed, "never, that's not it at all. I just want to be . . ." And then she began to laugh a little wildly. "There's the point, Maria, I don't know quite what I do want."

"Well, Jess," Maria said, rising and bearing the cups off to the basin, "it's a problem I'd give the world to have. That gentleman that told you as how it's a hard world for a woman alone wasn't half-right. Of course, if you play your hand well, it's all gravy. But I can't see you setting up as a Cyprian. And I can't see you going on alone, because it's clear you're not wise to the time of day, love. No offense, but I think you ought to just pick the best of the lot and get shackled. To that young fellow from your village. Or to that Alex you keep going on about. Seems to me you have a care for him."

"Lord Leith?" Jessica gasped, so overwhelmed at Maria's misinterpretation of her complaints that she forgot discretion. "Why, he's the worst of them all."

"Lord Leith," Maria asked, turning about to stare at Jessica. "Oh, that's flying high. Never say he's the chap you were complaining of?"

Caught by her hostess's glittering eyes, Jessica only nodded.

"Top of the trees he is," Maria said excitedly. "Oh, he's high as the Regent. One sees him everywhere. He's got that shrewd piece Libby Kenton in his keeping now. She puts it about that she's Lucille LaPoire, but she's no more a Frenchie than you or I. Friend of "Harry" Wilson's and as wise as owls, she is," Maria said enviously.

"In his keeping?" Jessica asked, forgetting her resolve not to mention any of her acquaintances to Maria, and only catching onto that one salient fact. "He has a female in his keeping?"

"Oh, Lord love you, Jess. You're green as sour apples. Of course, he does. All the Quality does. Don't you know anything?" Maria laughed.

And suddenly affecting a motherly air, Maria sat down with her young guest again. There, as the evening drew close, Maria sat at her small table and patiently explained the ins and outs of the world of the demi-rep to Jessica. She was flattered and pleased by having her young friend's absolute attention, and so she carefully explained the hierarchy of her profession to the rapt girl.

Jessica sat still, only silently moving her lips now and again, as though memorizing the information. Maria began at the bottom, telling wild tales of such low females as the infamous Flashy Nance, Dirty Suke, and Billingsgate Moll. These graceless females frequented the lowest sort of establishments and would sell their admittedly inferior persons for as little as a draft of Blue Ruin, or Giniver, Maria explained. Then she waxed rhapsodical as she detailed the exploits of such successful and admired harlots as Brazen Bellona, the famous Harriet "Little Harry" Wilson, and of Lucille LaPoire, and of their traffic with the gentleman of the Ton. She spoke lovingly of their jewels, their gowns, and their houses in the best part of town.

Only once did Jessica's instructor drop her gaze and look aside. And that was when she admitted that for the moment, she herself prowled the alleys alongside Covent Garden and other theaters, rather than actually attending the opera or theaters, as her more exalted sisters did. But, she then added cheerily, that was, of course, only for the moment, as her luck was sure to turn.

Jessica ignored these rosy visions and asked in bewilderment, cutting across ruminations about the change in fortune sure to be brought by fine false teeth, "But do all gentlemen have such females in their keeping?"

"Lord love you, Jess." Maria laughed. "No. But there's enough that do to make business for the likes of us. Now as to your fine Lord Leith," she commented, watching at how her young visitor's eyes would open at each mention of that gentleman's name and playing to her audience as only an ex-performer could, "he's had many a choice piece under his wing. And not all of them working girls, if you catch my drift."

As Maria began to prepare "for the evening," as she obliquely put it, by applying a heavy coating of unguents and salves to her already encarmined features, she rattled on to Jessica about the Society females—widowed, bored, or just "out for a lark"—who were known to accommodate wealthy lovers. By the time the sun had set and only a faint afterglow gave testimony to the vanished day, Jessica had amassed a quantity of information about the love lives of the Aristocracy.

Jessica had at first been embarrassed, then shocked, then curiously enraged by the foibles of the males of the Ton that had been so carefully detailed for her. The fact that Lord Leith had a famous mistress whom he visited as frequently as he visited his aunt, caused Jessica more difficulty than if she had been told that he had a wife stowed somewhere in the countryside. So it was with a mixture of self-righteous anger and shame that she prepared to at last return to Lady Grantham's home. She faced the fact that they would all be appalled at her disappearance for the day with stomach-churning dread, but clutched close the evidence of her prime antagonist's double life with a certain mean triumph. Let him rail away, she thought as Maria went to the door to spy out the land, never thinking of Ollie or Lady Grantham's or even Tom Preston's reactions, I now have ammunition enough to last through a week of warfare with him. And, she thought as she stepped out the door, Red Jack always said that well-armed is half-won.

Jessica had left off her bonnet and concealed her hair beneath a borrowed scarf of Maria's. As they walked swiftly down the low streets, Maria whispered reassurance. "Trade's picking up now. Mother Carey's got too much on her mind to seek out one stray female. Just walk beside me and keep your head down."

They had not gone too many streets when Maria nudged Jessica in the ribs, causing her heart to leap up as she looked wildly about her.

"See how you're costing me business." Maria laughed low in her throat as a poorly dressed fellow stared after the two of them, hesitated, and then walked on away from them.

"Not that I'd have anything to do with such a paltry fellow. But you have to walk alone to stir up business. Two's a pair, one's fair game, you see," Maria said.

Jessica ducked her head, but this time in shame as she recalled how she had fought for the freedom to walk alone, never knowing that it was not mere masculine prerogative that had caused her to be given that edict.

The evening was growing cool when the ill-matched pair finally reached a street that Jessica recognized. She was wondering at how she could dissuade Maria from actually walking her to Lady Grantham's door and also castigating herself silently for even thinking of such an ignoble action after all the older woman had done for her, when she heard her own name being called frantically. She flinched for a moment as the high-wheeled coach drew to a sudden stop at the curb and the driver tossed the reins to his tiger and leaped down to the pavement.

"Jessica!" Lord Leith shouted. "My God, Jessica, what has befallen you?"

She looked up and in the dim light saw nothing but deep concern and fear barely held in check upon his pale countenance. He had clasped her two hands in his own as his troubled eyes searched her face.

As she did not immediately answer, he went on gently, "What's happened, Jessica? Are you all right? We have been searching the streets all day. We were about to bring Bow Street in. What's happened, can you tell me?"

"I . . . went out to see about securing other lodgings and became lost. Miss Dunstable here, she, ah, sheltered me till now. For you see, my Lord, there was this woman, a Mrs. Carey, who meant me ill, and Maria here . . . Let me make you known to Miss Maria Dunstable, my Lord," Jessica went on, remembering her manners. After Lord Leith muttered "Servant" beneath his breath as his gaze quickly encompassed her companion and flew back to Jessica, she went on with a little less heart, "I had to wait till evening to be sure I was not followed. Oh, it's all been a mull, Alex," Jessica said on a frightened gulp, "but Maria did help me and I am all right. And very sorry," she added in a whisper, "to have upset anyone."

After a moment's silence, Lord Leith's face set into strong immobility. "I see," he breathed. "Very well, then," he said in a voice of command. "Jessica, please get into the carriage and I will see you home in a moment."

Jessica took a deep breath, turned, and said softly to Maria, "Thank you, Maria, for all your care." She put out one gloved hand and solemnly shook hands with the bemused Maria. "I shall never forget your kindness. Oh," she added as she was about to enter the carriage, "I wish you great good fortune. Tonight and every night."

As she disappeared into the vehicle, Maria looked up at the tall gentleman, and seeing his barely contained emotion, she laughed and said in a friendly low voice, "Never fear, my Lord, I kept her snug and safe as the minute she left you. She's a bright little article, but she oughtn't be let loose by herself. She's got no more idea of how to go than a day-old chick."

"Mother Carey had her eye on her?" he asked.

"Aye," Maria said, smiling, "but I outfoxed her."

"Then we owe you a great deal," he answered, and taking out his purse, pressed a quantity of notes into her eager hand.

"Lord!" she exclaimed, examining her bounty in the dim light. "And here I thought my virtue would be its own reward" She preened saucily, giving him the full splendor of her gap-toothed smile. "But perhaps you'd like to know my whereabouts so you can see what good use I've put to the windfall?"

"Thank you, Miss Dunstable," he said, permitting himself a rueful smile as well, "but I believe I'll have my hands full

enough as it is without another distracting female to contend with.''

Maria gave him a long appreciative look. Then she sighed.
''Nicely said, nicely done. I've never been turned down so
prettily. Jess don't know when she's well-off, does she?
Well, I thank you, my Lord. But go easy with her. She's only
a babe, you know.''

''I know.'' He smiled.

''And she has more of a care for you than she knows,''
Maria said slyly.

''Now, that I didn't know,'' he answered.

Maria gave him a wise look. ''For all she's a green goose,
she's got eyes, hasn't she?'' she simpered. And then she
bobbed a curtsy and, smiling radiantly, backed off the way
she had come, melting into the shadows as she hurried home
with her booty.

He stared after her for a moment and then entered the
coach. He gave Jessica only one cursory glance as he settled
himself. Seeing how she sat straight and silent in the farthest
corner, he only spoke once to her as the horses began to
move.

''We'll talk Jessica,'' he said softly, ''when we get
home.''

Jessica sat still, breathing shallowly, as she heard Lord
Leith conferring with Lady Grantham. When she heard that
good woman say, ''But, Alex, surely you can discuss it
another time, the child looks fagged to death,'' Jessica's
guilt rose and threatened to overbalance her.

But when she heard his reply, ''No, Aunt. There are some
things that must be thrashed out now,'' she steeled herself
for his entry into the room. She heard the mantel clock's
slow ticking and forced her breathing to match its reassuring
steady beat. So when he entered and closed the door quietly
behind him, she looked up at him and said staunchly before he
could utter any of the words she was sure he longed to say, ''I
know it was wrong. I know it was a damn-fool thing to do,
my Lord. But I've said I was sorry and don't know what else
to say.''

He stood silent and looked down at her. She could not
know what a pathetic sight she appeared to be, for she

seemed to him to be frightened beyond a mere show of tears, but her indomitable spirit kept her voice steady. He could not find it in himself to attack such gallantry. He only sat and said quietly, "Then I do not have to tell you how distressed we all were. Ollie has been sent word of your return, and when Preston comes back from his searchings, we will lay his fears to rest. Jessica, I know what terrors you must have felt, and I don't think I have enough funds in the world to ever repay Miss Dunstable for her efforts. You may not, even now, know fully what sort of fate you eluded. That is safely done with, thank God. But what caused you to rush off the way you did? Bartholomew said that you were as one bereft of your senses. Why did you tear out, unattended, to secure other lodgings? That made no sense to any of us?"

Jessica twisted her fingers in her lap. She had expected to find wrath and had fully prepared herself for it with counteraccusations and with equal anger. But she discovered only a certain sad patience in his affect, and she was overwhelmed. She said, without rancor this time, but with real hurt in her voice and sorrow plain in her eyes, "It was a dreadful day, my Lord. Perhaps the worst I have ever experienced. There was too much, you see. First, I discovered that I was not permitted to go to Brussels. And then I learned that my father had often been to London, without my knowing. And then, to cap it all, I discovered that all the while, you and Ollie and your aunt only intended to marry me off, like some simple unwanted baggage. I was determined to leave, you see. And then the manager of Stephen's misdirected me. Lud, can it all have been in one day?" She laughed shakily.

The tall gentleman nodded as though this incoherent roster of injustices had been crystal-clear to him. But he had spoken to many people that incredibly long day, as he had fearfully searched London for her. So he only said quietly, "Of course, we all wanted to see you settled, Jessica. But we thought that discretion was the better part of valor. I fear we were a little afraid of your reaction to our plans. But we were wrong, it seems. Still, Jessica, if we were so careful about even broaching the matter to you, how could you think we could ever get you to acquiesce to something you did not desire? No matter. It does not matter now. It was unpardonable in us to presume to influence your future, however subtly. And, as you know, equally foolish in the extreme for you to fly off as you did. Let us not refine upon the matter any longer tonight. I'm sure you are exhausted. If you wish, we'll talk about it another time. But if it makes you easier, I'll tell you what we have decided today. We think that perhaps the strain of a total immersion in London Society is not for you, as you yourself have always said. If you would like—and I make clear that it is up to you—we think it would be better for my aunt to repair to her country home. If you accompany her there, you can have some peace of spirit. And of course, more freedom than you would have in town.''

Jessica felt both relief and queer sense of disquiet at his reasonable forgiveness. Knowing that she had both disappointed him and acted childishly did not make being treated as a child any easier to bear. So she said after a moment's thought, ''And of course, along with the freedom and ease of spirit, I would also be unable to disgrace you further?''

He stood and said calmly, ''We are doing our best to hush the whole matter up.''

She swallowed hard and said bitterly, ''Would it not be best to simply wash your hands of me?''

''We cannot do that,'' he answered. ''And,'' he added, almost as an afterthought, ''you know we should not wish to.''

''I cannot see why not,'' Jessica cried.

''Have I not said we were friends?'' he asked, watching her carefully.

She bit back all the ready retorts at her disposal. There had been too much violence done to her emotions this day.

''I agree with your plans, my Lord,'' she whispered. ''I think a respite in the country would be best for me, but I dislike running counter to your aunt's plans for her own social life.''

''The Season is almost over, anyway, it will be no hardship for her,'' he answered.

He hesitated, as if to speak again. She seemed so diminished, so deflated, he almost wished she would flare up at him.

''Come, Jessica,'' he said with a strange half-smile, ''never say you are totally squashed. I'm sure we can come to cuffs again even in the vastness of the countryside.''

"Shall you come as well?" she asked with an eagerness that surprised even herself. So she was not quite a social outcast after all.

"Of course," he answered lightly, "and Ollie and Thomas Preston as well. It will be a repairing lease for all of us. And there is one other surprise. I had thought to tell you tomorrow when you were rested, but I think you need a happy thought to go to sleep on. Mr. Jeffers returned this evening with some rather pleasing news for you.''

"He has found my legacy, then?" Jessica cried out.

"No, only a part of it. He still travels to the Continent for your father's treasure. But, it appears, part of it has come to you already," he answered, closely watching her expression.

"Really, it has been such a trying day, I fear I'm not thinking clearly," Jessica said, passing a hand over her eyes. "I don't understand.''

Lord Leith returned to her side and sat again. There was nothing but gentleness in his gaze. "No, how should you think clearly?" he asked softly. "But it really is great good fortune. It seems that Mr. Jeffers came along with only a small part of your inheritance. But a charming, concerned part at that. He came up with your cousin, Anton," he said with the air of a man presenting a gift.

"My what?" Jessica asked stupidly.

"Your cousin, Anton von Keller," Lord Leith repeated, noting the stunned disbelief in her eyes.

"But there is no such person," Jessica stammered, "or at least there was never such.''

The tall gentleman looked deep into her wide and amazed eyes and then said gently, "But there is, Jessica, or at least there is now.''

11

When Jessica went to bed that night, she closed her lids only as a gesture to convention, for she knew she would not have a moment's sleep. Thus, when she opened her eyes what seemed to be only a second later, she was stunned to see her room flooded with broad daylight. Sitting up quickly, she noted from the clock upon the mantel that she had slept the dial around in deep and dreamless slumber. It could have been that she had taken refuge from all her confusion in the sound way of any healthy young animal, but Jessica thought it had more to do with the brimming glass of evil-tasting restorative that Lord Leith had pressed upon her. She had grimaced, for a vagrant memory of the concoction that Mother Carey was said to use crossed her mind. But Alex had claimed the brown stuff was only "Cognac," so she soon downed it all.

She sat up in bed and drew her knees up to her chest, crossed her arms about her knees, and pondered. For once Miss Eastwood was in no great haste to greet the day. Too much had happened too quickly and she felt the need for some quiet reflection before plunging back into the wakeful, worrisome world again.

There was no sense, she told herself, in going over the events of yesterday. She fully accepted whatever blame there was, and only made a sour face at the thought of what a donkey she had been. And since the mere thought of what might have happened if she had not been so lucky as to pause outside of Maria Dunstable's window was so fearful, she quickly cast the thought aside for reference on some less-demanding day.

The thought of the nightlife of her male companions was not so readily shoved away, and Jessica spent some moments pondering the duplicity of the masculine gender. But as those thoughts quite naturally led her again to thoughts of her father and his secret life, she soon gave up those ruminations as well. It was the present, she decided, not the irreparable past, that needed her fullest attention now. And the most pressing of those matters was the appearances of this spurious cousin that Alex had been on about.

For that this Anton was some impostor, she had no doubt. The only cousin of hers that she knew of was the odious Cribb, and if he had any relatives without scales, she could not think of them. And surely, she thought, Cribb would have told her of any, for he would have been fearful of anyone who might lay claim to Oak Hill in his stead. No, she thought, this "cousin" simply does not exist. Alex and Lady Grantham may have been cozened into thinking so, for they had both been full of smiles and charity for the fellow's manners and graces. But more than likely, she thought, narrowing her eyes against the bright sunlight, he was just a scrambler who had heard of her legacy and was in hopes of claiming part of it. As far as that goes, Miss Eastwood thought, tossing back her tousled, gleaming mane, he shall find I am not such an easy bird to pluck. And, much heartened, she pulled the bell cord to summon her maid to help her dress for battle.

A charming Nile-green frock was her uniform, a burnished coronet of braids became her war bonnet. Taking a serious peek at herself in the looking glass, Miss Eastwood was satisfied and told herself grimly that her native wit would have to be her ammunition and her ready tongue her only firearm. She would, however, she decided as she went to join her hostess, have to be wily as well, and she vowed to send a note around to Thomas Preston, requesting his presence when the impostor arrived, for even the boldest soldier requires reinforcements.

She slid into her seat at the dining table, head down and silent save for a muted good-morning to her hostess, for she did not wish to have to defend herself so early in the day. But Lady Grantham, instead of being angry, hurt, or offended at Jessica's activities of the previous day, as might have been expected, instead lay down her newspaper and smiled in the friendliest fashion at her guest.

Lady Grantham waited until Jessica took the first sip at her coffee. Then, she leaned over and lowered her voice so that the hovering footman could not hear her. "You must," she whispered urgently, "tell me all about it."

When Jessica turned a puzzled face toward her and wondered whatever her oddly animated hostess was on about, Lady Grantham sighed in exasperation. As soon as all the breakfast dishes were arranged to the footman's satisfaction, Lady Grantham sent the fellow away, telling him airily that she would ring when she required further service.

The moment he disappeared through the door, Lady Grantham inched her chair closer to Jessica and leaned so far forward that the younger woman feared the Lady would submerge her sleeve in the dish of porridge.

"Alex said you ran across Mother Carey, not to mention that you spent part of the afternoon and evening in the sole company of a low courtesan."

Jessica bowed her head unhappily and stammered out her carefully rehearsed apology again. Lady Grantham frowned and waved away her words, brushing the lace of her sleeve across a plate of kippers in her impatience.

"No, no," she said, "I know that. You had the most harrowing time, I'm sure, and I quite understand that you regret it. Well, it was a buffleheaded thing to do, but as you've come to no harm, there's no need to keep abasing yourself. But tell me, what was she like? Mother Carey, that is. Does she truly look just like any Society dame? And Maria Dunstable, whatever did you talk about all that time?"

Jessica began to slowly tell her hostess all that had transpired, and as she did, she noted with amazement that Lady Grantham hung upon her every word and attended her sordid tale with great fascination, interrupting every so often to ask pertinent questions. Heartened by such uncritical interest, Jessica unburdened herself almost completely, for she thought it best to leave out the part about what Maria had said about Alex.

"Well," Lady Grantham said with a satisfied sigh when Jessica had done, "what an adventure! Of course, I have heard about Mother Carey forever but never thought to actually speak to someone who had dealt with her. She never appears in public, you know, and one must depend upon rumor."

"You have?" Jessica asked in confusion. "Then you mean

that such activities are known to decent females in London?''

"Of course," Lady Grantham said, carefully applying jelly to her slice of toast.

"Then why is nothing done about it?" Jessica demanded.

"What is to be done?" Lady Grantham answered. "The woman is famous for her depravity. Imagine, recruiting her unfortunate victims from among the most unwary, those poor young things who come to London to seek their fortune. How simply dreadful," Lady Grantham said, but with something of relish in her tone.

"I think," Jessica said with some heat, "that she should be stopped, that there should be some sort of law against what she does."

"Oh, there is," her hostess said through a quantity of toast, "but there's the proving of it, you see. And anyway, most of the drabs in her employ are there willingly. It is those few that she gets by more unorthodox means that have given her a reputation.

"At any rate," Lady Grantham continued as she disposed of her egg, eyeing her guest's horrified countenance, "all decent females go in pairs in the street and only a simpleton would speak to strangers. Why, the lowliest parlor maid knows better than to strike up an acquaintance with any chance-met female."

Seeing the guilty start that Jessica gave at those words, Lady Grantham hurried on, "But imagine, Maria Dunstable living in a mean flat like any ordinary slattern. She was a dazzling creature in her day. How time passes. I was used to see her decked in jewels at the opera, with the likes of Torquay and Bessacarr. Lord, I am getting old." She chuckled with a reminiscent smile.

Jessica put down her fork. "You mean that respectable females know all about such liaisons?" she gasped.

"Certainly," Lady Grantham said, looking at Jessica curiously, "we are respectable, not deaf nor blind, you know."

"But then," Jessica rushed on, aghast, "you know of Lord Leith and . . ." But then she realized to whom she was speaking and let her words trail off, trying to disguise her speech by taking a large gulp of coffee.

"Lucille LaPoire?" Lady Grantham answered so calmly

that Jessica almost drowned in her cup. "Of course. It's quite a famous arrangement. But I cannot see why you are so shocked. He isn't married, you know. And one can hardly expect such a man to be satisfied with composing sonnets or dreaming about his future wife like some raw schoolboy. Now, Lord Wycliffe and that Turner woman, that is shocking! And he with five in his nursery and another on the way."

Jessica sat still and began to form an argument of the unfairness of gentleman being able to squire about legions of fallen females, while the young unattached females of their own class were considered fast if they entertained even respectable young men alone in their own parlors, but Lady Grantham put a stop to her high reasonings with a few careless, but artful words.

"But then," she sighed, watching Jessica's heightened color, "it has always been thus. And always will be, I expect. For a gentleman has to be sure that his heir is his own and none other's. And nature has seen to it that his lady must be the one to produce the heirs. But now, if a lady produces the requisite number and her husband is complaisant, why, then, the tables are turned right enough."

And for the remainder of Jessica's uneaten breakfast, Lady Grantham told her stories of the peccadilloes of the fashionable females in London, that not only matched Maria Dunstable's tales, but in some cases overshadowed them.

She spoke of the infamous Kitty, Countess of Auden, whose shocking indiscretions lived on long after she herself had gone; and of the aristocratic Countess of Oxford, whose children were called the Miscellany because of the assortment of fathers they were assumed to have; and of a score of other ladies of high degree and low sensibility.

By the time Lady Grantham had done and had rung for the footman to clear, Jessica was quite subdued. She waited for the visit from Mr. Jeffers and her false cousin dejectedly. For she had begun to think that she was, indeed, only a simpleton from the provinces.

For it was not that she had never known of such goings-on. Didn't she know of Thomas Preston and his dalliances with the slattern at the inn? And hadn't she heard the rumors about Mrs. White in town? But she never refined upon such matters at home. Either people in the country are far more moral, she thought miserably, or people in the city are far more honest. Or, she decided with as much honesty as she herself could summon forth, I have left far more than Yorkshire behind me in these past weeks.

But she soon left off her unhappy ruminations when Thomas Preston was announced. Jessica was so anxious for a private word with him that she scarcely noted that Lady Grantham was more stiffly correct with him than she had been in the recent past. When at last Lady Grantham turned to direct her butler as to the number of people who were to have tea with them, Tom had a moment to speak to Jessica alone. His face, she saw, was filled with concern.

"I could bite my tongue out," he said without preamble, "for having said anything that might have caused you to act so rashly. No wonder Lady Grantham is so angry with me," he sighed. "But Jess, why didn't you contact me? Why, I was mad with worry as I searched for you. Lord, Jess, never do that again. You know you have only to send me a note and I will act for you."

Jessica knew that time was short, and so she cut him off with a frantic whisper. "Never mind that, it's done, Tom. But what of this fellow who claims to be my cousin? I don't believe it, Tom. I believe he wants Red Jack's treasure and has made up the whole. I haven't any cousin, Tom."

A look of speculation crept into his light eyes, and his long face set in intense thought. "Then we'll have to watch him closely, won't we, Jess?" he answered as Lady Grantham turned toward them again.

"Oh, yes, Tom," Jessica breathed, feeling a little more secure now that she knew she had a concerned ally. While they seated themselves and made poor stilted work of a conversation about the weather, Jessica kept her gaze upon his determined face.

When Lord Leith was announced, Jessica performed the correct social amenities, but she could not bring herself to easy conversation with him. Rather, she kept her attention upon her one old friend, Tom, and discouraged any eye contact with Alex. Somehow, she felt uneasy in his presence, and even his puzzled expression as he noted her coolness did not change her affect.

It was only when Ollie had come, and the general conversation had died three natural deaths before being painfully resuscitated again, that Mr. Jeffers and Herr Anton von Keller were announced and all speech came to an abrupt halt. Mr. Jeffers came in expansively smiling and greeting everyone assembled. The young man at his side made his bows absently, but when his searching gaze fell upon Jessica, he stopped in his tracks. He frankly goggled and then shook himself as if awakening. He came toward Jessica with both hands outstretched, a look of fierce emotion upon his dark face. "Mira!" he gasped.

Now that, Jessica thought with rich satisfaction as she rose and extended one hand in greeting, proves it. He's nothing but a fraud. "The name is Jessica," she said calmly.

"But you are the image of your mother," he said in his precise, slightly accented English.

And that, Jessica thought on a smile, settles it. For she knew that she was the picture of her father.

The young man, Jessica noted dispassionately as she settled herself once again and he answered a question of Tom's, surprised her in at least one respect. She had thought that a fellow claiming to be a relative would have looked something like herself. But he was slight and swarthy, and being only of average height, he looked diminutive beside the other more sizable gentlemen. His clothing was as precise as his speech, but rather more colorful. His bright waistcoat, with its rich fobs, and the many jewels on his fingers were more lavish than even the most outright of the Dandy set's ornamentations. His hair was smooth and inky black, and his large black eyes, which he never turned from her for a moment, were ringed around with lustrous dark lashes.

As soon as he had answered Tom's question, which had to do with his lodgings in town, he turned to Jessica again. "Excuse me, Cousin," he said anxiously, "for my impertinence. But when I saw you sitting there, for a moment it was as if I saw your dear mama again. But now I see that you are taller, yes, and have a lighter complexion. Still, there is no doubt that you are her daughter. I had expected, from what I had heard of your papa, to see a real English miss, not our dear Mira again."

"That is a quantity of detail to have gotten from a portrait," Jessica said smoothly, cocking one eyebrow and bending a knowing look upon Thomas Preston. "But how did you ever discover my whereabouts?" Jessica went on, ignoring the slight frown upon Lord Leith's face.

"It is as I told Mr. Jeffers and everyone yesterday, when you were feeling unwell," Anton said, his great eyes searching her face. "My father had received a letter from Captain Eastwood, apprising us at last as to your whereabouts. It must be," he said solemnly, "as Sir Selby has said, that a soldier feels it in his bones when his day has come. We waited to hear from him, for he said that he would write again. When he did not, we set our own investigations into motion. And then we found that he had fallen and were very sorry."

Jessica inclined her head as if in acknowledgment of his sympathies, but really to hide the smile she could not help. Did he really think she was that green? She had heard better tales at her nursemaid's knee.

"And then, Papa decided that dealing through intermediaries was not enough. He delegated me to come to England to discover the matter myself."

"And," Jessica asked, barely controlling a sneer, "to reunite me into the bosom of the family?"

"It is our dearest wish," the dark young man said fervently.

"After all these years," Jessica mused aloud. "How very unexpected."

"Ah, no," Anton said uncomfortably, looking about at Mr. Jeffers as if for help, "not so unexpected. We knew of you, Jessica, but your papa never answered our letters before. In fact, he forbade all communication with your mama, as you must know."

"He never did believe in mediums, or the spirit world, Herr Von Keller," Jessica said sharply, growing impatient with the fellow.

"Jessica," Lord Leith began, but Anton, hurt showing in his large dark eyes, went on, "We do not blame him, Jessica. For none of us really knew him and your mama never spoke of him at all. It was as if that was a part of her life she did not wish to reexamine. But she fooled none of us. I for one, always saw the pain in her eyes when she looked upon a child. She never had another, you know."

"What are you talking about?" Jessica demanded, for the conversation was growing beyond her comprehension.

"But what else? Of Mira, your mama," Anton said in bewilderment.

Jessica rose to her feet. "And how can you speak of her when she has been gone for over fifteen years?" Jessica said in rage as a small niggling fear assailed her.

"Why, Jessica," he said, rising with her and taking one of her cold hands, "she was gone only from you. I thought Mr. Jeffers had told you. Your mama passed away not three years ago, but she lived not five kilometers from us until that time."

Jessica heard a great many voices above the loud buzzing in her ears. And when the annoying sound ceased, she found Lord Leith pressing a glass of liquid into her hands while Lady Grantham bent over her.

"Burnt feathers," the lady cried, while Ollie could be heard to insist that brandy would do the trick. Tom told her to put her head down and Mr. Jeffers tried to drown them all out by proclaiming that his wife swore by salts.

Jessica pushed the proffered glass away feebly and said peevishly, "I haven't fainted. I do not swoon. I only lost my bearings. I was startled, you see."

"You did not tell her?" Lord Leith asked his aunt incredulously.

"We were discussing other matters," Lady Grantham said weakly. "It quite slipped my mind."

The look the gentleman gave his aunt caused that sallow lady's color to rise, and she backed away to the fringes of the cluster of people gathered around Jessica.

"I am recovered now," Jessica said bravely, although her head still swam and she felt an icy knot in her stomach. But she never shied from the truth, so she turned her wide brown eyes to Anton. "Tell me the whole of it," she asked simply, "please."

It was a pitifully simple story, Jessica thought, so simple that she kept nodding her head as though in agreement for the whole of it. Her father had told her the truth: her mother had "gone" when she was in infant. But not to the great beyond, only as far as her original home in Austria. The two of them had fought, evidently, almost incessantly from the day the dashing Captain had talked the wealthy young noble-woman into eloping with him. Both Tom and Ollie verified that.

After one last convulsive battle, her mother had packed her belongings and left for good. Her father, returning from a tour of duty and finding himself and his infant abandoned, had turned his back upon the truth and had told everyone his wife had "gone." Even Ollie had not known then that her leaving had been only a physical displacement, rather than the ultimate journey to her maker he had assumed it to be.

Her mother, the beauteous Mira, had come from an influential family, and a legal divorce had been procured. The papers were, Mr. Jeffers admitted, discovered among Red Jack's meager belongings. She had married again, this time to a prosperous Austrian gentleman.

"But there was no issue," Anton said sadly. "You were her only child. As she was her father's only child. I am," he said with a little smile, "only your second cousin, but we are a close family."

"And her new husband?" Jessica asked almost fearfully, envisioning some portly mustachioed fellow swooping down and claiming her as a stepdaughter.

"Alas," Anton sighed, "the Baron left poor Mira a widow five years before her own passing. So you can see how glad we were to finally locate you, Jessica. And I tell you, you are Mira's own image. That hair, those eyes, that smile. Why, your mama was one of the greatest beauties of Vienna. How I admired her when I was a boy: always laughing, always bubbling, always dancing."

Something in Jessica's heart cracked a little when she thought of the beautiful dancing Mira, who could be so gay when her only child remained alone and lost across the Continent from her. But she only said softly, "I am said to resemble my father."

"So you do, Jess," Tom said into the silence that followed her remark.

"But there are so many portraits of her at home," Anton enthused. "You shall see them when you come. And then you will see what I say is true."

"But I don't intend to come, to leave England. Must I?" Jessica asked Mr. Jeffers at once.

"Why, no," Mr. Jeffers intoned. "You are in the care of Sir Selby now. But we naturally thought that you would wish to return to your family . . ." He broke off when Sir Selby interrupted.

"No, no, Jess. You may do whatever you wish."

"But we want you to come, Jessica," Anton said imploringly. "We are your family."

"Jess should do as she wants," Thomas said loudly. "She's no infant to be led about by the hand."

"I think," Lord Leith said in his rich deep voice, cutting over all the protestations and clamor that had arisen, "that it is far too soon for Jessica to decide what she wishes. This has all come as a shock to her. There is still the matter of her father's legacy to settle, before she decides upon her mother's. Time is the only remedy for such confusion."

"Yes," Jessica cried, holding on to that calm statement as to a lifeline, "just so."

"Of course," Anton said, looking deep into Jessica's distracted eyes, "I did not mean that she must rush off with me. I only meant to say that we not only offer her a home, but also do so with full hearts. Of course, she could not decide to leave with a stranger. She must get to know us."

"We leave for my country home within the week," Lady Grantham said thoughtfully, and then she exchanged a glance with her nephew. "Herr von Keller, should you like to stay with us? We are scheduled to leave for Griffin Hall by the weekend. But I would not wish to break up such a reunion with my plans."

"I could not so impose upon you, my Lady," Anton said sorrowfully.

"No imposition," Sir Selby put in. "It's a capital idea. We are all going and Jeffers knows that's where he shall find us."

"But, my dear Lady," Anton said, rising and bowing in front of Lady Grantham, "it is too much to ask that you shelter a complete stranger at such short notice."

"Nonsense," Lady Grantham said, happy to make amends for her forgetfulness. "It isn't the largest establishment in the Kingdom, but there are fifteen guest bedchambers, so I think you should have no compunctions. We shall be happy to have you."

"And you, Cousin?" Anton asked shyly, turning to Jessica.

"Of course," she answered automatically.

"Capital," Sir Selby said happily.

"What a good idea," Jessica said in a whisper, and wondered why, when she had so many new friends and it seemed relations as well, she should suddenly feel like weeping as the child who was left so many years ago might have done.

12

Anton was a delightful companion, there was no one who could deny that. He melted Lady Grantham's defenses with his sweetly earnest considerations in the days that passed after his introduction. For that Lady discovered that she could never enter a room without his huge dark eyes filling with anxiety as to her welfare or without his instant flattering interest in her appearance. But the fellow wasn't a coxcomb, Sir Selby had to admit, for all his airs and graces. He was, in fact, a regular out-and-outer, and his fencing skills were the talk of the exclusive club that he had been taken to as a guest.

There was nothing to dislike in him. He laughed at all of Thomas Preston's reminiscences about Captain Eastwood, agreed with every syllable uttered, and could not be prodded by any innuendo into any sort of disagreement. He was clearly impressed by Lord Leith's good Ton, and never let a moment pass without showing in some fashion how he admired that elegant gentleman's dress, manners, and style.

Jessica found him very diverting. For if Tom had said that Lord Leith's array of waistcoats showed that fashion was his consuming passion, she would have bridled and thought him a jealous fellow. But when Anton said, in his wondering innocent fashion, that surely Lord Leith must have a separate room for his waistcoats alone, since no one wardrobe could accommodate so many, she only dissolved into laughter at the possibility of that top-lofty fellow having a secret room in the attics just for his clothes. And if Lord Leith had drawled that Thomas had such a temper that he would have invented Napoleon just to have someone to vent his fury on, had that fellow not been born, Jessica would have thought him unconscionably snide. But when Anton mused upon that very theme one afternoon after Thomas had done with one of his war stories, Jessica had a bout of giggles, envisioning Thomas ranging the world seeking a suitably legitimate foe.

It was a relief to find someone who could make light of the two gentlemen Jessica had been most concerned with. Laughter both dissipated her uneasiness and reduced both men to a size where she could cope with them in her most private thoughts.

But she did not have time for too many private thoughts since Anton had arrived. For even as Lady Grantham saw to the preparations for their remove to the country, her town house was filled with company every waking hour. Thomas Preston arrived every morning to ride with Jessica and found himself riding with both Miss Eastwood and her diverting cousin. Lord Leith dropped by every afternoon to chat and discovered himself conversing with his aunt, her female guest, and her newfound cousin. Anton had become a staple of the household. It was as he had said, with his usual smile, that his whole object in traveling so far had been to acquaint himself with his cousin, and he must make every effort to make up for the lost years.

This was precisely what Jessica was attempting to explain to Thomas as they spoke after their morning ride. Anton, with his usual good graces, had gone to see to the stabling and welfare of their mounts, and Jessica thought that Thomas was being a great deal too hard upon her absent cousin.

"You don't understand," she said, more sharply than was her usual custom with Thomas. "He isn't forever hanging on my sleeve, as you say. Well, I suppose he is, but there's no harm in it. He is my cousin, after all."

"I know," Tom said as he ran a hand through his bright canary hair in exasperation. "But even though I have three brothers, you do not see them at my side each time we meet."

Jessica scolded him lightly. "Tom, just as you and I are comrades, so is Anton. Don't you see? Really, if you are to begin to resent his presence, where will it end? This isn't at all like you. You never minded when Ollie was about, nor even Leith. Has Anton offended you in some fashion?"

The fair-haired young man suppressed his agitation and gave Jessica a forced smile. "No, that isn't it at all. Never mind, Jess, I was just subject to a distempered fit. It is only that I tend to be jealous of my friends," he said weakly.

Jessica would have pursued the matter, but Anton entered the room and made further discussion impossible. It was not long before Tom bade them good-bye, saying that he had business to attend to. Although he shook hands warmly with Anton and made the best of bows to Jessica, leaving her with his broadest smile, it was a very disturbed gentleman that the butler saw to the door.

Once Tom had left, Jessica forgot the matter and turned her fullest attention to Anton. She bent a look of warm approval upon him.

He sat and went over the events of the morning in his usual fashion, as though they had been raised in adjacent cradles. Anton described his impressions of a fop they had encountered in the park, and Jessica's grin widened at his narration. At first, she had been alarmed by his claims to close kinship and by his pressing insistence upon friendship. But no longer, for he made no real demands upon her. For all that he was courtly and attentive, he never frightened her by speculative looks or even hinted that he wished for anything but cousinly affection.

He was a naturally warm person, she decided, watching his expressive face. So warm that one felt one could hold one's hands up toward him on a chill day and take the numbness from them. At first she had been confused at his constant need to sit close, to touch while speaking, to take her hands in his at every opportunity. But he had explained when he saw her withdraw in surprise that it was only the way of his people. Continentals, he assured her, were themselves surprised at how distant the English were with one another. Then he had solemnly promised to attempt to be more "British," as he put it, and ruined the whole effort by clasping her hands tightly in his own while he swore to try. He had been genuinely shocked when Jessica had dissolved in merriment as he so vowed.

Now, when she threw back her head and laughed as he mentioned the idiosyncrasies of the gentleman they had encountered, he stopped and said with a look of great awe, "So. Just so your mother would laugh. No, don't stop. When you laugh like that, I swear I see my Mira before me again."

"But I am not your Mira," Jessica said uncomfortably, "and I don't wish to be."

"There is nothing so bad in being like her," Anton protested, moving closer to her and taking up her hand. "You did not know her. I understand that you dislike being compared to her. Oh, I know," he said sadly, trying to look deep into her averted eyes, "that you do not like to speak of her. But, Cousin, I feel as a man with only one leg when you forbid me to speak. She was that much a part of my life. Of course, Papa and I agreed that you might feel anger toward her. But, Jessica, if you had only known her! She was not the sort of a lady to be able to fight your father for your care. She was too gentle for that."

"She would not have had to fight for me when she left," Jessica said soberly, "for my father was off to battle and she was alone with me."

"But, Jessica," Anton persisted, "those were dangerous times. Perhaps she was willing to endanger herself, but she could not bring herself to so expose an infant. I cannot say, for the subject of her baby was too tender for any of us to bring up to her. But I know that she would never, never have wished to leave you if she could have helped it."

Jessica sat silently for a moment. Anton's suggestion was one that had not occurred to her, and she turned and asked, "Do you think so, Anton? Truly, do you think that was the case?"

"If you had known her," he answered soberly, "you would not ask that of me."

"Of course," Jessica said rapidly, "it makes no difference now, for they are both gone. But to think that perhaps I had two loving parents, all the while . . . It is a comforting thought."

"That is what I am here for, Cousin," Anton said softly, "to bring you the comfort of a family. And now, too much serious talking," he said abruptly, his large dark eyes lit with laughter. "Now I must think of some way to divert you, Cousin, for when you frown like that, you are too British for me. No, I must make you laugh again, then I feel as though I have known you forever. Ah, but if I could see you dance, just once, I would know you were truly my cousin."

"Then you shall just have to wait till we attend a ball."

Jessica giggled, thinking that would be a rare sight, Red Jack's daughter waltzing and capering like a giddy miss.

"But there is no need to wait," Anton cried, catching her hand and making her rise with him. He placed a hand on her waist, never letting go of her other hand, and in moments he was circling the floor with her, humming the notes to the most popular new waltz from the Continent. After her initial surprise, she relented and they glided past tables, threaded their way through thatches of chairs, and wound about the room, dancing and laughing together.

This close to each other, the family resemblance, which had been superficially belied by their distinctly different coloring, was apparent, at least to one silent spectator. For though Jessica was fair when Anton was dark, they were of an even height and were matched in the delicate fine-boned structure of their faces and in their lithe grace.

Jessica tossed back the flaming hair that had escaped to cover one eye, and her long white neck bent back like a stem supporting the weight of an exotic showy scarlet bloom. Anton pulled her closer and his own dark head threw a shadow upon that snowy neck. How long they would have gone on there was no telling, but the humming and the laughter stopped abruptly when a deep laconic voice drawled, "Bravo!"

They stopped instantly in their tracks and looked to the door, where Alexander, Lord Leith, stood, his broad shoulders leaning negligently against the frame.

"No, don't stop," he said casually. "It was quite a performance. Are you practicing for some future party? I do hope I will be invited."

"We were only dancing," Jessica said nervously, pulling far away from Anton and looking as flustered as if they were indeed doing something as intimate as Lord Leith's set face and sarcastic tone implied.

"Jessica," Anton said earnestly, "is quite as good a dancer as her mother was."

"Is she?" the tall gentleman mused. "Pity I never got a chance to discover that. She refused me, you see, the only time I asked."

"I was only trying to prove to her that she had that talent," Anton said, now seemingly contrite as he gazed anxiously at the gentleman. "Have I overstepped good manners? Dancing is not considered fast at home, you see."

"Nor here either," Lord Leith said softly, "at a dance, that is."

Jessica cut through Anton's hurried apologies for any lapse in taste and said, "But we weren't expecting you, my Lord. That is to say, dash it all, Alex, why have you come?"

"*Very* hospitable," Lord Leith said.

"I don't mean that," Jessica cried in agitation, "and well you know it."

Her further flurry of explanations was cut off as he raised a white hand. "I only came to discuss travel arrangements with you, Jessica," he said calmly. "Have you forgotten we leave for Griffin Hall tomorrow morning?"

"*Also!*" Anton exclaimed. "I myself had forgotten. Can you excuse me, please, Cousin, my Lord? I must see to my valet and my packing."

"You needn't run off," Lord Leith said dryly.

But Anton, now all haste to go, said, "But there is need. I do not wish for your good aunt to have to wait a moment for me in the morning."

After kissing Jessica's hand and bowing to Lord Leith, Anton fairly flew from the room.

"Sorry to have routed your dancing partner," Lord Leith commented as he seated himself and cast one glance at Jessica's flushed face.

"There really was nothing to it," Jessica said defensively as she positioned herself in a chair across from him.

"Of course not," he said idly, inspecting the tip of his Hessians. "What could there be to it? Two cousins dancing? Do you think you will like it, then, in Vienna?"

Jessica sprang from her seat as though stung. "I am not going to Vienna, my Lord," she said. "Anton merely showed me how my mother was used to dance. Dancing with someone is not a commitment to anything."

"Calm yourself," the gentleman said with a trace of amusement, "I never said it was. Although, from the way you are carrying on now, I do begin to wonder."

Jessica sat and tried very hard not to show her rage. Why was it, she thought furiously, that he always made her feel she must justify herself? She paused and then said in a calm voice, "What time are we leaving, then?"

"Very good." He laughed. "No, don't fly up into the boughs again, Miss Eastwood. I'm only complimenting your good manners. I had no right to pull your leg. But what was I to think when I entered the room and found you two locked in each other's arms, dancing to unheard strings. Really, Jessica, I wondered if I had lost my hearing or you your wits."

"I must have," Jessica sighed, glad to hear his normal voice again, "but Anton is so persuasive."

"Indeed he is," Lord Leith said carefully, and then went on to discuss the arrangement of the carriages and the number of outriders for the next day's journey. They decided that Jessica would sit with Lady Grantham in the lead carriage, and that they would allow Sir Selby to ride alongside upon his favorite mount only long enough for him to prove he was still a hearty campaigner before they called him into the carriage. They laughed immoderately at the ruses they would use to achieve this end. Soon Jessica found herself completely in charity with her visitor again.

"I didn't know," she interrupted as he began to detail a ruined abbey they must plan to visit in July, "that you intended to stay so long. That is," she said as she noted his curious look, "I thought you were only going to see us settled in and then dash back to town."

"Do you think me such a town beau, then?" he asked. "No. I usually leave London for the whole of summer and often find I must force myself from the land when the leaves begin to turn. In fact," he went on, stretching out his legs, "I have been occupied with building a house for myself not two leagues from Aunt's for these past three years. It is almost done with now. We'll have to ride over one day and spend the night. All of us, that is." He smiled.

"But building a house?" Jessica asked. "I had thought that you would have had a family seat, you know, just as your aunt does."

"I did," he said thoughtfully, "but you see, it is my brother's now. I had to sell off my own meager property years ago. You remember I told you how shockingly expensive my brother was. Don't look so sorrowful, my estate was only a small holding, and as I never spent time there, it was no wrench to rid myself of it when the need arose. But now that I'm a gentleman of parts, I've occupied myself with providing my heirs a proper sort of home. And the advantage is that I've helped to design it all myself. The disadvantage is that when I discover a drafty chimney, I can't heap abuse upon some ancestor's head for its deficiencies.''

As he went on to describe his new home and the lake that lay beside it, Jessica watched him closely. It was curious that times such as these, when they were in harmony, were times when she felt the most wary of him. It was as though she could never be completely at ease with him, as she could be with Tom or her cousin. But why this was, she could not say. When he relaxed, his strong features softened, his gray eyes held no threat, and his curved mouth lost its arrogant contour. As she found herself watching that mouth and wondering at whether its color was actually a pale lavender or rather a soft rose, she realized the trend of her thoughts and jerked her head up so that she looked him in the eye. As that was no better, she fell to examining a fold in her skirts.

"And of course, the stables are well away from the house, and Lord, I'm boring you to flinders, aren't I?" He chuckled.

"No," she protested, "not at all. It must be a rewarding project to undertake."

"I've found it so," he said. "And do you know the best part?" As she hurriedly shook her head in the negative, he went on, "When I stood beneath its rafters for the first time, I had the most delightful notion. As the first occupant, I shall have the honor of being the first ghost. Well," he said with a smile, noting her shocked expression, "in any other great house, I should have to spend eternity shouldering aside all manner of previous occupants if I want to get up to a good night's haunting. But at Bright Waters, I will have seniority. Can you just imagine some future Lord Leith quaking in his bed as I rattle down the long hall I designed? Or some nanny in a far-off generation ordering my great-grandchildren to eat their porridge or old Alex will get them? Or guests being shown the head of the dining table with a quaking finger and being told, 'Here is where old Alex fell, stone cold dead after his last drink of port. On this very spot. And you can still hear him roaming the house on windy nights, looking for another glass.' "

While he laughed, Jessica could not. She suddenly felt great pity for the beleaguered boy who had to sell off his birthright and toil for years in a far-off land until he could build another home. She sorrowed for his loneliness, envisioning him standing in his unfinished house able to think only of his demise.

So it was in the spirit of trying to cheer him, and not, she afterward told herself again and again, to dispel the discomforting mood of intimacy that had overtaken her, that she said quickly, "But surely you will have someone with you," she blurted. "You are not going to leave Miss LaPoire all alone when you take up residence there?"

"Miss LaPoire?" he said, sitting up straight and glaring at Jessica. His mouth, she saw, was now rigid.

"Why, yes, your lady," she began, until she saw the look in his eye.

"How dare you mention her name!" he thundered, leaping to his feet and towering over her.

Jessica stood as well. Although he was enraged enough to cause her to catch her breath, his swift change of mood and his presumption in shouting at her caused her temper to flare. When she was angry with him, she noted fleetingly, she felt much better and on firmer ground.

"How dare you bellow at me!" she cried. "If she exists, I can mention her name. I did not think she was some sort of holy icon."

"It is not fit that a young woman speak of such females," he countered.

"And why not?" she shrilled, beside herself at the injustice of it. Her words tumbled out as they formed in her mind. "If you can speak of her, why can't I?"

"But I did not speak of her, I never would, to a young lady," he started to say, but she went on, "It is just ridiculous. If she is your mistress—yes, mistress, for I won't say lady-friend—after all, why can't I say it if I know it?" she asked, puzzlement beginning to take the edge off her fine fury.

"Proper young females do not discuss a gentleman's mistress," he answered, beginning to lose some of his anger as well as he realized how pompous he sounded.

"But I'm not a proper young female," Jessica said as

though explaining to a child, "and really, if a gentleman is notorious for having a famous mistress, he shouldn't become savage when she is brought up in conversation."

To her amazement, the irate gentleman before her began to smile. Soon he was laughing heartily. When he had done, he put both hands upon Jessica's shoulders and spoke in a reasonable voice, "Jessica, believe me. What you say makes perfect sense. But also be assured that it is simply not the thing for a young lady to discuss with a gentleman, even if it is true. Which it isn't," he added quickly. "Anymore. But you are not supposed to know of such arrangements, much less mention them. Was it your dear friend Tom who told you?" he asked.

"No," Jessica said, feeling the weight of his large hands upon her shoulders. "No, it was my good friend Maria Dunstable, and your aunt too."

He grimaced. "Ah, well," he sighed. "I am sorry I shouted at you, but it isn't something I care to discuss. At any rate, Jessica, a gentleman never asks such a woman to his home. Blast," he muttered, "I should not even be explaining it to you."

Jessica looked up at the elegant face before her and drew in her breath. It seemed that his hands tightened on her and that he was going to draw her closer. His gray eyes held a considering look. She closed her own eyes for a moment, thinking he was going to embrace her again as he had another time when he could not explain his point. That thought sent shivers of what she felt were sheer terror through her, and she wrenched away from him.

"It is not fair," she said bravely, looking anywhere but into those eyes that could drown her resolve so quickly, "that a gentleman may take as many mistresses as he can, but that a lady cannot even mention them. And no," she went on, "it is not fair to think that one sort of female cannot know about another. We are all females, after all. Would you shout at her if she mentioned me? But that would be nonsense too."

He stood and looked at her, and then said quietly, "Jessica, this is not seemly. I'll leave you now and see you in the morning."

As he turned to go, she whispered, "But can't you see? It is ridiculously unfair, is it not?"

And because for the first time he realized that it was, he could not answer. He only bowed and left a sorely troubled young woman gazing after him.

There were many things that Lord Leith had thought to do with his afternoon, many details that he had to clear up before he left the city. One such matter he had thought to take care of in the evening; he now decided, as his long legs took him far from his aunt's house, he would have to see to it right away. For he was not in the habit of lying, if he could avoid it, to any man or woman.

It was a short walk to the house, and a shorter step into her bedroom. But he felt as though he had come a long way.

"My Lord," she cried when she saw him, "so early in the day? I am delighted. We shall have hours and hours of joy before us."

"I'm afraid not, Lucille." He smiled. "I'm off to the country tomorrow and I've only stopped by to bid you adieu."

"*Au revoir*, surely." She laughed. She looked very well, he thought as she approached him in her misty-blue dressing gown, with her dark hair in artful disarray. But when she began to wrap her arms about his neck, he stepped back.

"No, no, my dear," he said, "I speak the truth. I must not tarry today. But I have a little present for you."

He withdrew the bank check from his pocket and handed it to her. Although she tried to make it seem as though she only glanced at it before she set it on the table, he saw her eyes widen as she saw the figure written upon it.

"But surely there is no need for such generosity," she said, giving up all attempts at ignoring the sum.

"But there is," he said, "for it is not only to compensate you for the time I will be gone. There is enough there, I believe, to give you ample leisure to select a new companion."

She sighed softly. She had known that this moment was coming from the infrequency of his visits of late. She had been sure of it the night he had gone off into riotous laughter when she had drawn back the curtain from the mirror over her bed. Mistress LaPoire had been in her profession long enough to know that though laughter might be the sweet balm of love, it was a death knell to fascination. But still, it was hard to let him go. There would be others, many others; she did not depend on youth or looks for her continuing career. But she was loath to part from him.

"I suppose," she said coquettishly, "it is that scarlet-haired young pretty you've been escorting around the town. I imagine you decided it's time to set up a nursery. But really, my Lord, even so, there is no need to completely sever our pleasant association."

He cut her off with an upraised palm. "My dear," he said harshly, "it is not a proper thing for you to mention, is it?"

But he did not hear her reply, he was so startled to hear the echoing of his own words in his mind.

"No, quite right," she said with uncharacteristic spite. "Mustn't acknowledge her existence, must I?"

But she recovered herself quickly and only said in a placating manner, "Well, then, I thank you, my Lord. Should you care to stay on for a while today?"

"No, no, thank you, Lucille," he answered brusquely, bedeviled by his own thoughts and by the strange cold way he could say farewell to someone whom he had shared such intimacies with.

They parted as good business associates should, he thought, with a handshake so firm that it would have gladdened Miss Eastwood's heart.

It was only when he was on the pavement again, heading in the direction of his own house, that he thought, with a sense of wonderment, that Miss Eastwood had been quite correct. It was ridiculous. All of it. And he was growing heartily weary of it.

13

As Griffin Hall was only a day's ride from London, Jessica first saw it as glorious sunset wreathed it with rosy light. But it didn't need that spectacular assist from nature to give it stature. She thought it the most imposing home she had ever seen. It stood upon a grassy rise, huge and white and serene. It looked almost, she thought fancifully as she peered from the coach window, like some sort of hallowed ancient temple. But unworldly though she was, even she could clearly see that this particular ancient temple would have easily housed a hundred Druids without letting the hems of their ceremonial robes touch.

"Of course," Lady Grantham said as she watched her awestruck young visitor's face, "it isn't in the latest mode. It's been in the family for generations and hasn't half the flash or modern conveniences that the great edifice Alex has been about erecting these past years has got. But," she added comfortably, "we like it."

Jessica wondered what there was that anyone could not admire about such a place. It was more of an artistic composition than a mere dwelling. Even the sunset seemed no fortuitous accident, but rather part of the original plans for the place. The towering trees appeared to have been carefully set in their places by some giant artist's hand just so that they could cast the proper shadows upon particular verdant stretches of lawn, and even the several peacocks parading in the park like animated lady's fans seemed to have been judiciously arranged to lend an extra dash of color to the whole.

This was not a thing like the rustic country home Jessica had envisioned and she wondered that her hostess had thought she might have more freedom and relaxation here. For, she decided as the coach went sedately along the long and winding gravel drive, Griffin Hall, at first stare, seemed more intimidating than London itself had been.

The physical part of the journey had been easy enough, but it could not have been said to have been a truly pleasant day. Lady Grantham and Ollie had been their usual selves, but none of the others had been quite natural. Thomas Preston had ridden alone and apart from the others, the only bright thing about him the sunlight glancing off his erect golden head. Anton had seemed happy to be upon his sleek gray mount, so happy, in fact, that he did not cease chattering all the while, even calling light comments to them each time he rode past their window. And Lord Leith had so busied himself with the details of their travels that he had no time or word for any of them. When they had broken their journey at a wayside inn for lunch, the unspoken tensions had put an end to any idea of easy camaraderie.

So it was a much-subdued Miss Eastwood who stepped forth from the carriage with her hostess to be shown to her rooms.

Once Anton and Tom and Sir Selby had gone off with various manservants, Lady Grantham removed her hat and let out a vast sigh of relief as she unceremoniously sank to a divan in a sunset-filled sitting room.

"Lord, Alex," she puffed, "never again, I vow it. What an uncomfortable journey. I chattered like a magpie to dispel the gloom until Ollie was staring at me as though I'd lost my wits. And so I should have, if we had gone a pace farther. Thomas Preston sat mute as a thundercloud brewing upon the horizon, but he couldn't have gotten a word in edgewise if he had wanted to, for all the babbling Anton was doing. And as for Jessica, she acted as though she were being taken to perdition rather than to Griffin Hall. And you, my dear boy, played least in sight through the entire affair. What has gotten into everyone? If this is the way we mean to go on, I'd as lief pack it in and turn around for town again."

"Never fear," her nephew said, smiling, "I am convinced it was a momentary aberration. Some people show their nervousness by rattling on, as Anton did. He is, after all, in the tenuous position of being a foreign gentleman invited to a virtual stranger's country home. Some become shy, as undoubtedly Thomas Preston did. Jessica likely felt uneasy about being taken here so soon after her adventuring in town. And, Aunt, this great mound of yours is a bit staggering at first glance. I'm not sure that any of your guests have ever passed a night in such a place. When I was young, I used to think I was visiting the palace whenever I arrived. I distinctly recall always whispering for the first day, for fear of waking the King.''

''Nonsense,'' Lady Grantham said irritably. ''You came from just as pleasant a home. And anyway,'' she went on hurriedly, suddenly remembering the true condition of her nephew's childhood home, when his father began to sell off all the family belongings to pay for his eldest son's indiscretions, ''they were behaving oddly even before they clapped an eye on Griffin Hall.''

''I am convinced that all will be well when they grow accustomed to their surroundings,'' her nephew said calmly, as though the problem had already left his mind.

Lady Grantham noted his boredom and said with some acidity, ''Well, they never shall if you don't come out of the clouds. You scarcely had a word for anyone all day. Joseph knew the road as well as his own palm, there was no need for you to hover about him constantly. And as there are no brigands about in broad daylight, I cannot see why you rode guard as though we were carrying the Crown Jewels in the baggage.''

''I shall mend my manners straightaway,'' Lord Leith replied, but with such patent disinterest that his aunt literally threw up her hands in disgust.

The tall gentleman chuckled at that and then went up to his rooms to arrange things, as he said, and to dress for dinner. But, he thought even as he left her, the things most in need of ordering were his thoughts. He had deliberately not spoken a great deal while they were in transit. It was not as though he were so simpleminded that he could not ride and speak at the same time, he told himself with a self-deprecating grin as he rested his hands upon his window's sill and gazed down at the tranquil approaching evening. It was that he had grown into the habit of thinking a thing through before he took any action. That was a lesson he had learned in a hard school during those years abroad.

He had undertaken the task of educating Ollie's protégée

into the art of acceptable feminine behavior at first out of a sense of obligation and then because the entire effort amused him greatly. But as is so often the case when one immerses oneself in a task completely, amusement soon gave way to real interest. Miss Eastwood was the most uncommon female he had ever encountered, but he recalled with a frown, he had realized that from the first.

As he had gotten to know her, he had come to admire those very things that made her so unfeminine: her lack of vanity, her courage, her forthrightness, and her gallantry. She might have made a fine young fellow, but he had the uneasy feeling that she might make a finer woman someday because of those very attributes that he was supposed to discourage.

Damn, he thought in annoyance, I like the baggage just as she is. But it was clear to him that she was in the process of changing even as he thought of her. What he had set in motion was gaining a momentum of its own. The fine clothes he ordered did not make her preen like one of those strutting peacocks, he watched it only made her delightfully aware of her own attractions. The attentions he made sure she received in London had not turned her head, but only helped her make the sad discovery that most people judged mostly by appearances.

The two gentlemen who now hovered about her were ingredients of her education, but he had not requested their services and he could not yet fathom their impact upon her. Thomas Preston was at least open about his intentions. He wanted her for her forthcoming fortune. And that, the tall gentleman decided, his face growing still, he would never permit. Surely she deserved better. Anton, that delightfully amusing, facile fellow, seemed to want no more than to clasp her to the bosom of her long-lost family. But he had seen a considering look in Anton's eyes at odd moments, and he wondered if that was the only bosom Anton wished to clasp her to.

These thoughts still nagged at him as he turned to summon his valet to help him change for dinner, for he decided that he had dwelt upon the subject long enough. He was not, after all, her father.

The fact that she was becoming uncommonly desirable

was, admittedly, often disturbing. But there was nothing new in that. He had known innumerable desirable females and yet remained wise enough to sate desire only with those whose state or station precluded marriage. So far as matrimony went, he felt it could continue on is way without him. Lord Leith's brother may have gotten the title and inheritance, but his own birth as second son, plus the wages he had earned in his years of exile, had given him the freedom to wed where he would. But he would not.

Yet the odd Miss Eastwood most decidedly did not want the services of either husband or lover. In fact, he thought with only a little annoyance, she seemed to dislike any physical contact with him.

The slight sound of his valet tapping upon his door eased his thoughts from their deepening channels. He would, he decided as he absently requested a bath be drawn, look after her interests as a brother should, for he was only trying to secure her happiness in much the same way that he would for any young person he had grown fond of. He decided with relief that he felt it such a paramount, pressing duty only because of the trials he had suffered because his own brother had not so exerted himself for him.

When Sir Selby's valet, freed for the task by his employer, knocked upon Mr. Preston's door to offer his services, he was politely told that there was no need for him.

"In fact," Mr. Preston said, "you know we old army fellows can take care of ourselves. Unless," he added, giving the man his best white-toothed grin, "we come into a title, of course."

The valet had accepted the lighthearted answer and taken himself off to the kitchens for some gossip to fill his unexpected free time. It was because of such proclivities that Mr. Preston had disdained his help in the first place. Because, he told himself as he shut the door and went back to the task of dressing himself, it was bad enough to have to watch one's step every moment without one's missteps being the subject of idle servants' banter as well. Although he had come from a good family, there were leagues of differences between a country squire's establishment and a palatial home such as the one he now found himself within.

He washed and dressed quickly, with a neat economy of motion that left little time wasted. Thus, when he had done and examined himself in the glass for faults and found none, he discovered that he had time to spare. As it would be socially incorrect to lounge about belowstairs as though he were so hungry he could not bear to wait for dinner, he sat in a chair in his room until he judged it would be late enough to make it seem as if he had just recalled the hour. But he did not relax.

There was so much latent energy in his trim frame that he appeared to be poised for some more dire activity than a pleasant country dinner. He was a man of decision and he could scarcely bear to wait to put his most recent decision into action. Events had taken him far in time, place, and mind since he had struck his bargain with the noxious Cribb. He still planned to wed Jess, he thought with a grim smile, it was only that unexpected impediments had come into play against him. But if he knew anything, it was the maneuverings of war, and if it were to be a battle, he was the man for it.

That Leith disapproved of him was no matter, for Jess herself did not entirely approve of Leith. And it would be the work of a moment to show Jess that she was only a passing interest of the tall gentleman's, and an obligation rather than an interest at that. No, it was Anton who troubled him. For he could not explain that young man's motives at all. Was it cousinly affection that glued him to Jess's side, or was it something more? And if something more, why?

It was true that Jess was becoming something quite out of the ordinary in looks, but not even her dearest champion could claim that she had a patch on some of the great Society beauties that a gentleman like Anton had access to. She had none of the graces, wiles, and fascination of those females. She was still in many ways, no matter what the costumes she now affected, more lad than lass. But lass enough for him, Tom thought, a rare real smile softening his tight lean face.

He had few illusions about her gender. He had a need for females, but he fulfilled that need as he would any other appetite. And he would no more refine the next day upon any female he had spent a most enjoyable night with than he would rhapsodize and moon over an excellent roast he had partaken of the night before. In much the same way that, if no gourmet repast presented itself when he grew hungry, he would devour inferior dishes, he placed no high premium upon any bed companion. He liked to think of himself as a practical man. But he never actually thought of females as a class, as being precisely human. He had little interest in them aside from the bodily pleasures they presented.

But Jess was different. For all her new trappings, he had almost to remind himself at times that she was not just another bright young fellow. She would suit him perfectly. And, he decided, rising now that the twilight shadows were forming, for as an ex-army man the sky was a surer clock for him than any Swiss masterpiece, he would have her. He would no longer sulk or hide when Anton came upon the scene. Upon reflection, it was he himself who held all the cards. He knew her father and the bond that had been forged between them. He knew just how strong that bond could be, and he could remind Jess of it whenever she thought to lapse. And best of all, he thought as he went to join the others, he could do all with a clear conscience. For with all her fortune, he was clearly the best man for her, for hadn't he been told often enough that he was a man's man?

Anton von Keller heard the door to the next room open and close, and his valet, from his place by his own half-open door, whispered to tell him that Mr. Preston had gone down to join the others. With a sigh of satisfaction, Anton stood. A glance in the mirror told him that all was well. He had spent the better part of an hour dressing, but it was well worth it. He smiled as he thought of how Jessica would be impressed with his good appearance, and as he had taken care to be the last to arrive before dinner, she could hardly miss noticing. It was odd how she did not sum up a man with her eyes as all the ladies of his acquaintance did. But then, he shrugged, she was English, after all. But only half-English, he reminded himself.

It was very good, he thought as he stepped from his rooms, that she was lovely, a copy of her mother. And even better than she had never lost her heart to anyone. The cold Lord Leith had no interest in her. The anxious Mr. Preston had too much. As Papa had predicted, it had been a worthwhile journey, even if it had taken him from his loved accustomed pastimes. But to have a wife who was the image of Mira! That was well worth any arduous travel. And if she did not as yet acknowledge that link, he would be sure to remind her.

Blood will tell, he told himself as he sauntered down the long stairs, and if it will not, he thought gaily, I shall.

Lady Grantham was well-pleased with dinner. It was a great success. The food, of course, did not matter. But the conversation was sparkling. Alex was at his top form, amusing and gracious. Ollie was clearly enjoying himself. Mr. Preston had come out of his blue dismals and was most congenial. Anton, of course, was a superb dining companion, as usual. But Jessica was transformed by their turnabout. She was in great spirits and looks. It was too bad, Lady Grantham thought as she and Jessica rose to leave the gentlemen to their port, that such occasions could not be pressed between the leaves of a book, to be taken out and savored in some fashion long after they were over and done.

She smiled at Jessica as they sat in the music room and awaited the others. The girl was blooming, she thought with almost maternal pride. Her countenance was clear and open. Her magnificent hair had been arranged a la Sappho, and its high color exquisitely set off the periwinkle-blue gown she wore. And bless Madame Celeste, but the chit's high tip-tilted breasts were clearly defined by the clever cut of the gown, which Jessica had put on only because she deemed the neckline high enough for propriety. We'll get her hitched in spite of herself, Lady Grantham gloated as she tried to turn an unremarkable face to the girl.

"We couldn't bear to leave the lovelies alone," Sir Selby chortled as he entered the room, as he always did, bless him, Lady Grantham sighed.

"No, indeed," Anton echoed, "for this custom of drinking alone when there are delightful ladies by themselves is quite . . . British," he faltered. "Which is not to say that it is not a very delightful custom," he went on hastily, "but in my homeland, we should never leave such beauties alone, for fear of losing them."

"It is a vast place," Lord Leith said reflectively, "but to my knowledge we have never lost a guest. Some have strayed, to be sure, but none have actually been misplaced."

"But they could be stolen, it is not so?" Anton said with a great show of slyness, as amid the general laughter he sat down next to Jessica on the divan.

"Not Jess," Tom said heartily, "for it would take a whole regiment to carry her off if she did not want to go."

Jessica laughingly agreed and motioned for Tom to come and sit at her other side. Lord Leith stood and chatted with Sir Selby. Lady Grantham was content to relax in a comfortable chair and enjoy the company. But Jessica soon found that her neck was growing strained with having to turn first to Anton and then to Tom. For, though she sat back far enough so that the two gentlemen could converse, neither seemed to have any interest in talking to each other and both tried to keep up separate conversations with her.

As Tom awaited her reply as to plans for riding in the morning, and Anton bent closer to hear what she thought of the weather, Jessica's gaze chanced to fall upon the pianoforte.

"Oh, Ma'am," she breathed in a sort of desperation to Lady Grantham, "do you think you could prevail upon Lord Leith to play at the pianoforte? For he is the most excellent musician."

Lady Grantham raised an eyebrow. "Been showing off, has he? That's rare, for he usually don't play for company. He always begs off. Well, what do you say, Alex? Here's a request you can't say nay to."

"But how churlish do you think I am?" her nephew replied, breaking off his conversation. "Of course I shall play upon such a sweet request. But not a solo piece, I'm afraid. I'm far too shy for that. I shall want an accompanist."

Sir Selby threw out his chest in pleasure, for he was known to have a fine, deep baritone. Anton smiled gaily, as his dulcet tenor was usually in great demand at home. Thomas Preston steeled himself, for although he was accounted to have a fair voice, he knew only music-hall tunes and barracks ballads of the sort that could not be rendered in polite company.

But all three gentlemen drew back in surprise when Lord Leith, seating himself at the piano, said, with a wicked arch smile, "And, of course, if I accede to such a charming request, I shall expect my request to be met with the same good grace. Come, Jessica, and sing for me."

Lady Grantham frowned. It was very bad Ton for Alex to corner the child that way. With her upbringing, it was unlikely that she could sing a note. She noted Thomas Preston's growing pale about the lips while the other two guests smiled in anticipation. She was about to volunteer to sing herself, although she had been told often enough by those even nearest and dearest that her voice alarmed crows, when she was forestalled by Jessica's saying, "Of course, my Lord. I am honored."

She did not look honored, Lady Grantham thought uneasily. As she rose and strode to the pianoforte, she looked as though she might put paid to Lord Leith's career not only as a pianist, but as a living man.

As Jessica stood beside the pianoforte she glared at her accompanist. She did not wish to sing, had never sung in company before, in fact. But she knew a challenge when one was issued, and had never turned from one yet. Though she would far rather have supped with the devil than open her mouth to sing in public, she would not cry off as a craven.

"You need not, you know," her tormentor said in an undervoice. "I was merely teasing you. Let Ollie do the honors. His breast is swollen with stoppered song. Go," he added kindly, "none will think the worse of you. It was, after all, an ill-mannered jest. Aunt was right, I don't usually play for company and I expect I was only exacting revenge.

But the kindness in his tone signified condescension to Jessica, and she would not back down. "It's quite all right," she said with admirable control, "I should like to. I do not know many popular tunes, nor any opera. But," she said as he was about to release her from the bargain again, "I do know many folk tunes. The music is not written down anywhere that I know of. But if you think you can manage without a music sheet, I should be delighted to sing," she concluded sweetly.

The tall gentleman bit back a smile and answered humbly, "I can but try."

The song that Jessica sang, "Fine Flowers in the Valley," was an old one, about a deceitful woman, a murdered infant, and a wise child. Heavy stuff, indeed, Lady Grantham thought. But Alex had either heard it or in his remarkable fashion learned it quickly enough to provide gentle accompaniment. Yet the surprise was neither in the subject of the piece nor in the piano rendition. It was in Jessica's voice. It was an intimate breathy voice, soft, throaty, and true. It was not suited to a concert hall, but rather brought to mind the gentle whispering of trees or half-remembered strains hummed at a cradle's side. Jessica had to sing three roles, and for each her affect subtly changed. Soon her audience was enraptured.

Lady Grantham sat back in contentment. The girl was acquitting herself well. The elder lady looked over toward Ollie to see him beaming with fatherly pride. But she saw Thomas Preston at his side, looking at Jessica with a determined devouring stare. Anton too was gazing at the unknowing singer with a look of such greedy possession that Lady Grantham was startled. She chanced to look to Alex to see what he made of all this, and there surprised such a look upon his face as she had never thought to see, for he was watching Jessica with a peculiarly fond and tender gaze.

Good heavens, thought Lady Grantham, so shocked by what she alone had seen that she did not even join in the applause at the end of the rendition. This shall not be a restful vacation, after all.

14

Although midsummer's eve had passed, the skies remained light until after ten in the night. Yet there still did not seem to be enough hours in each day that Jessica spent at Griffin Hall. Bright mornings passed as if in a moment with riding; afternoons fled as lawn games were played, or picnics enjoyed, or excursions were joyfully taken. Dinners did not end the day as they had at home, rather they signaled the beginning of long laughter-filled hours of light gaming, music, and conversation. Even inclement weather did not still the jocund company. By the time Jessica prepared for bed each night, she was too worn out with merriment to lie awake a moment to ponder her new circumstances or the changes they had wrought upon her.

Anton had become a dear and delightful playmate. He had an almost childlike capacity for enjoyment and never allowed her a moment's seriousness when he was in her vicinity. Thomas was an amiable companion, becoming solemn and silent only when he waited for a fish to follow his lure or was deciding upon which card he should next play. Lord Leith was a relaxed and entertaining comrade. He kept Jessica roundly amused with his droll commentary and impressed her with his unexpected prowess at sports she would have thought he had left behind in boyhood. Lady Grantham was the best of hostesses, and she and Sir Selby pleased themselves by watching their younger guests at play. The countryside seemed to have worked a faerie magic upon them all, and Jessica sometimes laughed in the rare moments when she was alone at how she could have ever seen Griffin Hall as forbidding or formal.

This day the elder pair were seated on the lawn in the dappled shade of a spreading beech, watching their four junior guests playing at lawn bowls. Sir Selby was guffawing at Anton's antics as he pretended to find himself incapable of getting up from the grass where he had been awaiting his turn. But there was not the faintest hint of amusement upon his companion's thoughtful face.

"There's a storm brewing," Lady Grantham finally intoned as Sir Selby wiped his eyes and chuckled.

"Nonsense," Sir Selby replied, quickly scanning the azure sky. "It's a bit warm, but there's not a cloud above us. It's the fairest day we've had yet."

"Not that sort of storm, Ollie," Lady Grantham said pensively as she watched Thomas Preston's set face as he in turn watched Jessica weak with laughter at Anton's clowning.

"Don't speak in riddles, my dear," Sir Selby said irritably. "You know how I like plain speaking." He turned from his observations to look at her. "Why, you're not jesting! What's troubling you, my dear? You've got the grimmest look about you. Has anything happened?"

"Not yet," Lady Grantham said cryptically. Then, noting her companion's confusion, she bent forward and sighed. "Ollie, leave off laughing for a moment and really watch that lot out there."

Sir Selby did as he was bade to do. He saw Thomas Preston take up his position in the game; saw Anton confide something to Jessica, who threw back her head in an arch flirtatious gesture as she laughed; and saw Alex, his jacket thrown off and in his shirtsleeves, watching Anton and Jessica with alert, evident interest.

"I've seen them," Sir Selby said in bewilderment, "and they seem merry as grigs. What are you going on about?"

Lady Grantham saw Jessica called up to her mark by Tom, his turn done, and saw her straighten her back and march to his side, all traces of coquetry gone. She saw the flaxen and the fiery heads bent close together for an instant, and she noticed the beginnings of a frown upon her nephew's face, which vanished the moment Anton recalled him to his surroundings with a jest. She sighed again, so heavily that Sir Selby frowned as well.

"Never mind, Ollie, but mark me well, this cannot last."

"I suppose not," he said. "It's been uncommonly good weather and we're due for a good dousing. But it's nothing to take on so about," he complained. And then, shrugging at the inscrutability of all women, even his boon companion, he turned with pleasure to watch the game go forth again.

When they had done with the game, Lady Grantham accepted Sir Selby's arm as they strolled back to the Hall to rest before preparing for dinner, for the hour had grown late.

Anton, noting his elders leaving, made his bows, picked up his jacket from the grass where he had thrown it, and after a parting jest, hurried along so that he could have ample time to prepare himself for the evening as well. None of his fellow game players were surprised, for it was well-known by now that Anton prized his correct appearance above all else in life. Although they had dined together every evening for a fortnight, no one could recall seeing the fellow with a hair out of place once or with a similar getup twice, they often joked.

Although Lord Leith offered to escort Jessica back to the house, as he often did, she hesitated, for Thomas seemed to be searching for something in the grass.

"I'll wait for Tom," she explained brightly as she did not take his proffered arm.

He shrugged, smiled down at her, and whispered, "Probably searching for his aim. I never saw him so off his game before. Even you beat him to flinders this time, Jessica."

"Even I?" Jessica said haughtily, then grinned. "You're right, I fair routed him, didn't I?"

As he stood and watched her, with a bemused smile upon his lips, she said conspiratorially, "I'll help him look for whatever it is he's lost, and gloat a little over my victory as well. Just a little," she added with a mischievous smile.

Lord Leith seemed to shake himself from reverie, and then muttering, "Wretch," he left her laughing again as he went back to the house. His long legs had taken him far up the lawn when she turned and went back toward Tom.

"Whatever have you misplaced, Tom?" she asked merrily. "Alex is of the opinion that it's your mastery of the game."

She waited for an easy reply and was shocked when he turned a deadly serious face to her and answered bluntly, "No, it something far more valuable than that."

She dropped to her knees by his side at once and said in alarm, her eyes searching the even green turf, "What is it? May I help? Where did you last see it?"

He rose to his feet, helping her up with him in one fluid

movement. His gaze was stern as he said softly, "I last saw it in Yorkshire, Jess, and I fear it is irrevocably gone. But yes, perhaps you can help me find it again."

Her eyes were wide with startled confusion as he took her arm and led her to the chairs that Lady Grantham and Sir Selby had just vacated. She sank to a seat, watching his forbidding visage. There was no trace of jest in his cool blue eyes, and every line in his hard young face was set and pronounced.

"Jess, Jess," he breathed, shaking his head slightly, "how can I put it? I only stayed behind so that I might have a private talk with you. I haven't had the chance to speak with you apart from the others since the day I set foot in this great cavern of a palce. There is always someone at your side. But I have stayed and watched and listened, and I cannot stay still a moment more."

"What is it, Tom?" she whispered, though there was not a soul in sight and only the slight rush of wind through the trees to compete with the sound of their voices.

He took one of her hands in his. And this was unusual, for while Anton was forever holding her hand, Tom had never so much as touched her since they had met again in London. His hand, she noted irrelevantly, was not plump and warm as Anton's always was, rather it was cool and hard. But it held her tightly as he spoke, his eyes never wavering.

"Jess, can you not see? Do you not know? I came to London and found you transformed. But it was a good change, for you seemed to at last have grown up. You were lovely, Jess, truly lovely, and as I said then, your father would have been proud of you."

"But what has changed, Tom?" Jessica asked. "I've bought no new frocks since then," she said thoughtfully. "What is the problem?"

"Can you not see what you have become?" he cried in agitation as she drew back at the vehemence in his tone. "Batting your lashes, simpering, tossing your hair about, posturing. Good Lord, Jess, you are become like some music-hall caricature of a giddy female. I grieve to see the alteration in you. You used to remind me so much of Red Jack, you were so straight and true. Now . . . ." He made a gesture of despair.

Jessica gaped at him. Then she drew herself up, snatched her hand from his, and spat, "Where? When have you ever seen me act so? Have I ever simpered at you, Tom, or fluttered my lashes? You're speaking nonsense, my good fellow."

"Oh, no," he said dourly, "never to me. To me you are just as you always were. But you are a chameleon, Jess, for when you are with Anton, you are transformed."

Jessica sat with an arrested look upon her face. It was true, she thought suddenly, that association with Anton had altered her in some way. But then, he was always encouraging her to smile, to flirt, to laugh, as her mother had supposedly done. And when she behaved so, it sent him into transports of delight. It pleased her to please him, he took such an eager delight in the memories she brought back to him. But now the innocent imposture that she had done for her cousin seemed somehow shameful. So she said angrily, "And where is the harm in a jest, Tom? I have not changed at all, and if I occasionally behave a bit differently, where is the fault?"

"Jess, Jess," Tom said mournfully, "where would be the harm if I suddenly began to behave like a coxcomb, or to preen like a peacock to delight some young female? None, I suppose, but if I were to do so, or to languish and pen poetry and try to do the pretty like some fop, would you not have a concern for me?"

"I'd think you'd lost your wits," Jessica confessed. "Oh, Tom, have I made such a fool of myself, then?" she gasped, rising and wringing her hands in consternation. She envisioned herself as having behaved like a strumpet, a bawd, and was deeply ashamed and frightened.

He rose and drew her up with him. He clasped her close to himself, holding her securely and perfectly still. She felt his smooth lean cheek against hers and the long tight length of him against her body. Then his lips strayed to her forehead and he whispered, "Never a fool, Jess. But I have a deep care for you and only worried that I had lost my little Jess altogether."

"I am still myself," she half-said, half-thought.

But then, as they stood so closely enwrapped, she began to realize that he was not, after all, so cool and contained. She could feel the subtle warmth of his person and became slowly aware that his hand had commenced a slow stroking motion upon her back. She dared not turn and look into those knowing clear light eyes. Instead, she pulled away and turned away from him.

"I shall endeavor to remember what you have said, Tom," she said in a low voice, keeping her head downcast.

He made no move to hold her again, but only said, "I mean it for the best, Jess. You know that. You have no truer friend than I."

Now at last, she could look at him. He stood, hands at his sides, tense and awaiting her answer. She forced a smile. "I know it, Tom," was all that she could say as she began to walk toward the Hall.

When she left him to speedily achieve the privacy of her own rooms, she wore an abstracted, distressed expression. But her blond companion wore a very satisfied smile as he watched her door close behind her.

Anton made every effort to cheer his cousin that night at dinner. He did such amusing things that Sir Selby almost overset his soup. His jokes wrung a wry smile from Lord Leith and even drew a grin from Tom. But Jessica sat and picked at her food, and when rallied for being such a dour puss by her hostess, she pasted such a patently artificial smile upon her lips as to distress everyone at the long table.

"I suspect," Anton said owlishly as the gentlemen sat alone and sipped at their port, "that it is a difficult time of the month for my dear cousin."

The sudden shocked silence that followed his artless comment caused Anton to look up in surprise.

"This is not a correct thing to say?" he asked guilelessly.

"Not very," drawled Lord Leith with the hint of a smile.

"Most peculiar," Anton mused, "for we understand such things about the ladies at home."

"We understand such things about females, yes," the gentleman replied languidly, "but we do not discuss such things about ladies."

"Most peculiar," Anton sighed. "You will explain this to me, yes?"

Sir Selby rose and began to quickly speak about it being time to join the ladies.

"Later, yes." Lord Leith smiled, noting how the dark young man's precise English always faltered when he thought he had made a faux pas.

"But that is most likely just the problem," Anton insisted as they left the room and Sir Selby began to babble about what a lovely night it was.

Whatever the problem, Jessica made poor work of the rest of the evening. Anton could have stood upon his head during charades for all the response he could elicit from her. Thomas Preston kept looking at Jessica in a concerned fashion. Lady Grantham watched her young guest with growing discomfort. And when the time came for a song, Jessica rose and sang laments about lost lovers, abused orphans, and drowned sailors until Sir Selby had to search for a new handkerchief to wipe his eyes with. Lord Leith resolved to have a talk with the forlorn Jessica before the night was out.

And so it was that when everyone had bade each other an early good-night, the tall gentleman took up a position in a shadowy recess by the grand staircase. He saw his aunt and Sir Selby take the stairs in deep converse. He frowned to see Tom Preston, once he thought he was out of sight, lose his caring expression and skip up the long stairs like a boy. And his own face grew grimmer when time passed and he did not see either Jessica or her animated cousin appear on the steps.

Jessica had risen to leave with the rest, but Anton's omnipresent hand upon her wrist had restrained her. When everyone else had left the room, he nodded in satisfaction and confronted her alone.

"Now," Anton said with determination, "what is this, Jessica? Hmmm? Suddenly you are a weeping willow, yes? What has happened? I tell my best stories and I cannot get even a little smile from you, so there must be a thing I do not know about."

He held her fast, and she could see from the determined look in his dark eyes that he did not mean to let her go until he had an explanation.

"Oh, Anton," she said at length, "it is really a very silly thing, and difficult to tell."

"So," he said adamantly, "it is not difficult to listen. I am your family and you must tell me."

"It's very foolish, really," she prevaricated, but then she said in a rush, "It is only that I have been told, for my own good, of course, that I have appeared to be very giddy, very blatant in my recent actions."

At the look of incomprehension writ large upon his dark face, she went on desperately, "I've been told I've been carrying on like a trollop, with all the giggling and flirting I've been doing."

Anton's expression cleared. "I see," he said at once. "This must be a very English thing. But I assure you, Jessica, you have been behaving perfectly. Who was it, the icy Lord Leith, who told you this? Or the silent Mr. Preston? It makes no matter. I tell you, Jessica, you have been behaving like a lady, and a charming one. Just like your mama."

When Jessica averted her head at his words, Anton seemed to grow angry. He stationed himself in front of her. "You cannot help but be like her, Cousin," he said angrily. "With all that they try to make you otherwise, it is in your blood. You are your mother's daughter. And where is the harm in a little gaiety? Must all of life be so . . . English?" he protested.

She laughed at that, and he reached out and took her by the shoulders. As they were of a height, she could see directly into his sincere, deep dark eyes.

"Better," he whispered, "better still. You are very special to me, Jessica, just as you are."

There seemed to be a certain heat in his eyes that she had not seen before. She stepped away and laughed again, with the little toss of her head that he so admired.

"You are good medicine for me, Anton. But now you must leave me and go to your rooms, or else all the English will think we are up to no good."

"Ah, would that were so," he sighed with a mock despair that made her laugh again. But he left her. And her laughter ceased the moment he did. She stood in thought for a long while until she heard a light tap upon the door. Looking up, she saw the long figure of Lord Leith as he stood in the shadows of the room.

"Is it so bad, then?" he asked softly.

When she did not answer at once, he walked up to her and tilted her head up with one long finger. When she gazed back at him with an abstracted stare, he smoothed back a strand of her flaming hair and said quietly, "I give excellent advice, you know."

"I know," she answered distractedly, "but I've had too much advice already. It seems some people advise me to be light and gay, and others to be what I was before. Only I can't recall what that precisely was. Oh, I'm not making any sense," she concluded, shaking her head in despair.

"Oh, but you are," he answered. "And I think the answer is to be whatever you want to be, and damn to what others want."

"But what it that?" she whispered. And then, although he had taken no step nearer to her, nor touched her again, she looked up at him and realized that they were alone and very close in an otherwise-empty room.

"Good night, my Lord," she said suddenly, and took to her heels as though he had menaced her.

He stood alone after she had gone and then muttered a curse that would have brought the house down about his ears if there had been anyone to hear it.

Jessica would have spent the morning abed, brooding over the new single cloud upon her heretofore spotless horizon, if it were not for Amy treading heavily into her room and drawing the curtains back vigorously. The little maid bustled about the room, bumping into furniture and rattling her tray of chocolate and cups with gusto until Jessica could no longer pretend sleep. The moment she opened her eyes, Amy sniffed with satisfaction.

"Oh, miss," she said at once, "there's such news! Your solicitor has come. Only think, he's all dust-covered. He rode straight from the docks, he says. And he's got your treasure, he says. Every bit of it!"

It was lucky that Amy was in the room with her, or Jessica would have flown down the stairs in a night shift. As it was, she could barely contain herself long enough for the maid to do up her buttons and brush out her hair. Though it seemed like hours, it was only moments before Jessica was able to throw open her door and hurry downstairs. And it took every bit of fiber she possessed to slow her steps and calm herself before entering the sitting room, where she heard excited voices talking together.

Jessica's eyes widened when she entered. For though it was still an early hour, all of the guests were assembled in the room, and even Lady Grantham, who seldom stirred before noon, was sitting awaiting her. But Jessica had eyes only for Mr. Jeffers and the square black case he had upon his lap.

"My dear," Mr. Jeffers said happily, rising to greet her and leaving the box upon a chair, "you look wonderfully. And I have wonderful news. I have located Corporal MacKenzie and he has entrusted the item your father left with him to me. He had some reservations about my papers," Mr. Jeffers went on, although no one was attending to him, "but in time he came to see that I was to be trusted. He had not opened it since the day it was given to him. As you see, it is still sealed. Now, if you will sign the necessary papers, and you as well, Sir Selby, I can turn the box over to you."

"Be damned to the papers," Sir Selby cried, quite forgetting there were ladies present. "Let's have a look at it, man!"

Mr. Jeffers looked about him in growing alarm. He was, it seemed, the center of avid attention and he felt very much like the sole survivor of a shipwreck in a sea boiling with sharks.

"But," he protested, unconsciously backing up a bit, "it's not at all how it's usually done. Shouldn't you like to be alone, my dear, and open the box in private?" he asked, appealing to Jessica to do the correct thing.

"As to that," Jessica said tightly, "there's nothing about me or my family that hasn't been better known to everyone else in this room than myself. There's no reason to become secretive now. Ollie's right," she declared, forgetting her old friend's title in her excitement, "we have waited long enough."

As Mr. Jeffers watched, appalled by the intensity of avarice displayed by the nobility, Sir Selby took up the box and applied a fruit knife to the tight wax seal that fastened down the lid. Lady Grantham stood gazing in fascination as he struggled, until Lord Leith produced a sharp hunting knife from a desk drawer and applied himself to freeing the other side. Anton and Thomas stood waiting expectantly as the two men prized off the seal. Then, as if by common consent, both men stepped back and smiled at Jessica.

"There you are, Jess." Sir Selby beamed. "Now it's only right that you open it yourself."

Jessica stepped forward and took the box in trembling hands. For a moment she closed her eyes. She thought of her dear Red Jack sealing the treasure in to await her touch. She thought of his concern, his love, and his face seemed to appear before her, smiling encouragement. Then, the sound of someone in the room giving out a little nervous cough caused her to open her eyes again. She slowly lifted the lid off the box.

There was nothing but a worn black velvet drawstring bag within. She took the bag out cautiously and gently pulled the strings apart. It had been in the box so long, she fancied she could even breathe her father's last exhalation as the pouch slowly drew apart. Then she carefully reached in and drew out the object that had lain concealed for all these past weary months since her father had fallen. And then she gasped.

"It's only a comb," she cried. Then, unable to carry the jest further, she said, "Only look!" her voice shaking with relief and awe.

And they looked, even as she did. Then she laughed and handed it to Sir Selby, whose face instantly wreathed in smiles.

"Knew he'd do the right thing," Sir Selby shouted. "Red Jack always honored his debts if he could." He passed the treasure to Lady Grantham and soon it was going hand to hand about the room as the laughter and glad cries grew louder.

For it was a treasure, Jessica thought with wild exultation. Only a comb, yes, but what a comb! For surely it had been made to dress a Princess's hair. Two rows of gems stood out in bold relief above the intricate silver filigree of the comb itself. The first row was of bright-green translucent stones, the second tier of clear, dazzling, sun-catching gems.

"Diamonds and emeralds," Mr. Jeffers said as proudly as if he had manufactured the piece himself. "So Corporal MacKenzie said your father told him it was. Nine fine emeralds and ten fine diamonds. Your father came by it in France a few years ago; doubtless it was worn by the Queen or the Empress herself.''

But Jessica could not hear his tale of how her father had acquired the comb. Her knees were suddenly weak and she had to catch on to the side of a chair to stand upright. She beamed at Sir Selby and he wrapped his arm about her shoulders. He began to congratulate her, and tell Lady Grantham, with high enthusiasm, how he and Jess had been vindicated. His old friend had been a Prince, after all.

Jessica was so absorbed in her joy that she did not note the other reactions to her treasure. Thomas Preston held it in his hands and watched its faceted jewels gleam with such a naked look of wonder that it was only when Lord Leith lifted it lightly from his palms that he realized he should have passed it along for inspection long before. He was so chagrined at his gaucherie that he did not see the tall gentleman hold the comb up to the light and frown darkly. Nor did he see Anton take it up when it was his turn and inspect it carefully and dispassionately. For a second, the dark young man frowned as well, but a moment later, his expression was one of unholy glee.

"Now come, Jess," Sir Selby chortled. "Everyone's seen it. You must wear it."

After much good-natured jesting, Sir Selby took up the comb again and, as ceremoniously as a King dubbing a knight, placed it upon Jessica's ruddy locks. She touched it once with shivering fingers to make certain it was secure, and then ran lightly to the glass upon the wall to be sure it was set right.

She did not see Lord Leith take Mr. Jeffers aside and began to speak earnestly with him in low tones. Nor did she see Mr. Jeffers' expression change to amazement and then in turn to ire, then to acceptance. She faced the company with misted eyes and tried to make a mock processional march among them, her head held high. The sunlight streaming in through the long windows made the green gems dance with light against her glowing hair, the diamonds spit back sunlight until it seemed she was crowned by supernatural fires.

"Of course," Mr. Jeffers' voice cut in to all their clamor, "you must give it back to me, Miss Eastwood. For I have to take it straight to London to have it appraised and have the necessary papers drawn up to protect and insure your ownership.'' At the groans that were set up, he added, ''Then, of course, you may wear it anywhere.''

''But today, Jess,'' Sir Selby cried, ''wear it in to breakfast.''

And dipping and swaying, Jessica took her guardian's hand and led them all into the breakfast room, so glad in spirit, so excited and absolved that she did not see her solicitor lag behind. Nor see that Lord Leith tarried with him. And as she had led in their little parade, she of course could not hear Lord Leith's cautionary whisper to Mr. Jeffers as they followed, ''But she must never know. Upon my soul, Jeffers, this must be so.''

15

That night the music room in Griffin Hall rang to the strains of a laughter it had never contained before it all its long years. For though it had held many sorts of parties, surely none was so full of gladness and relieved celebration as this one was. Jessica drank far too much wine in her exultation, but rather than making her dizzy or sleepy, it seemed each cup was only a drop and her joy was undiminished. Sir Selby capered like a boy and Thomas Preston unbent so far as to even risk singing some of the songs he had heretofore deemed unfit for the company.

Lady Grantham, her nephew, and Mr. Jeffers had a long talk early in the evening, and now they watched the merriment, even joining in from time to time, but there was no way that their participation could equal that of the others. It was curious that Anton, who had been their quasi-official court jester until now, was overshadowed by the outrageous hilarity of the others. But, if anyone chanced to think upon it, it was only natural, after all. He had not known the gallant Captain Eastwood, and he could not feel the surge of happiness in knowing that the fellow had come through at the end. And then, too, he was sophisticated enough to realize that he was a visitor and that this night was made for others to make much of.

The hour had grown so late that even trained footmen were hard put not to stifle their yawns, when Lady Grantham dropped a quick word into Sir Selby's ear. He reluctantly rose and interrupted Jessica and Tom as they discussed, for the fifth time that night, how clever Red Jack had been to purchase the comb from a fleeing émigré.

"All good things," he intoned, taking care not to slur the words, "mus' come to 'n end. 'Our revels now are ended.' 'S time to go to bed, don't y' know?" He chuckled.

When Jessica and Tom turned disbelieving faces toward him, he went on plaintively, "Why, jus' look at the dear Lady. She's dropping 'n she's too p'lite to say it. Mus' go to bed," he proclaimed, a bit mawkishly, in his present state almost ready to drop a tear for his hostess's bravery in the face of exhaustion. " 'S late, don't you know?"

Jessica rose and giggled. "Oh, I'll go," she said happily, "but I wish this night would never end. But you're right, Ollie, it is late. But I shall go," she went on, wondering why she could not seem to come to the end of her statement. "But," she added more brightly, remembering what it was she had to say, "I shall wear my comb all night. I shall wear it for the rest of my life. Always. Even in the bath," she confided loudly to Tom.

Lord Leith smiled down at her. It was odd, she thought, how he just seemed to appear from out of nowhere, for the last time she had looked, he had been lounging against the mantelpiece, watching them.

"I'm afraid not, Jessica," he said slowly, but clearly and distinctly enough for her to hear even over the peculiar fogging in her ears. "You see," he said gently, "Mr. Jeffers needs to take it to London tomorrow, very early in the morning. And we don't wish to wake you at that hour, and I'm sure you don't wish it either."

But as Jessica only raised a hand in a protective fashion to touch the comb, he went on, "It's only a day's ride there, Jessica. Give us two days to complete the business, and a day's ride back again. And then you shall have it forever, even to wear in your bath. We must have the proper papers filed," he added reasonably, seeing her standing immobile, one hand upon the comb in her hair. "You don't want your cousin Cribb to get it, do you?"

At that Jessica gasped and tore the comb from its anchoring, spilling a cataract of gleaming red hair across her horrified face as she did so. She pressed the comb into his hands and blurted, "Take it. Take it, then. But please don't lose it."

He laughed as he pocketed it and said easily, "Never fear. I shall accompany Mr. Jeffers, for safety's sake, and we shall even take two other men to guard it from harm."

At that Thomas Preston looked up warily. "I should like

to go with you," he said ruefully, "but you've sprung this on me. You shall have to give me some time in the morning to recover from my excesses this night."

"And I," Anton put in excitedly, "shall come too, but I do not know that I shall be of much help. I am very good with a saber, but do your highwaymen here use those? For I'm not a great good shot with pistols."

Lord Leith paused a moment, watching his two reluctant volunteers, and then caused relief to be apparent on both faces when he drawled, "Gentlemen, I assure you I had no intention of asking you to leave this pleasant party. There is no need, after all. We'll take two stout footmen, and as there are very few daylight robberies on the main London Road, content yourselves, we shall be safe enough. We will be back, Jessica, I promise, within the week."

"Thank you," Jessica said very mistily, thinking both of what a good fellow he was, and also, now that she was standing upright, of how very tired she suddenly was. She was grateful for Lord Leith's help as he escorted her from the room. She was even more gratified by his strong arm, which became necessary for support as she negotiated stairs that had taken on the nasty habit of fading away just as one was about to set foot upon them.

"Good night, Jessica. Do not worry," he said after he had summoned her maid to help her to bed.

She looked up at his steady gray gaze and found herself about to weep over the extent of his kindness. As Amy urged from very far away that she come to bed, Jessica found that some other person within herself had caused her to reach up on tiptoe and press a quick kiss upon one of Lord Leith's high cheekbones.

"Sandalwood!" Jessica exclaimed, leaning upon her door-jamb. At his lifted eyebrow, she explained earnestly, "You smell delightfully of sandalwood, Alex."

He laughed and steered her to a clucking Amy. "Good night, my dear." He bowed. When her door had closed, he paused a moment. And then felt a large hand clapped upon his shoulder.

"Be ready in the dawn," Sir Selby said confidentially. "Shouldn't miss it for the world. Bring m' pistols too. Show those highwaymen a thing or two, I shall m'boy."

"Sleep well, Ollie old friend," Lord Leith said firmly as he walked Sir Selby to his room, "and do not disturb yourself. All will be well."

The rolling blue and gray dawn mists covered the verdant fields, making the two gentlemen in the swaying coach feel as though they were traveling across some weird wide sea. It was the elder of the two who eventually broke the ruminative silence.

"You are sure, my Lord, that you are doing the correct thing?" he asked.

"Absolutely sure, Mr. Jeffers," the younger gentleman replied sternly. "Have no doubt. There is no crime in what we do, nor any penalty attached to the deed. It needs must be done, though, and promptly."

Mr. Jeffers glanced across at the other man. It was a confident, assured face, he thought. Refined, yet strong. The tumble of light-brown curls bespoke relative youth, but there was nothing but determination and sagacity in the cool gray eyes. He sighed. "So be it," he said at length.

Lord Leith's firm mouth twitched. "Come, Mr. Jeffers, it is extraordinary, but it is legal. I shall not lead you to the hangman by this day's work."

"A great many things can be made legal," Mr. Jeffers said ponderously.

"And I only ask this one thing of you," came the calm answer as his companion gazed out at the rising day.

Jessica awoke to a mixture of remembered joy and unaccustomed pain. For though she leaped up to meet the day, it was not long before she sat back down again and frowned at the ache in her head. But it was Amy, who, from long experience with a bibulous father, restored her to health to match her spirits again. After a thorough dousing with cold water and a few sips of a herbal concoction, Jessica was ready to don her clothes and greet the bird-loud morning.

She breakfasted alone, as she was informed by a discreetly smiling butler that Lady Grantham and Sir Selby were breakfasting in their rooms. Along with her eggs, she was served the information that Mr. Preston had gone for an early gallop and that her cousin had not yet come down.

Jessica hummed to herself as she strolled the paths that surrounded Griffin Hall. For once she did not stop to admire the roses. Instead, she walked aimlessly, totally preoccupied with a different sort of beauty. She could, she reasoned as she stepped through the knot garden, simply keep the comb intact and have it as a reminder of her father's love for all her days. By the time she meandered through the boxwood maze, she had also decided that he would surely understand if she had to sell off one or two stones so that she could be free to leave Cousin Cribb forever, and when at last she seated herself on a stone bench beneath the terrace wall, she had determined that she might have to exchange another few so that she would not have to hang upon Sir Selby's sleeve forever.

But though it was a vexing decision, it was a good sort of problem to have, so that when her cousin came upon her, he discovered her sitting alone with an engaging smile upon her lips.

"Such a lovely morning, Cousin," he saluted her. "I do not wonder at your smile. But do I dare presume that it is all for me?"

Jessica made room for him on the bench but noted that, as usual, he sat as close as possible to her. Although he was dressed in country buckskins and a light brown jacket, he was so immaculately turned out that one might be pardoned for thinking him on the way to dinner instead of a morning's stroll.

"I'm always happy to see you, Anton," Jessica said. "But in truth, I must admit I was still thinking about my father's legacy. I cannot get over his forethought. I have been waiting and wondering so long, you see," she explained.

"And now that you have discovered it," Anton said earnestly, "what do you propose to do? For I understood that you would stay with dear Lady Grantham only so long as it took to find your inheritance. What do you do now, Cousin?"

Jessica paused as she was about to explain her plans for the dispersal of the gems. For although she had been thinking of independence and security, she had not thought at all of where she was to go from this place. She would not go back to Oak Hill, now that she knew she had no need to. And it was true that there was no further reason for staying on with her hostess.

"Why, I don't know," she answered with truth, turning her great brown eyes upon her cousin. "I hadn't thought it through. I expect I shall collect my things, and my old dog Ralph, and set up on my own somewhere," she added weakly.

"But, I do know," Anton exclaimed. "Now you can come back home with me! Ah, Jessica, you will love our home. You will truly come into your own there and will wonder how you ever thought not to leave this cold land."

As he had possessed himself of both her hands this time, Jessica could not pull back. Rather she shook her head in the negative, and said gently, "Not immediately, Anton. I am sorry, but I hadn't planned on travel just yet."

He looked at her with the traces of a smile and said, "But I do not speak of travel, Cousin. I speak of marriage."

Jessica's eyes flew wide and she gasped. But now he pulled her closer and said rapidly, falling over his words in his enthusiasm, "I have waited so long, as is proper. First, so that you might know me better, and now, at last, there is no better that you can know me. There is no more to know. And second, till this matter of your legacy was cleared. And now it is. But I have known from the first. Jessica, marry me."

She stared at him as though he had run mad, and stammered, "But, Anton, I had no idea. I never thought you were interested in me in . . . in such a way."

"I have been too proper," Anton agreed, nodding vigorously. He pulled her toward him quickly and fastened his mouth upon hers.

At first, Jessica was too amazed to protest, and he took her passivity for approval. His mouth opened against hers and his hands pressed her close and roved about her, clutching at her hips and breasts. He made love as he made conversation, with great rapidity and total involvement.

Jessica felt as though she were drowning in some suffocating envelope of flesh. His mouth was hot and wet, his hands busy and thorough, his body so intimately gripped to hers that she could feel both his furnace heat and growing arousal.

Thoroughly alarmed and revulsed, she fought to free herself. But it was only after she had managed to bite down hard upon his soft lower lip that he let her go.

He touched his lip and asked her in hurt surprise, "You did not like that?"

"No," Jessica said, smoothing down her dress with shaking fingers. "It is not your fault, Anton," she added, upset by the distress in his eyes. "It is just not what I expected or wanted."

"Then," said Anton happily, reaching for her again, "you show me what you expect and want."

"No," she cried, jumping up with haste. "You don't understand. I like you very well, Anton, but not as a lover. I don't wish to hurt your feelings, but I simply cannot think of you in that way."

And it *was* odd, she thought, how he could be so very good as a friend and so very distasteful as a lover.

He sat quietly for a few moments, so still that Jessica, after she had righted her frock, felt safe enough to sit beside him again. She hardly knew what to say to cheer him when he at last looked at her. There was no laughter in his eyes now, and in some strange way, without his omnipresent smile, he no longer looked recognizable to her.

"So be it," he breathed. "It is time to talk facts." He looked straight at her, his dark face now composed and his voice staccato. "I would have liked to make love to you, Cousin, but if you feel nothing for me in that way, that is regrettable, but a fact. Perhaps, in time, you will change. But I do not discuss that now. Let us be frank. You have no parents. You live only on the good graces of your friend Sir Selby. That is no security at all. As for your other friends, the lofty Lord Leith is only entertaining you as a favor to Sir Selby and his aunt. He has wealthy and worldly beauties at his disposal. You are nothing to him."

Anton waited a moment until the import of his words registered upon Jessica, and then nodding, he went on, "Your friend Thomas Preston has not a penny to his name. He was awaiting your legacy as anxiously as you, Cousin. But I do not think there is enough there for two. Now, I am your cousin. If you do not desire me, at least you do not detest me. I have a great deal of money. And I am family. What better future do you have, Jessica?"

She sat still, as though she had been slapped. But then after a pause, her head came up and she looked at Anton directly. "No," she said softly, "it will not do. I cannot marry you, Anton. Where there is no love, it would be a travesty. Thank you, but my parents made a capital mistake in their union. I shall not follow suit."

"That is because they were not logical," Anton replied calmly. "They thought of love first, and reason afterward. We shall start with facts. You do not have to love me, Cousin. In fact, it would be extraordinary if you did. That is not the way marriage is thought of in my circle. Your mama was not madly in love with her Baron either. But she was happier with him than with your father. And you are very, very much like your mama. In fact, after we have a son, you may love where you will. It is the way things are done and exactly the way your mama went on."

Jessica drew in a painful breath. Before she could speak, Anton continued, "No, I was not her lover. She thought me too young. But many were. And if she had lived longer . . ." He shrugged. "It was my ambition."

"Is that why you wish to marry me?" Jessica asked in horror.

"Not at all"—he laughed—"for there were many beautiful women who were my ambition."

"Then, why?" she breathed. "For I do not think you love me. And surely it cannot be just because we are cousins. And," she went on, trying in some small way to repay him for the enormous hurt he had given her in telling her about her mother, "you have said I have little to offer materially, and few prospects."

"Ah," said Anton smoothly, "but there you are wrong. It is time you were told the truth. I have promised Mr. Jeffers that I shall tell you before he returns. I begged him for the right to the felicity of telling you. He is, in fact, angry with me for delaying so long. I wished to wait for the right moment. I had hoped to tell you sometime when you lay in my arms, content after love, but you English . . ." He laughed bitterly.

"Cousin," he said, leaning forward, "you do have prospects. Great prospects. Your mama was a wealthy woman. She left almost all of her estate to you. But," he said with a wry smile as soon as excitement sprang up in her eyes, "your mama was still very angry about your dear Red Jack. And so she made it plain. You receive her fortune on your wedding day, but only if your husband is an Austrian. If not"—he shrugged—"there will be a party at Saint Gertrude's Orphan School on your twenty-first birthday, for then they will be very, very wealthy little orphans."

Jessica sat and tried to assimilate all that he had said. Anton remained silent, watching her. Finally, she asked quietly, "But, Anton, if you are already wealthy, why should you want more?"

He laughed. "Our family is wealthy because we have always wanted more. Papa said that I should come to Britain and wed you and bring you home. He is a reasonable man. He was right. If you think on it, you will agree."

"I don't agree Anton," Jessica said, her anger rising. "I cannot see how you were prepared to marry me without ever having seen me. What if I were an object of disgust to you? And how do I know that I am not?"

"*Liebchen*," Anton said coldly, "do not play for compliments. If you were an ugly woman, it would have been a business arrangement. When I saw you, I knew that I could mix business with pleasure. Still, if you do not share my tastes, as I said, you may eventually go your own way."

"I do not have to marry you for that course," Jessica replied. "I cannot, will not, shall not marry you."

He looked at her consideringly, not at all downcast by her words. Then, he clapped his hands together. "Yes, I see. Cousin, I think you speak from a false position. There is one other thing you should know before you make your final answer. If you are thinking that your father's gift will be your security, I tell you now to unthink this. The comb, that beautiful comb," he said mockingly, "it is nothing. Do you hear? Not that it is worth little, it is valueless. Diamonds and emeralds? I tell you again, our family has dealt in gems for centuries, it is strass glass and rock crystal. Oh, once it may have been a treasure. But someone, your dear Red Jack perhaps, has taken out the gems and substituted glass. Perhaps you can sell the silver— that is real enough—and buy yourself a handkerchief."

"You lie!" Jessica cried.

"And does your correct Lord Leith lie? For I overheard him tell Mr. Jeffers last night while you were dancing with joy,

'Her father must have prized out every gem to pay his mistresses and back debts.' "

"But," Jessica asked, fearing his answer, "why has it been taken to London, then?"

"To sign papers, most likely, swearing that no one here has stolen the jewels and substituted glass, in case you decide to go to the courts with your worthless legacy. Or, more likely, to hurry it away from my eyes before I saw and knew. For they hope you will wed me, you know, and hoped I would think it a fine dowry. Why do you think they asked me here and threw us together?" he asked triumphantly.

Jessica did not answer. She stood, head down, and pondered. Her comb was no more than a gaudy trinket. Somehow she knew that in this, at least, there was unmistakable truth. It was as though she had always known, for she had felt no real jolt of surprise at what he said. When she at last raised her eyes, there were tears upon her cheeks, but her voice was steady.

"Go, Anton, go home. Without me. I had nothing before I came here, I will leave with nothing. And at that, I think I am far richer than if I left with you."

"Do not think, Cousin," he sneered, "that you can come to Vienna and catch another husband with the right ancestry for your mother's will. For I shall spread such tales about you, if you do, that even a dustman would not offer for you."

"Go," Jessica said through clenched teeth, "and congratulate the orphans for me."

He arose, bowed precisely, and strode off.

Jessica stood, as though rooted, until a passing groundskeeper saw her and hesitantly approached to ask if she were well. Then she took to her heels and rushed over the lawns to the solitude of the park.

Thomas found her, at last, sitting upon a grassy hillock overlooking the grounds. He swung off his horse, tethered it quickly to a tree, and dropped to one knee beside her. He asked, as soon as he had gotten his breath back from his mad search for her, "Jess, what has happened? The place is in an uproar. Anton marched in, demanded his valet to pack his bags, and is about to leave. He will not say a thing to us, except farewell."

He searched her face. She seemed unmoved by what he said.

"Are you all right? He hasn't hurt you or offended you, has he?" he asked on a rising note of anger.

"Why, I suppose he has," Jessica said slowly, and then stayed him with a light touch upon his knee, "but only by asking me to marry him."

"Oh," Tom said on an explosion of breath. He sat beside her. "And did you accept?" he asked carefully.

"Oh, no. Never." Jessica laughed weakly. "Do you think he'd be leaving in such high dudgeon if I had? I'm not that bad, you know. No, I expect he is very offended. And if so, I am very glad, for I as much as let him know I would not have him for love nor money."

She gave a peculiar laugh, and then, seeing Tom's bewildered look, she took a deep breath and slowly explained all to him. All, except for the matter of her jeweled comb, for she could not bear to voice her tumultuous thoughts on that head as yet.

"You are well rid of him even for a thousand fortunes," Tom swore when she had done, his lean face a composition in earnest anger. But she had not failed to note the brightening in his eyes when she had first spoken of her mother's legacy.

"He was never the right sort for you, Jess," Tom said after a brief silence. "Why, you even behaved artificially when he was about. Just see, you will be yourself again once he has gone. But, wait, what am I thinking of? Did he insult you in any way, Jess? I mean physically," he said as though he were prepared to leap back on his mount and race off to thrash little Anton.

"No," Jessica said weakly. "He only kissed me. And I found that abuse enough. But, Tom, stay," she commanded as he tensed to spring up, "for a kiss is a small thing and no battling matter. Let him go, as soon as he is able."

Tom stilled at that. But soon he spoke again. "Jess, he is a foul fellow, but there is right in one thing he said. What are your plans now that you have Red Jack's treasure?"

"Oh," Jessica replied with a sad little smile, "I expect I'll stay on with Lady Grantham for a space, and then I'll go home, where I belong. If I could handle Cousin Anton, no doubt I shall be able to cope with Cousin Cribb."

"Jess," Tom said, rising up upon his knees to face her, "you needn't, you know. Damnation, but this is not the time nor the place, but, Jess, you must know how I feel."

He drew her very close to her, so close she could feel the tension in his arms and see the sunlight glancing off his light eyes.

"Say good-bye to all of them, Jess," he urged, "and come away with me. No, don't look surprised, for, I swear, if you think, you'll see that it was always meant to be so. Did not Red Jack himself always bring you to me when you were but an infant? Have you not known me forever? Why do you think I am here at all?" he scoffed. "For Lady Grantham's musical evenings?

"As I knew your father and respected him, so have I always thought of you," he said with passion, "for you two are very like. I only waited for you to grow up. Ah, Jess, marry me and be damned to the lot of them."

While Jessica stared at him as though he had run mad, he gave a muttered oath and embraced her. It was not at all like Anton's moist embrace. His lips were cool and hard, and his hands only held her comfortingly close. But there was not the shiver of unbidden sensation that she had experienced all that time ago at home, or the curious shaken reaction she had felt for another man's mere gesture of annoyance. Instead, she found herself waiting for a response to well up within herself. But all she discovered was numbness and her own cool patience for him to be done.

When he took his lips from hers, rested his fair head against her cheek and murmured, "Jess, ah, Jess."

And then she said quite calmly, as though explaining a lesson to a schoolboy, "Tom, there is no legacy from Red Jack. The comb is set with glass. It is worth nothing, you know."

He drew back and stared until she thought his clear eyes glittered brighter than the sham diamonds had.

"It is true," she said sadly, and told him at last all that Anton had said—all of it, except what he had said of Tom's own intentions.

When he remained silent after she had done, she said softly, "So, go, Tom, and I shall not mind. For there are so many females out in that wide world that can offer you more, and indeed, we both know you deserve more. Do not confuse your friendship with Red Jack for love of me.''

She dared to reach out and smooth his flaxen hair tenderly and said again, "I shall not mind. We both know, after all, that I am not cut out for marriage. Go now, Tom, we'll talk as old friends later and never mention this moment again."

He got to his feet quietly, never taking his eyes from her. He opened his lips to say something and thought better of it. He backed to his horse and remounted, and then, with a sad smile to match her own, he turned the animal and rode off deep into the parklands.

He rode on mechanically, letting his mount choose its own way, for he was too wrapped in his own shocked thoughts to guide the beast. He rode on for a very long time until he recalled himself and stopped. And then he sat, head bowed like some glowing, drooping sunflower's head in the darkness of the trees' shadows, and thought again. At last, when the dappled light had faded from gold to gray, he straightened, and giving his horse an exultant prod, he galloped back toward Griffin Hall.

He had been right, he thought as the sound of his released laughter rose above the pounding of hooves, he was altogether right. For they were made for each other and had been destined for each other forever. Where else could he find such a female? Red Jack's legacy be damned, he would marry her anyway. She was half a lad, but honest and brave as no female he had yet encountered.

And she had grown to be beautiful. He did not fool himself into thinking she desired him, but he could teach her that. She needed him, poor girl, as no other woman had, there was that too.

At last permitting himself to be acutely aware of the truth that he rode upon a borrowed horse, through another man's land, he hastened to be with the one thing in the world that he could call his own, Jess.

Although twilight was coming on, he knew she would not yet have returned to the house; she would have waited for Anton to be gone. When he saw her slowly walking toward the Hall, he gave out a great cry, leaped down, and slapped the horse's flank so that it would find its way back to the stables by itself.

"Jess, Jess," he half-cried, half-laughed, catching her up and swinging her around, until her hair came loose from its moorings, "what fools we both are! The treasure be hanged. We'll place it on the mantelpiece for our children to laugh over. It's you I want, Jess."

He put her down carefully and held her fast. She looked back at him levelly. So he spoke as honestly as he knew how.

"I haven't a cent, Jess, and you know it. But neither have you, my girl. So we're even, aren't we? Ollie said as how he'd provide a dowry for you, but," he added hastily, seeing her face cloud up, "we needn't touch it at all. There's nothing for us here, Jess, but there's a whole world awaiting us. There's America, where a smart fellow can make his own fortune. Or Australia . . . or anywhere where an honest fellow and his honest wife can build a future. It won't be easy, Jess, but you're the sort of female who has the bottom to make it. You don't give a hang for fashion or comforts. You think more like a man than a fine lady. What do you say, my girl? It's what your father always wanted. It's the sort of chance he'd jump at," he added desperately, seeing how his words had failed to ignite her. There was something new in her aspect, a calm, a maturity that hadn't been there only a few hours before.

"And as for the lovemaking part," he said with embarrassment under her steady gaze, "that needn't be a problem. You'll come to it in time. Till then, be my own straight soldier, Jess. Answer me. Marry me."

"Oh, Tom," she whispered as though uttering those simple words were enough to break her heart.

"I'm your best friend, Jess," he swore.

She reached up and linked her arms about his neck. "Yes, Tom, I know." She smiled, though clearly she was weeping.

16

Although the employees of Peterson's considered themselves members of a staff far too exclusive to hurry for any custom that walked into their jewelry shop, when the tall gentleman strolled into their establishment that morning, they could justly be said to scramble. His appearance caused the manager to fairly scuttle over to his side. Though there were others pricing rubies, or negotiating sapphire pendants, within moments of his entrance Lord Leith was snug within the proprietor's private office being tempted with tea and being welcomed with bows and smiles. For he was known to be a man not only of taste and decision, but one who would come down heavily for any bauble that suited his purposes.

The proprietor contained himself from actually rubbing his hands together in anticipation of this day's business, and only asked politely when the necessary greetings were done. "And how may we be of help to you today, my Lord?"

Lord Leith withdrew a worn velvet pouch from his pocket and placed it upon the smooth mahogany desk.

"You can appraise this piece for me," he said laconically.

The jeweler eagerly withdrew his magnifying eyepiece and tenderly eased the silver comb from its confines. His initial look of delight faded as he gazed upon it, and soon he seemed insensible to his visitor as he minutely inspected the piece with his glass. At last he put the comb down and, recalling his customer, pasted a suitably mournful look upon his face.

"But, my Lord," he said sorrowfully, "it is worthless. It is cleverly done," he hurried on, "and one can see how anyone might be deceived by it. But it is composed of several types of imitation gems. There is Strass glass," he said, pointing as he spoke, "and Ravenscroft glass, and even Bristol diamond—that is rock crystal, my Lord. And the green stones are all different sorts of crystal, some with foil backings and some with slivers of real emerald affixed to their bottoms. In fact," he said encouragingly, for he thought the usually astute nobleman had won the piece in a game of chance and wished to soften the blow of his estimate of it, "one might say that it has some worth simply because it is such a compendium of excellent forgeries. It is," he mused, "a veritable museum of false gems and, as such, might have some value to a collector of such trifles. But not much," he hastened to added.

"I thought as much," his visitor replied calmly without batting a lash. "Would you say it was designed to be so?"

"Oh, no!" the proprietor said with shock. "It is clear that the comb itself was destined for higher purposes. In fact, I distinctly remember seeing such a piece many years ago, in France, being worn by the Comtesse de Lorraine, who was a great favorite of Louis himself. No, no, it is clear that it was once an item of great virtue. But the actual gems have long since been sold off."

"All at once, would you say?" Lord Leith asked with a bit more interest.

"No, that is doubtful," the other man said, picking up the piece and holding it to the light, "for each substitution is quite different from the others. I should hazard to say that it was done randomly, as the occasion demanded, at different times, and, indeed, perhaps even in different lands. This stone, for example, is of English construction, and this is decidedly of French devising. It is often so, my Lord," he sighed, "for when a person comes down in the world, they often refuse to accept the truth, and only sell off their treasures piece by piece in denial of their true state. They attempt to cover their circumstances even from themselves by such substitutions."

This the manager knew well enough, for he had often helped gentlepersons from Lord Leith's own set to do precisely the same.

He began to replace the comb in its pouch when the nobleman's next words caused his hands and very nearly his heart to freeze in excitement.

"Very well," Lord Leith said, "then, if you please, put it back the way it was."

"I beg your pardon, my Lord?" the jeweler said, not daring to believe his ears.

"I should like you, with all possible speed, to replace the false gems with true ones," Lord Leith said patiently.

The proprietor had to wait a moment for his blood to begin to flow again. Then with admirable calm, he asked, "With what sort of gems, my Lord? That is to say, there are all grades of stones—"

But the cool gentleman had already risen to his feet and cut him off by saying, "With the best sort of gems, Mr. Peterson, the sort that belong in such a comb."

"Certainly, my Lord," the other man agreed breathlessly.

"And, oh, Mr. Peterson," Lord Leith added as he reached the door, "by tomorrow evening, if you please."

"Tomorrow evening?" the jeweler cried, so aghast that he forgot to add "my Lord." "But that would be—"

"Possible, I do hope," his customer said coldly. "Or, if it is not, I should have to patronize some other establishment in Regent Street."

"Tomorrow evening," the other man said thoughtfully. "I shall have to send runners throughout London, I shall have to call upon some favors owed, but it shall be done, my Lord. But it will be, I hesitate to say this—"

"Expensive," Lord Leith provided. "I don't expect it to come cheaply. But I do expect a fair reckoning, Peterson."

The jeweler nodded, for he knew well that this was a sharp gentleman, quite unlike the run of the nobility in his business acumen.

"And, of course," Lord Leith said in parting, "it is to be carried out with utmost discretion."

"Of course, my Lord," Mr. Peterson agreed, though privately he was surprised, for it was usually in the dispensing of gems that his silence was called upon, not in the acquisition of them.

Lord Leith sketched a bow and was gone, leaving the jeweler to a moment's deep thought and then to hours of frantic activity.

Alexander, Lord Leith, took to the pavements with a light step and found himself in an unconscionably happy mood for one who had just contracted to part with a great deal of money. But how, he asked himself in justification of his pleasure with the deed, could he not have taken the course he had? If the girl had not been so ecstatic over the blasted piece, if it had not come to mean more to her than mere money, perhaps it would not have mattered so much. But he recalled her face when she had seen it and remembered the sheer glory that had shone from her countenance all that night as she celebrated her acquisition of it. It was hard to think of what her state might be had she discovered the truth.

Of course, he amended, it was not simply for her, for he was not Father Christmas, visiting gifts on every worthy child. It was for Ollie, of course, he corrected himself. So that Ollie would never know and thus could hold on to the belief that his dear old friend had been a worthy man, after all.

Damn Red Jack Eastwood, Lord Leith thought with unaccustomed vehemence as he strolled toward his club for luncheon. He had never laid eyes upon the man and he was long gone, but his shadow still rested upon all those who had loved him. What a feckless, dastardly fellow he must have been. No doubt he had been a delight to be with. But all such charming wretches always left chaos in their wake when they had gone on their brief sparkling way. See how he had left his only child, Lord Leith frowned, quite unintentionally decomposing the doorman at his club, penniless, portionless, and ill-equiped to deal with life.

But later, as the tall gentleman toyed with his luncheon, he thought that perhaps Captain Eastwood, all unknowing, had done the right thing, after all. For Jessica was unique. It was not at all a bad thing, he thought, grinning a little at the mere remembrance of her, for a female to value such masculine traits as valor and bravery. He lay his fork aside and left an excellent cut of beef to congeal on its plate as he contemplated the matter.

None of his mistresses had ever shown such traits, he mused. As pleasurable as their company always was, or indeed, as intelligent as some of them might have been (for he never had interest in mere vessels for his convenience, no matter how exotic they might appear to be), still none of them had ever dealt with him as an equal as Jessica always attempted to do. But how could they, he wondered now, when he was, in effect, always in the position of being an employer they had to please?

All the correct young ladies of fortune or title whom he had met in his time always treated him with shy acquiescence and constant approval. They, in fact, behaved toward him as though he were a member of some superior species. While that was undoubtedly flattering, it was also undoubtedly flat. Which must be why, he thought all at once, he had never been tempted to offer for any of them. For though he had always thought it was because they valued his purse, it was now clear it was also because he had the sneaking suspicion that they were all as false toward him as the crystals in Jessica's damned comb.

It seemed to be only the older women, who had no apparent designs upon his sex, whom he could be totally easy and honest with. Should he then have to wed a grandmother? he thought with amusement. For how could a man be willing to spend the remainder of his life with a mate who was in constant accord with him? Who took his every word for holy writ, his every desire as command? It would be intolerable. This was such a revolutionary thought that Lord Leith sat frozen at his table in such arrested fashion that his waiter feared he must have found a rodent hair in the butter.

It was with great relief that Lord Leith found himself hailed by some acquaintances from across the room. He was well-pleased to join them and catch up on all the tattle he had missed while out of town. He listened to tales of routs and wagers, indiscretions and mad romps, and assemblies and scandals. While his companions roared with glee and listened with delight, he found to his own perplexity that none of it was amusing in the least.

When he left his club, he hastened to his town house, for the hour was advanced and he had promised himself to Mr. Jeffers for dinner. There was only time to instruct his valet to lay out his clothes and then to quickly wash, and change his garb. But he was several moments late, for all his good intentions. While drying his face, he had suddenly become aware of the strong aroma of sandalwood from his soap, and had chanced to remember the tipsy Miss Eastwood, leaning against her doorway and complimenting him wonderingly upon his scent. Sandalwood, he paused to reflect, the fragrance he had become so accustomed to in India. While she, he remembered, always bore the faint enchanting aura of herbs.

The only scent he was aware of when he joined Mr. Jeffers in the private dining room of that gentleman's residential hotel was that of the heavy snuff Mr. Jeffers was partial to. The solicitor was in an expansive mood this evening, his original trepidation at taking part in the deception of his client Miss Eastwood having been effectively lulled by Lord Leith's urgent arguments and by the extraordinary sum he had earned by his compliance.

Mr. Jeffers was a man who feared the consequences of not doing a thing the way it had always been done. But upon sober consideration he had decided that deceiving a client in a client's favor could not actually be construed as true chicanery. He had also spent the better part of the afternoon rummaging through stacks of law books for references to back up his position, should he ever be called to account for his part in the affair. Since he had found several very ambiguous rulings that could shore up his position, he was now quieting the last of his conscience by converse with the noble perpetrator of the scheme and with several bottles of excellent claret as well.

He unbent so far by the time a flaming dessert was borne in as to comment pleasurably, "And so now our dear Miss Eastwood shall be a truly well-situated young female for life. That is very well, my Lord, for she is withal a most engaging young person."

"I should not call the possession of one jeweled comb exactly a snug sinecure, Mr. Jeffers," his companion refuted.

"Why, no." Mr. Jeffers smiled, pouring himself yet another goblet of the '97. "But with that, plus the portion she will receive when she weds her young cousin, she'll do, my Lord, she'll do."

The deathly silence that fell after this pronouncement, coupled with the blazing look in his companion's eye, made Mr. Jeffers, even fortified as he was, acutely aware that he had made an enormous mistake.

"What?" Lord Leith demanded, putting such force into that single syllable that Mr. Jeffers quailed.

"Nothing, my Lord," he temporized. "Or, rather, something that I am not at liberty to divulge. Part of my client's private affairs, don't you see? Professional confidence that cannot be violated," he finished weakly.

"Mr. Jeffers," Lord Leith declared, and placed two tightly clenched fists upon the tabletop, "you will tell me the whole."

The unsaid words, "Or die," were so implicit that Mr. Jeffers swallowed hard. And before his dessert had time to cool, he was unhappily pouring forth the entire state of Miss Eastwood's affairs, from her mother's will to her cousin's plans for her future.

As Lord Leith rose to leave, Mr. Jeffers caught hold of his sleeve and mournfully pleaded, "But, my Lord, you must never divulge your source of information. It would not be proper."

"It was not proper," the gentleman replied, shaking his arm free, "for you to keep the information from Miss Eastwood in the beginning. It was not proper for you to leave it to her cousin to unfold to her. And it is not proper for you to presume to play matchmaker. Good evening, Mr. Jeffers."

Lord Leith was still shaking with rage when he arrived at his town house and still wondering whether he ought to have landed the fellow a facer, when he prepared for bed. It was only when he had lain brutally awake for hours of fury that the thought that he was behaving very strangely finally fell ponderously upon him. He left his bed then, his strongly muscled body gleaming in the moonlight, and sat upon a chair in his room.

It was, after all, he had to confess, not such a bizarre arrangement that a cousin should wed another, or even that she should do so for profit. But the thought of Jessica wedded to Anton disturbed him profoundly. He had known many men such as Anton—glib, superficial, and worldly. The idea of such a man taking Jessica to wife, to bed, froze his blood. And when he thought of the sort of man who should be entitled to such a person as Jessica, he felt his entire being suffuse with understanding at last. Then, in the depth of the night, he laughed.

He ought to have known, he thought, shaking his head in amazement at how he could still confound himself, through all his thoughts and actions. She had occupied him completely, from the moment they had met. He wanted her in every way that he had ever wanted a woman, and in ways that he had never known he needed a female. He wanted her for a life's mate, for a wife, not just an amusing friend.

He desired her and understood that one night, one week, or one month with her would not be enough for him, even if such a thing were to be possible. As she had run contrary to all other females in behavior, so it would always be with her. Just as his appetite for most of her gender diminished with each union, he was sure that the joys of intimacy would increase with every encounter with Jessica. She would unfurl herself to him more completely each time and would grow more enticing with familiarity.

But, he reminded himself, it would not be easy to win her. For though she liked him very well as a companion, he knew that she had no desire for him as a man; indeed, he wondered if she could ever be brought to that desire after her strange upbringing. And unlike Thomas Preston, he would never be content with having only her comradeship. Still, he thought as he stretched his long frame to greet the dawn, nothing he had ever wanted had been easily come by. And if he could have suffered seven long years of exile to achieve one goal, he could surely take the rest of his life in pursuit of another.

She was still very young. In time, if he were to be constant, she might grow into the womanhood that he knew awaited her. And he must only needs be there at that precise moment. He would wait, he thought, content at last. But as he rang for his valet, the idea of whether or not she would be content to wait occurred to him and filled him with unaccustomed dread. Anton was very persuasive. Thomas Preston also had her friendship. And he was here in London while they were at Griffin Hall with her.

Thus it was that when Mr. Peterson came to unlock his shop, with his assistant in tow, he found Lord Leith awaiting him upon his very doorstep.

"It must be ready by this day," that imperious nobleman announced in tones that brooked no argument.

Mr. Peterson looked up to the determined face above him, bowed his head, and sighed. "Of course, my Lord. I excel in the impossible."

* * *

Another lovely sunset backlighted Griffin Hall as the solitary rider reined up in front of it. The groom who ran to take charge of the mount was astounded to see the usually impeccable Lord Leith covered with the dust of the road. He had ridden long and hard, the groom thought knowingly, eyeing the blowing horse, which was also not the usual way of the languid gentleman. But the rider, instead of appearing fatigued or worn, dismounted jauntily and took the steps to the house as though it were cock's crow rather than eventide.

"Aunt," Lord Leith called merrily, "where is everyone? I'm arrived sooner than planned, I know, but this place seems more of a museum than ordinarily. Where's Ollie? And Thomas and Anton and Jessica?"

Lady Granthan sat alone and silent in the front parlor. She seemed so uncharacteristically crestfallen that he took alarm.

"Come. What's toward?" he asked anxiously.

"Everything," she replied softly.

"Please, Aunt," he asked, "don't speak in riddles."

"Anton is gone," she said absently, "Ollie is resting up for dinner. Thomas has gone off riding. And Jessica is wandering about the grounds. I've had a long talk with her this day, Alex, and I am not happy. We had no right to meddle in her life, Alex, no right at all. All we have brought her is unhappiness."

"What has happened?" he repeated, his gaze searching her face for a clue to her distress.

"I think it best that you ask her that," Lady Grantham said primly.

"But I am in all my dirt," he replied as he tried to gain time to think.

"Go anyway, Alex," his aunt said sternly, "for you are as responsible for her state now as anyone."

"I?" he asked, confounded. But he did not wait for her answer. He turned at once and left to seek out Jessica.

She was roaming the paths near the herb garden and he made her out by the glow that the last light struck from her cream-colored frock and from her impossible hair. He came up to her and noted with surprise that this day, for the first time, she wore that lustrous burden of hers loose and that it coiled down upon her shoulders like random fire.

"Jessica," he said tentatively, "I've returned before time."

She looked up at him and said in a small quiet voice, "Hello, Alex."

He matched his stride with her soft pacing and said as noncommittally as possible, "Aunt seems most disturbed. What has occurred whilst I've been about your business?"

"Everything," she answered quietly, echoing his aunt.

"Blast it!" he cried, gripping on to her shoulders and turning her to face him. "I cannot go creeping about and asking forever while all I am given are cryptic little answers. What is going on? This is not like you, Jessica. What has happened? Has there been a murder? A death? Good Lord! Ollie is well, isn't he?"

"Oh, yes, Alex," she answered quickly, "everyone is well. I'm sorry we have all been so mute, but really it has been a most unsettling time. And you are right, it isn't fair to you."

He relaxed his hold on her and said in what he hoped was a light tone, "Then out with it, Jessica, or I shall think you have a corpse put by about the place somewhere."

She laughed up at him at that, in more of her old style. But yet, he thought, there was a difference about her. There was a subtle, indefinable difference in this girl that he had thought of so constantly since he had left her side. She grows, he thought, eyeing her grace and her new tranquility, she grows with every moment that passes.

"That is," he said, strolling on with her, "most illuminating."

She laughed again and then said, idly snatching up a bit of trumpet vine as she passed it, "I'm sorry again. But you see, Alex, I know now why Anton came to England. I know about my mother and her spiteful bequest. She left me a true fortune, you see. But it can only be mine if I marry one of her countrymen. Anton included the information in his proposal to me."

The elegant gentleman halted abruptly. But before he could bring himself to frame the question, her soft voice went on almost prosaically, "I refused him, of course."

"Of course," he echoed as they resumed their walk.

"He wanted me both for the legacy and because I reminded him so much of my mama. Do you know, Alex," she said wonderingly, "now I am glad that she abandoned me as she did. For I think we would never have gotten on together. And I did not love him," she added as an afterthought.

He kept pace with her and after a time she said, "He was quite a different person than I thought. He was never honest with me. And so I told him, among other things. And so he left. I've whistled a fortune down the wind, Alex," she said on a half-laugh.

"It was never yours," he said calmly, "and you still have your father's treasure."

"Oh, as to that," she said, "I know just what sort of a treasure it is now. Anton told me, you see. And I told Thomas, and do you know he rode away from me when he learned the truth?"

Her companion stopped now in his tracks. He could not think at once of what to say, but her next words cut off the train of inventions he was quickly devising.

"But then, after a long while, he came back and said he wished to marry me anyway. Even though Red Jack's legacy wasn't worth a farthing. He said that he was my best friend."

"And you said?" Lord Leith asked, hardly believing what he was hearing.

"Oh, I agreed," she said softly.

It was lucky, he thought, the light had grown so dim that she could not clearly see his face as he turned aside. For he knew it must be such as he himself would not wish to look upon. He paused a moment to at least gain fleeting control. There would be time enough, he told himself savagely, for grieving later, when she had gone.

"Ah, yes," he said.

When she realized that he was immobile, she paused and returned to him. "Whatever is it, Alex?" she asked with concern.

"Well, then," he said briskly, "then I come in a good time. For I've got your inheritance all sorted out. Anton was wrong, you know. It is worth a fortune. It was appraised very high. See for yourself. What a paltry fellow your cousin turned out to be.'' He laughed brittlely. ''For it was only a ruse on his part. The comb is a true treasure. See for yourself.''

He fumbled the pouch from his pocket and handed it to her.

But she only laughed lightly as she took it. ''Alex, how should I know a true gem from a false?''

''See,'' he said harshly, taking the pouch and tearing its strings apart. He held the comb high so that the last rays of light caught its lucent fire.

She gazed up at it and then he placed it with shaking hands as a crown upon her crown of hair.

''It has been valued highly enough to give you and Thomas an excellent start. It is a plentiful dowry,'' he said woodenly, stepping back to view his handiwork.

''Thomas and I?'' she asked. ''A dowry? But I did not accept him.''

''You said you agreed,'' he accused in confusion.

''I said I agreed that he was my best friend,'' she answered with some asperity, in more of her old style. ''I could never marry Thomas. He is a friend, right enough, but that sort of affection is not enough for marriage. And so I told him, although it hurt me to deny him so. At any rate,'' she added absently, ''I think he only wanted me because I reminded him of my father. Poor Thomas, he doesn't know whether he values me as a man or as a woman, and that certainly would make a poor basis for wedlock. But, Alex, I know that this comb is worthless. And if you say that it was appraised so . . .''

She took the comb from her hair and held it in front of her. Even in the dying light she could see the emeralds were like starlight upon spring grass, and the cold blue stare of the diamonds winked back at the rising moon. The difference, even to her untrained eye, was as vast as the gap between any truth and any falsehood.

''It's been altered,'' she cried, ''it is not the same. Oh, Alex, never say someone's thrown away good money to save my feelings? Was it Ollie? Oh, this is dreadful. You must return it straightaway.''

He began to quickly tell her about Anton's ill intentions

and the lies a man might spread to gain his ends, but she cut him off as quickly as he had begun.

"No," she said simply. "There is no need for that anymore. You see, in the last days I have had to face up to many things, Alex, and the foremost among them is that my father was not what I so desperately wanted him to be. I invented him, Alex, and that was never fair. He was a carefree, thoughtless fellow. And whatever his original intent, he could never have left such a source of funds as this untouched. Not even for me. I see that now. I loved him dearly for what I wanted him to be, but I think I might have liked him anyway, for what he was. He was never, however, the sort of man to leave such a legacy. Take it back, Alex."

"Jessica," he said desperately, hating the sorrowful acceptance in her voice and wanting the fiery Jess Eastwood back again, not this imitation of a wordly-wise ancient that was speaking so placidly, "take it yourself. Why do you think I went to such lengths? It was what your father wanted you to have, really. He purchased it for you, whatever he was forced to do later."

"So it was you," she said suddenly. "Why, Alex? Please tell me the truth, I am so tired of deception. Everyone about me has been deceiving me, for my own good or their own good, it hardly matters anymore. Please."

Because he was tired of deception too, and because he could no longer play the patient game he had thought to, he carefully placed the comb upon her hair again, dropped his hands, and said simply, "Because I happened to discover that I love you, Jessica."

As she stared at him and as he could no longer read her expression in the soft evening's light, he went on, as if to himself, "I know that you are not ready for love and I do not know if you will ever wish to love me. But there's the truth of it. I found I loved you when you were a brave imitation of your father. And I loved you even when you tried to be what Anton told you your mother was. Whether you were Miss Eastwood, Jess, or Jessica, it made no matter. And I think that whatever you become in time, I shall love you. But," he said with a hint of laughter, for he felt free after speaking so freely, "I also know that you are yet the 'babe' that your friend Miss Dunstable titled you. I am content to wait. I only wanted you to know. And if you decide against me in time, I will endeavor to accept that too. Understand clearly, Jessica, that I want you as a friend and as a lover, for I will not allow either of us to live half a life together. But I shall wait.''

"Alex," she said, her voice so filled with emotion that he could not tell if it was gladness or sorrow she spoke through, "I too have come to a realization. Do you recall that a while ago you gave me good advice and told me about the Red Indians and their tactics for warfare?''

He put his head to one side, for he could not comprehend what she was going on about, and he feared for her reason after all the shocks she had suffered.

"But I recall a story my father told me about them," she went on. "He said that they do not let their infants go about with leading strings as they learn to walk, as we let ours do. He said that they swaddle their babes and carry them about on their backs, never letting their feet touch the ground long after they should have commenced to toddle. But then, on the day that they feel a child is old and strong enough, they unwrap him and set him down upon the earth. And do you know, Alex, within a day, before the sun sets, he is running about as any child of that age might do.

"Oh, Alex," she cried, throwing her arms about his neck and coming into his amazed embrace, "I am like that! For I feel as though I have grown years in a day. I've had hours to think, and primarily of you. I am not my father," she whispered against his neck. "Nor am I my mother," she confided as his lips touched her cheek. "I am myself, and thus I am yours. For I find that I do not wish to grow older without you. And," she said on a husky half-laugh, "even after that, I find my dearest wish is to help you haunt your new home, down through all the centuries.'' Then she only sighed as he found her yielding lips.

She could not analyze his kiss as she had other men's, for she was too lost in the sheer joy of his clever mouth. And when he gently touched her breast, she took no alarm, for she only wanted to offer herself more completely to him.

When at last he drew back to gaze into her eyes to convince himself that this was all real, she threw back her head and laughed. "Oh, Alex, your aunt will be so pleased. For she told me when I confided my feelings for you that I should not worry. She told me that she thought you had a care for me.''

"Had a care?" he breathed, and took her back again to lose himself in the impossible sweetness of her mouth.

"Jessica," he said at length in an altered voice, taking a step back from her, "I think we ought to be married at once."

"At once," she agreed, trying to wedge herself back into his arms.

"Within the month," he insisted a moment later.

"Within," he eventually groaned against her lips, "a week. At St. George's," he finally said firmly as he released her.

"At St. Gertrude's," she jested gaily as he led her back to the Hall. "For surely all the Austrian orphans will want to celebrate with us," she explained with a boyish grin.

17

The room was as dim as he had remembered. The wizened man behind the enormous desk, however, leaned forward, in excitement this time, as he strode into the study.

"Well?" the older man said eagerly. "Let's have it. Here's your second payment," he rasped as he flung a purse of coins onto his desktop. "Now let us see if you've earned the third."

"Yes," the blond young gentleman said softly, "oh, yes, Mr. Cribb, you were entirely right. Red Jack did leave a legacy. One beyond all our imaginings."

"I knew it! I knew it!" the other man cried.

"But it is not one that you can get your hands upon," the fair-haired man answered.

"Let me be the judge of that." The older man laughed as the huge woman who sat beside him roared with joy as well.

"Now," Mr. Cribb said happily as he threw a matching purse upon his desk, "let's have it. Where is it?"

"Why, I gave it away not two days past at St. George's in London," Thomas Preston said in a matter-of-fact voice. "Or, rather, I helped give it away, for it was Sir Selby who actually did the deed; I only assisted."

"Gave it away?" the older man gasped. "Well, I shall get it back again, never fear."

"I think not," the younger man said, "for it was all quite legal."

"Out with it! To whom did you give it?" Mr. Cribb shouted in vexation.

"To Alexander, Lord Leith. And I think, from the way he accepted it, that he will never let it go," his visitor said in a pensive tone.

"What was it?" bellowed the enormous woman, speaking for the first time as she heaved to her feet.

"Why, Red Jack's only treasure, and his truest one," Thomas Preston replied. He smiled and then turned on his heel and left the room, the two raging persons within, and the two bags of coins where they were, in the darkness.

Once out into the day again, he mounted his horse and pointed its head southward, to the coast. For he intended to ride to the shoreline to find a ship to take him to a land of opportunity for a fourth son, to a land where he might make his fortune.

But whatever treasure he found there, he thought as he rode away, it would never match the one that Lord Leith had been gifted with days before, the one he had let slip through his fingers. And humming a sad old song about a wise child that he had once heard, he rode toward the sea.

About the Author

Edith Layton has been writing since she was ten years old. She has worked as a freelance writer for newspapers and magazines, but has always been fascinated by English history, most particularly by the Regency period. Ms. Layton lives with her physician husband and three children on Long Island, where she collects antiques and large dogs. Her previous Regencies, THE DUKE'S WAGER and THE DISDAINFUL MARQUIS, are available in Signet editions.

More Regency Romances from SIGNET

*Prices slightly higher in Canada

**Buy them at your local
bookstore or use coupon
on next page for ordering.**

Other Regency Romances from SIGNET